NOBODY HEARD A THING

ANGELA HENRY

Storm

Ebook ISBN: 978-1-80508-732-8
Paperback ISBN: 978-1-80508-730-4

Cover design: Lisa Horton
Cover images: Trevillion, Shutterstock

Published by Storm Publishing.
For further information, visit:
www.stormpublishing.co

ALSO BY ANGELA HENRY

The Perfect Affair
Her Pretty Lies
The Family Lies

Kendra Clayton Series
The Company You Keep
Tangled Roots
Diva's Last Curtain Call
Schooled in Lies
Sly, Slick & Wicked
Doing it to Death

Xavier Knight Series
Knight's Fall
Knight's Shade

Maya Sinclair Thriller
The Paris Secret

Middle-Grade as Angie Kelly
Labyrinth Society: The Versailles Vendetta

PROLOGUE

AVA AND BROOKE

July 2000

Two little girls sat on the swings in the nearly empty playground eating their ice-cream cones, oblivious to the person who had been watching them for half an hour. Ava Hammond and her best friend Brooklyn Peters were ten years old and lived down the street from each other. Currently, their favorite thing to do was hang out at the Pleasant Street Park playground, a block from their houses, and race on the swings. Brooke was the current champion, having been able to get her swing so high she was in danger of wrapping herself around the swing set's top bar. Ava would watch her friend screaming with laughter as she pumped her legs faster and faster, pushing her swing as far as it would go. Ava would never admit it, but she didn't like the swing races nearly as much as she liked hanging out with Brooke. Brooke was fun and fearless. She was the leader to Ava's follower. Ava always knew that when she was with Brooke, fun and adventure was sure to follow, and she needed all the fun and adventure she could get to distract her from her parents' divorce.

Six months ago, Ava and her mom were supposed to be moving to Seattle to join her father who had gotten a job there. Ava hadn't been happy. She'd prayed and prayed that God would let her stay in Elmhurst so she could still be friends with Brooke. God answered her prayer but not in the way she had hoped for. Being able to stay in Elmhurst, Ohio, the only home she'd known, meant she had lost her father. He had met someone else in Seattle who he'd decided he wanted to be with more than he wanted to be with her and her mom. And now her mom was sad all the time, sometimes lying on the couch sleeping all day long with empty bottles of wine sitting on the coffee table next to her. Ava had become just one more thing she had to deal with. So, her running off every morning to hang out with Brooke was a godsend to her mom in the midst of her emotional breakdown.

"Are you almost finished? Hurry up, I have to be home in fifteen minutes." Brooke glanced at the half-finished chocolate ice-cream cone still in Ava's hand.

Ava could tell Brooke was impatient to get started on their last race before they both had to be back at home. Not that Ava's mom would care whether she was home or not. She also knew there would be no dinner waiting for her when she got there, and she'd be heating up instant mac and cheese in the microwave again.

"You know I can't eat ice cream as fast as you," whined Ava. "I'll get brain freeze."

"Then throw it away," commanded Brooke. When Ava continued to take small licks of her chocolate ice cream, she snatched it out of her hand and rushed over and tossed it into a nearby trash can.

"Hey! Why'd you do that?" Ava jumped up from her swing. "I wasn't finished." Tears sprang into her eyes. She'd been looking forward to that ice-cream cone all week since she only ever had money to get ice cream from the truck once a week. She already had so few things lately to look forward to.

"You were taking too long. Now, come on so we can race, and I can beat you again."

Ava's tears were quickly replaced by anger, and even she was shocked when her hand shot out and she shoved Brooke so hard she stumbled backwards and almost fell.

Brooke, momentarily shocked that Ava had shoved her, pushed her back even harder, causing Ava to fall on her butt.

"You're no fun! I don't know why I hang out with you. Even your dad doesn't wanna be around you. That's why he left. To get away from you!"

Ava sat in stunned silence. Tears filled her eyes as she watched Brooke stomp off towards the grassy field between the playground and the parking lot. She already worried her parents' divorce was her fault and now her favorite person in the world was telling her the same thing.

She slowly got to her feet. By the time she'd finished brushing playground dirt off the seat of her jean shorts, Brooke was halfway to the parking lot. She wasn't alone. She was talking to someone. Someone Ava had never seen before. A strange man dressed in baggy black warm-ups and a blue baseball cap pulled low over his face was saying something to Brooke and gesturing towards a car parked at the edge of the parking lot, a beat-up old blue car with patches of rust on the hood. Ava stopped what she was doing to listen.

The man was looking down at Brooke and smiling. "Do you want to see some puppies?"

"What kind of puppies?" asked Brooke excitedly as she looked beyond the man to the car.

"Black Lab puppies. Come on and I'll show you."

Ava also noticed another person behind the wheel of the car, but she was too far away to tell if it was a man or a woman. All she saw was a brown hand draped over the steering wheel. Ava instantly got a knot in the pit of her stomach. This felt all wrong. Neither one of them were allowed to talk to strangers. Both of their moms reminded them constantly – at least her mom used to before her dad left.

"Brooke! Come back! I'm sorry."

Brooke briefly glanced over her shoulder at Ava, who was quickly walking towards her and the man, and rolled her eyes.

"Go away!" said Brooke, stopping Ava in her tracks.

But then the man also looked back at Ava. The only thing she could focus on were his eyes which were hard, dark, and angry. Mere seconds ago, he'd been smiling down at her best friend, but when he turned to look at Ava, his entire face changed. The smile was gone, and his lips were pressed into a hard, thin line as he glared. Before Ava could even open her mouth to tell Brooke to stop, the man grabbed Brooke by her upper right arm and dragged her the final few feet to his car.

Startled, Brooke yelped as she pulled back frantically and screamed. Ava jolted into action and ran towards the car, but it was too late. The man yanked the back passenger side door open and forcibly pulled a flailing Brooke and shoved her into the back seat of the car, slamming the door shut before he jumped into the front passenger seat. Ava screamed and yelled, "Stop," as the car peeled out of the lot.

That was the last time Ava ever saw Brooke.

ONE

AVA

Present Day

I was sitting at the back of the Elmhurst County courthouse fighting tears. Unlike most of the tears I hadn't allowed myself to cry lately, these were happy tears. I'd been invited to the adoption ceremony of six-year-old Kaden and his four-year-old sister Marlee by Charles and Gracie Benton, the foster family I'd placed them with two years ago when their mother died of an overdose. It hadn't been an easy road. The couple had taken on two scared and traumatized kids who'd lived with their mother's lifeless body for two days before four-year-old Kaden used his mom's cell phone to call 911. He told them he couldn't wake up his mommy and he and his sister were hungry, but the couple didn't hesitate to open their home and their hearts, and now two beautiful children were getting their forever family today. As happy as I was for all the parties involved, I couldn't help but feel my own heart break just a little, but I managed to successfully push my own sadness aside to congratulate the Bentons after the ceremony.

"This never would have happened without you, Mrs. West," said Gracie, pulling out of the big hug I'd given her after the judge had declared the adoption official.

"Hey, I thought I told you to call me Ava. I just put the process in motion with the placement. You guys were the ones who changed those kids' lives. Kaden and Marlee are so very lucky to have found you. You guys are natural-born parents."

Gracie mouthed *thank you* and gave me a big smile before she rejoined her husband and the kids. I watched the new family leave the courthouse, thinking how Gracie Benton and I had more in common than she knew. Gracie had suffered numerous miscarriages and had never been able to carry a pregnancy to term. At least she'd been able to conceive. I couldn't even do that. After my last failed Clomid treatment, I had pretty much resigned myself to the fact that I would have to take a different path to motherhood. I wanted to adopt, but the only thing standing in my way was my husband Evan. He wanted his own biological children, and no argument that I presented to him in favor of adoption would sway him. We were at an impasse, and I had absolutely no idea what to do about it. As a result, Evan, who owned his own construction company, worked long days and when he was at home, he avoided me. Things were not good, and I didn't know how much longer we could go on like this.

Later, I sat across from my mom, picking at my chicken Caesar salad as she stared at me with a look of concern.

"You alright, Ava? Because you were the one who invited me to lunch, and you've barely said ten words to me since I got here. What's up? Everything okay with you and Evan?"

"Why wouldn't it be?" I didn't mean for it to come out so snappy, but Evan was the last person I wanted to talk about. Mom raised her eyebrow at my tone, and I instantly sat up and gave her an apologetic smile.

"Sorry, Mom." I briefly told her about the Bentons and the adoption, and her expression softened.

"Your time is coming, honey. I promise. It just may not look like what you thought it would." She reached out and squeezed my hand, and I squeezed back.

I wasn't so sure I believed her and really didn't want to get into Evan's views on adoption. He and my mom had a tenuous relationship at best. They weren't exactly besties but made sure to be polite and civil to each other when they were around me. Maybe it was his tattoos or the fact that he'd been to prison. Whatever the reason, she never really warmed to him. Then again, she was also super protective of me.

"I thought maybe you were upset because it's almost that time of the year."

Between my infertility issues, what was going on in my marriage, and attending an adoption ceremony watching other people get to be parents, I had pushed that time of the year out of my mind momentarily. Here it was, back again, and this time it was a milestone year. Next month was the twenty-fifth anniversary of the abduction of Brooklyn Peters, my childhood best friend. I tried to be super busy on the twenty-four anniversaries I'd lived through since that horrible day. Once we were married, Evan did an amazing job keeping me distracted with trips or excursions when that day rolled around every year. Though I knew this year would be different and I'd most likely be alone.

"I'm good. It's not like it hasn't been twenty-five years. It's not anything I'll ever get over, but I'm definitely used to it coming around every year. So, don't worry about me, Mom. I'm fine."

A look of indecision flashed across my mom's face, and she reached for her purse which was hanging on the back of her chair, opened it, pulled out a business card, and slid it across the table to me. I picked it up and saw that it was a white business card with black lettering that read *Lia Quinn*, with a phone number and an email address.

"What's this?"

"She came to the house looking for you. She's doing a documentary on Brooke's abduction. I told her you wouldn't be interested in contributing, but I promised her I would give you her contact information in case you wanted to talk to her."

"Why does she need to talk to me? Everything she needs to know about Brooke's case is public knowledge and has been written about a million times in the last twenty-five years. There's nothing I can add that will be anything different than what's already been written." I took the business card, ripped it in half and tossed it on top of the table.

"I know that, honey," she said with a sigh. "That's why I told her I would give you her contact information. And I have."

I hated that my mom was walking on eggshells around me about this. Even after all this time, what happened to Brooke still caused a visceral reaction in me. It was easily the worst thing that had ever happened to me, seeing my best friend abducted right in front of my eyes and not being able to help her. If there was one silver lining from what happened that day, it was that my mom, who had been well on her way to becoming an alcoholic after my dad left her, snapped out of her spiral and realized how fortunate she was that I hadn't been abducted that day along with Brooke. I lost my best friend, but I got my mom back.

"You know," she said casually after taking a sip of her iced tea. "I've often wondered if the reason why you still have such a hard time with this is because you've never allowed yourself to really talk about it. Survivor's guilt is a terrible thing to have to go through alone, Ava."

This was another not-so-subtle attempt to get me back into therapy. It wasn't like I was against therapy. I was a social worker and suggested therapy all the time to the people whose cases I worked on. I knew I wasn't strong enough to relive that day over again with a therapist asking the questions that have haunted me for twenty-five years. Why Brooke and not me? Or more importantly why Brooke and not me, too. Whoever had taken her could've just as easily grabbed me, too. Why didn't they?

I was so traumatized right after it happened that I was sent to a child psychologist that I saw for a few years, and once I entered puberty, my rebellious streak hit and I refused to go anymore. I think my mom thought that, after a few years, she could convince me to go back, but I never did. Everything was made worse by the fact that Brooke's family disappeared as well. Two years after her abduction, Brooke's mom and her older brother Sam moved in the middle of the night. I hadn't seen or heard from either of them for more than two decades. I even look for them on social media every year on the anniversary, but have never found a trace of them.

Back then my twelve-year-old brain had convinced me that Brooke's mom, Julia, who never once made me feel guilty about what happened that day, must have secretly blamed me. Because I sure did. If I hadn't shoved Brooke over an ice cream cone, she wouldn't have walked right into the path of the men who abducted her. Of course, that was faulty logic. If they had really wanted to take Brooke, they would've found another way. Still, I stuffed those memories down as far as they would go and did the best I could to move on with my life.

Every anniversary that passed and every request I got from the media to talk about it just made me all the more determined to forget that day ever happened. Now, I felt like the past was having an effect on me physically. I had never told Evan this, but I felt like it was my fear over what had happened to Brooke that was preventing me from conceiving. Why would I want to bring a child into a world where they could be taken from me at any moment, making me worry who might be lurking around every corner?

"Well, promise me you'll at least think about it. She even mentioned something about paying you," said my mom, snapping me back to reality.

"I promise I'll think about it." I grabbed the two halves of Lia Quinn's business card from the table and made a show of putting them in the side pocket of my purse. But the look my mother gave me told me she knew beyond a shadow of a doubt that I would do anything but.

. . .

I came home to an empty house because Evan was out of town supervising the building of an office complex in Columbus. To be honest, I wasn't up for dealing with him when I knew all he'd do was come home, ask me how my day was, inhale his dinner, grab a beer from the fridge and disappear into the basement where he would watch TV and fall asleep on the couch while I went to bed alone. In other words, going through the motions. I knew he was doing all of this extra work to get money to start IVF treatments, but after I'd told him I just couldn't put myself through it emotionally right now, and had mentioned adoption in passing, he'd been giving me the silent treatment. I had taken a leave of absence from my job as a social worker for Elmhurst County Child and Family Services to go on this journey. We'd hit a brick wall.

I knew I needed to get back to some kind of daily routine. Since I'd gained a little weight, I felt bloated and not like myself. So, instead of my usual after lunchtime nap, I changed into leggings, a tank top and trainers, and headed out for a nice, long walk through the park two blocks from our town house. The Black Eyed Peas commanded me to "Pump It" through my earbuds as I made my first lap around the pond in the center of the park. I was mainly focused on the path ahead, momentarily looking around every half mile or so, and I'd just made my third lap around the pond when I spotted him. About fifty feet away near a tree by the parking lot stood a man dressed in a black baggy warm-up suit with a baseball cap pulled low over his face. I froze.

My stomach knotted up as shear panic gripped me. I was rooted to the spot as beads of sweat popped up on my forehead. Logic told me this couldn't be the same man who'd taken Brooke. It had been twenty-five years. What would he be doing here now? Was he following me? Did he still have Brooke? My fear quickly melted away in the muggy July heat and I was just about to rush over and confront him. Much like before, I couldn't get a good look at his face. Suddenly, a hand clamped onto my left shoulder and I let out a shriek that would wake the dead. I whirled around to see a young, red-haired white woman staring at me in alarm. I looked back towards the tree near the parking lot. The man was bending down to pet a black Lab, taking the ball from its mouth and throwing it. He was just some guy playing with his dog. I felt like a paranoid idiot.

"Oh my god, Ava. I didn't mean to scare you. Are you alright?" said Kerri Sikes, a former coworker of mine at Children's Services. Kerri had left a year ago after getting her master's in social work and now taught at Elmhurst Community College. I hadn't seen her since her going-away party. I instantly pulled the earbuds out of my ears and gave her a smile.

"Kerri. It's so good to see you." I purposefully didn't answer her question because I felt like a fool.

"I was headed back to my car when I saw you just standing here. You sure you're okay? What were you looking at?" She glanced in the direction I'd been looking and then back at me in confusion.

I noticed Kerri was wearing biker shorts, an Ohio State T-shirt and expensive-looking running shoes. Her red hair was pulled into a messy bun. It was then I remembered she'd been a good fifty pounds heavier the last time I'd seen her a year ago.

"Look at you," I said, taking a step back and giving her a good look up and down. "You look amazing."

"Thank you." She blushed and quickly held out her left hand to show me the emerald cut diamond solitaire on her ring finger. "I got engaged a few months ago and we're getting married this fall. Got to get in shape for the wedding. I'd just wanted to lose a few pounds, but I fell in love with running and now forty-seven pounds later I feel like a new woman."

"That's wonderful, Kerri. Congratulations. Who's the lucky guy?"

"He teaches math at Elmhurst CC. We met at work. It's been kind of a whirlwind romance."

I knew all about that. I'd met Evan online and after a magical first date we'd become inseparable, getting married after only six months of dating much to the horror of my mom and friends. Had that really been eight years ago? Given the current state of my marriage, maybe they'd been right to feel like I was rushing things. Evan and I both wanted kids, but clearly, I should have asked more questions about what his definition of being a parent meant. I believed family meant more than just blood relations. He didn't.

"What about you, Ava? Patrice told me you took a leave of absence?"

Patrice Nelson was the Children's Services gossip, and I could tell by the way Kerri was now glancing at my stomach that Patrice had told her why I'd taken a leave of absence, which was confidential information. I was instantly annoyed knowing my coworkers had been gossiping about me, but quickly pasted a smile on my face.

"My husband and I decided now would be a good time for me to cut back so we could start our family. It's still very much a work in progress." I quickly added to let her know that I wasn't a mother yet.

"How long will you be out?"

"I go back next month. Why?" I didn't even want to think about going back to work. Not because I didn't love my job, but I knew a mountain of cases awaited me. My boss hadn't been thrilled when I'd taken a leave of absence because it meant she'd had to take over some of my caseload. I knew she was counting the days until I came back.

"Well," she said, giving me a sheepish look. "If you're ever bored and looking for something to do, I volunteer at that new women's shelter over on Conrad Road. We could really use your help. It would only be a couple of times a week when we do intake."

"You mean Haver House?"

"Yeah, have you been there?"

"Not yet. I've heard nothing but good things about it."

"It's a beautiful facility, a renovated Victorian Mansion. It currently houses about thirty women, and we've got a waiting list of about fifty."

I had wanted to get back into some kind of a routine, and volunteering a couple of times a week would not only get me out of the house, but it would also help me focus on other people with much bigger problems than me.

"Sounds great, Kerri. I'd love to help."

"Oh, thank you so much, Ava. I've got to go, but I'll give you a call tonight with the details. Is your number still the same?"

I nodded yes and watched her go, then put my earbuds back in and headed for my final loop around the pond. This time, when I looked over by the tree, nobody was there.

TWO

Three Months Earlier

Hurrying through the kitchen, she took off her apron with one hand while tugging open her employee locker with the other, cursing as the lock failed to click open. Sweat was already beginning to trickle down her back and she knew it wasn't because of the heat of the kitchen she'd just been working in. How had they managed to find her? She'd been so careful, or so she'd thought. She'd been living in Dayton, Ohio, for five years without incident. She kept her head down and did her work and rarely socialized except for the occasional dinner or movie with someone from work. She didn't even date and never dressed to attract any kind of attention, opting for no makeup and clothes two sizes too big to hide her slender figure.

When she'd first arrived in town, she'd even worn a wig but now wore her hair short and natural, so unlike the long hair of five years ago. Yet, when she'd served her last table, she'd seen him. She'd know him anywhere no matter how he'd tried to hide himself in a far corner of the restaurant. His eyes even locked with hers as she walked past his table. It took everything in her not to flinch under his gaze and stare right through him like she'd never seen him before, but she knew he'd recognized her because why else would he be here? She quickly shrugged out of her apron, tossing it into her locker, and grabbed her coat and purse.

"You okay, Cindy?" asked her supervisor Mr. Cox with a look of concern. She knew she probably looked like she'd seen a ghost because she had. No, that wasn't right. He wasn't the ghost. She was, and had been for twenty-five years.

"Migraine," she said in a low voice, like she was afraid the man sitting out in the diner would be able to hear her. "Sorry," she told her boss. "I'm gonna go home."

"No problem. You go on home and rest up. Let me know if you need to take tomorrow off, too."

She merely nodded and watched him go back out to the front of the diner. Then, when she was sure he wasn't looking, she slipped out of the employee locker room and across the hall to Mr. Cox's office where the safe was. Feeling horrible that her boss had trusted her with the combination since she was the one to deposit the diner's money in the bank each morning, she emptied the safe of twenty-eight hundred dollars. As an afterthought, and feeling guilty as hell, she left a note apologizing and promising to pay the money back.

Once she was behind the wheel of the ten-year-old Hyundai, she had to relax and let out a breath because she was gripping the steering wheel so tight her fingers hurt. Once her breathing got back to normal or as close to normal under the circumstances, she'd had a realization. She'd gotten way too comfortable, too complacent. She should have known he'd never stop looking for her. How long had he known where she was? And how did he find her? She'd been using a new identity and lived a life so far under the radar she may as well be dead.

With a heavy heart and a last look at the diner where she'd made some of the only true friends she'd had in years, she started her car with every intention of leaving Cindy Ford behind, wondering who she was going to be next. The thought overwhelmed her, and she turned off the ignition. She was tired of running, tired of hiding, and so very tired of lying. She couldn't remember the last time she'd told anybody the truth.

As she sat there contemplating her next move, she looked up to see the man in question. She froze, her eyes never leaving his car as he drove past without even glancing in her direction because he was on his phone. Then it hit her. Shuddering through her like an electric shock. Anger. Blinding white hot anger. Why did she have to keep running? Never feeling safe and having to start all over again multiple times over the past twenty-five years while the man who was behind her pain got to live his life. Maybe, she thought as the anger drained away, leaving her spent, it was time the hunted became the hunter. Maybe it was time she took her life back. Without thinking about how stupid and dangerous what she was planning to do was, she turned on the ignition and followed the man who had ruined her life out of the diner's parking lot.

THREE

AVA

I arrived at Haver House women's shelter three days after I ran into Kerri in the park. I agreed to meet her there for a tour before I started my training. The brick mansion with a porch that wrapped around the entire house sat on about an acre of land with a parking lot behind the house. Wicker porch furniture sat on both sides of the double front door which was inlaid with stained-glass panels. Before going inside, I saw a sign mounted next to the doorbell instructing me to ring the bell to be buzzed in. I was just about to do that when laughter caught my attention. Glancing to the left, I saw a playground thirty feet from the side of the house and noticed two little blonde girls in pink sundresses sitting side by side on a swing set. They were younger than Brooke and I had been. The girl with pigtails looked about five and the other girl with the long blonde braid down her back looked about eight.

My whole body tensed as I started to panic. Were those little girls out here all alone? Anything could happen to them. I was just about to head over to the playground when both girls jumped off the swings and yelled, "Grammy!" The girls ran to an older, white-haired woman sitting on a bench nearby, who I assumed to be their grandmother. I continued to stare as the woman took both girls by the hand and headed in the direction of the slide. Satisfied they weren't in any danger, I turned to press the doorbell when someone abruptly exited the house, knocking me sideways.

"Sorry," said a brown-skinned black woman who looked my age with short natural hair. She was wearing faded jean shorts, flip-flops, and a black tank top. The woman didn't bother looking back as she rushed down the front steps of the porch and headed down the long, winding driveway.

"Ava," said Kerri who'd emerged from the house behind the woman, looking beyond me at the retreating figure. "Welcome. Come on in. You're a little early."

"It's okay if you're not ready for the tour yet. I can wait. I brought a book."

"No, it's fine." She held the door open, and I walked inside.

I walked into a brightly lit foyer with a staircase on the left. To my right was a small office that had probably been a hall closet in its former life. Inside was a desk with a couple of chairs in front of it and a row of filing cabinets on the back wall behind the desk. A heavyset, older white woman with black horn-rimmed glasses and graying brown shoulder-length hair sat behind the desk. She smiled as Kerri and I walked into her office.

"Ava, this is Adele Mackie, our admin assistant and the person who keeps everything running smoothly around here. Adele, this is Ava West, our new intake volunteer."

Adele stood up and stuck her hand out. "Well, I don't know about all of that, but it's so nice to meet you, Ava. And boy, are we glad you're here because we really need the help."

"Nice meeting you, Adele," I said, shaking her hand. "I'm happy to help. I've heard so many good things about this place."

"I'm going to take Ava on a tour and then I'll hand her over to you for training."

"Don't forget to take her to the kitchen. Mrs. Brady whipped up a batch of lemon bars this morning," Adele called out as we headed out of her office.

. . .

For the next half an hour, Kerri showed me around the entire house, starting with the first floor TV room with a large flatscreen against the wall and three couches and about half a dozen leather chairs. There were a few women there watching a soap opera. The living room opened up into the dining room with a long narrow table down the center where a group of four women played cards and another woman sat coloring at the opposite end. One thing I noticed right away was that although the house had been an elegant residence to a wealthy family around the turn of the century, it wasn't anymore. The walls were stark white. The hardwood floors and stairway banister were polished to a shine, but age-scarred, and the furnishings were sturdy-looking but well-worn and mismatched. The house was very clean and yet I could detect the slightest hint of mildew beneath the smell of household cleaners. Somehow this only added to its charm.

"Are meals served to the residents?"

"Yes. We provide three meals a day. The residents are not required to eat here if they don't want to and they're even allowed to have their own food in their rooms as long as they clean up after themselves. Since we're currently at capacity, we have staggered mealtimes in the dining room, so everyone has a seat at the table if they want, and also to accommodate the women who have jobs."

Next, we headed into a large industrial-style kitchen where, true to Adele's word, there was a plastic container full of lemon bars. Kerri opened the container and the smell of lemony goodness wafted out. She held the container out to me, and I took one, taking a bite of the sugary delight and closing my eyes with a sigh of contentment. They tasted like heaven.

"You're not going to have one?" I asked.

"I shouldn't since I'm trying to fit into my size seven wedding dress, but I wouldn't want to be rude and let you eat alone." She snatched a lemon bar from the container before firmly putting the lid back on.

"How many other staff work here?"

"Aside from Mrs. Brady, our cook, and Adele," she said around a mouthful, "there's Selma Ross, our director and the rest are volunteers who work anywhere from two to three days a week for about four hours a shift. Sometimes longer if they're available."

"How often do you do intake?"

"Twice a week. Tuesdays and Thursdays. Sometimes, we have emergency cases that come in on days other than Tuesday and Thursday, but not often. We're still pretty new and residents usually get placed at the more established shelters first before they're sent here."

"What are you two doing messing around in my kitchen?" An older, black lady walked into the kitchen. She was dark-skinned, and rail thin, wearing a short, curly black wig.

"Eating your delicious lemon bars. Mrs. Brady, this is Ava West, our new volunteer. Ava, this is the illustrious Mrs. Brady, our fabulous cook."

Mrs. Brady looked me up and down and then crossed her arms and gave me a big grin. "Are you Natalie Hammond's girl?"

"Yes, ma'am." I didn't know this woman from a hole in the wall, but I shouldn't have been surprised she knew me because of what had happened to Brooke, so everyone in town also knew my mom.

"What's she been up to? I used to see her at church every once in a while, but she stopped coming."

"She's just fine. She got a promotion at work and that means she's on the road a lot more." My mom worked as a sales rep for a medical supply company and was on the road at least once a month.

"I'm so glad to hear that. I think about the two of you often. I know it's been a long time, but you're doing okay, aren't you?" The concern in her eyes was genuine, but I quickly looked away.

I should've known this was coming. Kerri had been born in Elmhurst but didn't grow up here and didn't know about my past. She glanced from Mrs. Brady to me with a quizzical look on her face as she shoved the last of her lemon bar into her mouth. It was time to cut this short. I didn't enjoy talking about what happened twenty-five years ago with people I knew well. So, I definitely wasn't going to talk about it, or how I was doing, with a stranger no matter how well-meaning she appeared.

"Doing just fine, thank you for asking. I think Adele is probably wondering where we are, don't you think?" I directed the last part to Kerri who nodded and then looked at her watch.

"I've actually got a class in about twenty minutes, so we probably need to get you back to Adele so you can start your training."

"It was nice to meet you, Mrs. Brady. Your lemon bars are amazing," I told the older woman, who smiled and nodded. From the look in her eyes, I could tell she understood.

For the next few hours, I sat in Adele's office with her as she went over the policies and procedures for Haver House, with an emphasis on intake procedures. There were a lot of things to remember and I'm glad I brought a notepad to take notes.

"Do you have any questions?" We'd been at it for at least two hours at that point and my eyes were starting to cross.

"Not right now, but I'm sure I will." Nothing she told me sounded too complicated. It was just a lot to remember. But, working in the social work field with so many laws and regulations I had to follow, this job should be a piece of cake.

"Well, I'm usually around, so if you have any questions, don't hesitate to ask."

Then a question came to me when I thought about the two little girls in the playground when I arrived. "How many children are living here?"

Adele paused to think before answering. "Currently we have four kids here, aged fourteen, nine, seven, and five."

"I think it must've been the seven- and five-year-old I saw in the playground with their grandmother when I got here."

"You must mean Callie and Caylee Burns. Blonde hair?"

I nodded.

"They live here with their mom, Hannah. Their grandmother, Vivi, watches them while she works. Hannah's lucky her mom is willing to watch them. Most of our residents with kids aren't so lucky. The plan is to have an on-site daycare here sometime in the future for residents because many of them can't work without childcare. Though that won't be for a few years at least. Do you have kids, Ava?"

"Not yet, but my husband and I are trying." I couldn't meet her eyes as I lied.

Did I still want kids? Of course I did. What I didn't want was for it to be so hard. Maybe that was the whole point. Maybe I was being tested to see how badly I wanted to be a mother. I'd managed to ruin my own good mood and Adele noticed.

"Everything okay?"

"Excuse me?" I feigned confusion.

"All the light just went out of your eyes. Are you feeling okay?"

"I'm fine, just a little overheated." It was sweltering in the tiny office where the small rotating fan on Adele's desk did nothing but blow hot air around the room. My sleeveless silk blouse was plastered to my back with sweat. "How about you? Do you have kids?"

Adele let out a laugh that almost sounded bitter. "No. My husband James and I tried for years, but it was never in the cards, but just because I never gave birth doesn't mean I've never *mothered*." She gave me a big smile, and I smiled back even though I had no idea what she was talking about.

"Are you and your husband from Elmhurst?"

"I am. James is originally from New York City. We met when he moved here looking for work. Then we got married and three years later we moved to Indiana and that's where we were until six months ago."

"Really? What brought you back to Elmhurst?"

"We own a property in the area that we've been renting out and the person who was managing it for us died. Since it's grown so much in value, we just decided it was time to come back and put it up for sale."

"What does your husband do?" I picked up a brochure from her desk and started fanning myself. I couldn't help but notice

Adele suddenly seemed very uncomfortable and I realized I was being nosy.

"Sorry about that," she said, giving me an apologetic half smile and nodding towards my makeshift fan. "This house is a bear to heat and cool. Central air wasn't in the budget I'm afraid. Here." She reached beside her desk on the side nearest the window that looked out onto the front porch and grabbed a bottle of cold water from a dorm-sized fridge and handed it to me. "Why don't you go outside and take a break for fifteen minutes? There are just a few more things I need to go over with you before I turn you loose."

I took the bottle with a smile of thanks and headed out onto the porch, surprised it was cooler outside than it was inside. A refreshing breeze swept across the porch as I drained half the bottle of water, and I was suddenly ashamed. In less than an hour I was leaving to go back to my air-conditioned town house. I didn't have to worry about having a roof over my head or money in my pocket like the women that called Haver House home. Granted my problems were apples and oranges in comparison to these women, but having basic needs like food and shelter weren't among them. In that instant I resolved to be grateful for what I had even if it wasn't everything I wanted. I had it so much better than so many people.

I'd finished the last of my water and was about to head back inside when the black woman with the short natural hair who I'd collided with when I arrived appeared at the bottom of the porch steps. This time she had a gray backpack and was pulling a rolling suitcase, which she left at the bottom of the porch steps before disappearing around the corner, returning a minute later with a large plastic laundry basket.

"Hey, do you need some help?"

She hesitated for a few seconds before replying, "Yeah, that would be nice. Thanks."

Once again, she barely looked at me, but I got a good look at her this time. She was pretty. Petite with big brown eyes and full lips. She wore no makeup but didn't need it because her skin was flawless and glowed with a sheen of sweat from the muggy heat.

Since she still had her hands full with the laundry basket, I grabbed her rolling suitcase and together we walked up the wide porch steps. I walked in ahead of her and held open the door.

"Where is your room?" I asked, planning to help her get her things to wherever in the house she was going to be staying.

"Not sure yet, but I'm good. You can just leave my stuff here and I can get it to my room myself. And thanks, I appreciate it."

"You're welcome. By the way, I'm Ava West. I'm going to be volunteering here." I held out my hand.

"Dana Shields." She gave my hand a brief hard shake before turning away from me and heading into Adele's office to get checked in, obviously having already gone through the intake process.

I pushed down the handle on her rolling suitcase and left it near the staircase. I was about to sit on a chair in the hall outside Adele's office so she could finish up with my training when she was done with Dana, but froze when I saw Dana take her backpack off and set it on the chair next to her. She was wearing a tank top, and I could see her exposed shoulders. On the back of her right shoulder, I saw something that made my blood run cold. It was a raised star-shaped birthmark. I recognized it instantly, although I hadn't seen it in more than two decades. It looked like the exact same birthmark Brooke had.

FOUR

LIA

"No, I haven't heard from her yet, but I have a good feeling she's going to get back to me."

"And if she doesn't?"

I could tell by the way my co-producer Ray's voice had dropped an octave that he wasn't happy. The only reason he'd agreed to co-produce a documentary about the abduction of Brooke Peters was because I'd assured him that I could get an interview with Ava West, the only witness to the abduction. She'd refused all interview requests the last twenty-five years, but lying to Ray had become second nature. It was a necessary evil especially when the one person that could make or break this documentary hadn't gotten in contact with me and probably never would, despite the money I'd told her mother about. I thought everyone had a price. Maybe Ava West was different.

"She'll get back to me. I promise. Look, I've got another call coming in. I'll call you later with an update. Bye." I hung up quickly.

I'd practically cornered Ava's mother in her driveway after following her home from the grocery store three days ago. I told her what I was working on and that I would really love to talk to her daughter Ava. The woman was understandably wary, especially of the media. I'd heard what Ava and Brooke's mothers had gone through after the abduction, being castigated and judged by the public for letting their little girls go to the park by themselves. They were hardly the only ones in their neighborhood who were letting their kids go to play in the park unattended. The public needed someone to blame in the absence of a kidnapper, and the only targets the public had access to were the girls' mothers, especially Brooke's mom, Julia.

I'd been awarded a large grant to make this documentary and already had to dip into the grant money to supplement my income when I lost my full-time gig writing for a women's magazine when they shut down. What was I going to do? I was pretty sure that if Ava West truly wanted to talk to me, she would have called by now. I guess I could've gone to her workplace to try and catch her in person, but she was taking a leave of absence. At least that was what I was told when I called the Elmhurst County Child and Family Services hoping to talk to her.

I'm not really interested in the details of the abduction. I wanted to talk to Ava about her friend Brooke. What was Brooke like and who was she as a person? What was her favorite color, TV show, favorite thing to eat? I was planning to do a human-interest angle. Ray had already shot down that angle because he said it wouldn't interest viewers. The only other person who could possibly make this story acceptable to Ray would be Brooke's mom Julia Dodson, but Julia and her son Sam left town two years after the investigation into Brooke's abduction went cold. Nobody I talked to who'd known them had the slightest clue where they'd gone, nor had they heard from them in twenty-three years.

I didn't have any more money to offer Ava, but I'd heard one interesting detail that miraculously hadn't made it into the newspapers at the time. Granted, it was probably just a bunch of gossip, but if I contacted Ava West and repeated what I'd heard, I could actually get her to sit down and talk to me to either confirm or deny the allegation. Even if she met with me to just cuss me out, it would still be more than I currently had, which was nothing. Suddenly, I was feeling a lot more positive about this story. Now, all I had to do was get Ava West on board.

FIVE

AVA

I was in the kitchen making spaghetti, lost in thought, when Evan arrived home looking tense and tired. He was wearing paint-splattered jeans, work boots, and a dingy white wifebeater which showed off his muscular arms, each covered with a sleeve of tattoos. It was funny how I could look at my husband and still find him incredibly hot but not have the slightest desire to sleep with him. Our fertility issues had pretty much killed our sex life and now intimacy with my husband felt more like a chore with both of us racing towards more than an orgasm. We'd lost all our spontaneity because of scheduling sex sessions to coincide with when I was ovulating. At first, it had been fun because our sex life had gotten kind of predictable and boring. At least back then I knew it was because we both wanted each other and that was it. Trying to get pregnant changed all that, and when we realized it wasn't going to happen right away, that just made things even worse.

"Hey," he said, walking over to me and planting a perfunctory kiss on my cheek, tickling me with his goatee. "How was your day?"

I watched him grab his after-work bottle of beer from the fridge, open it and drain half of it. I knew he couldn't have cared less how my day had been. I doubt he'd know how to respond if I told him I'd met a woman at the homeless shelter I was volunteering at with the same birthmark as Brooke. At least I thought it was the same birthmark. I only got a quick glimpse before the two little blonde sisters, Callie and Caylee, came flying through the door chasing each other and screaming with laughter, trailed by their annoyed-looking grandmother. By the time I turned my attention back to Dana, she'd already finished up with Adele and had her backpack on. Evan was watching me and waiting for an answer. So, I gave him one.

"Started volunteering at Haver House today."

"Really? How'd it go?" I was just about to say fine when I noticed he wasn't even paying attention and was staring past me out the window into the backyard.

"Dinner will be ready in half an hour," I said instead and watched him head down the steps to our basement.

I remembered a time when he'd have helped me cook dinner as we each shared our day with each other. Tears filled my eyes as I watched this stranger I was sharing a house with walk out of the kitchen like he couldn't get away from me fast enough. How did we get here?

We'd only been eating for five minutes when he brought it up. I knew he would eventually but just didn't know when.

"So, that's it then? We're just going to give up on having kids?"

"What are you talking about? Who said we're giving up?"

"You go back to work in a few weeks and now you're volunteering at some shelter. Looks to me like it's a done deal." He tossed his napkin onto his plate in disgust, making me wince.

"Me going back to work doesn't mean we're giving up. I just told you I needed a break before we explored IVF. It's expensive, Evan. Our insurance won't even cover half the cost."

"I told you not to worry about the money," he insisted, but couldn't quite meet my gaze.

"What is that supposed to mean? Where would you be getting

this money?" My pulse started to quicken, blood pounding in my ears.

When I first met Evan, he was very upfront about his criminal past, having spent time behind bars for theft. Smash and grabs he and a crew pulled off at high-end jewelry stores until the walls came tumbling down and they got caught. A former member of the crew who'd been arrested for a different crime had snitched on them all in order to get a lighter sentence. Evan called it no honor amongst thieves. I called it karma. Evan had a good lawyer who got him off with minimal time and he'd been on the straight and narrow ever since.

After prison, he started his own vending machine business which earned him enough to start West Construction. He was already a successful businessman by the time we met, but business wasn't as booming as it was when we'd first met, and he was having to go further afield for jobs. I couldn't quit my job because we needed the money and I was carrying our health insurance, hence the paid leave of absence. Now, he was pushing for IVF which we couldn't afford. How far was he willing to go to become a father? What was he willing to do?

"Did you land that bid contract for the new housing development out in the county? What's it called?"

"Bristol Estates. And, no," he said, pushing his empty plate away and leaning back in his chair. "They went with a big company out of Cincy."

"Then where is this money going to come from?"

"Why can't you just trust me?"

"Why can't you just tell me?"

"I'm going to rob a Brinks truck. Is that what you're expecting me to say? Thanks a lot for having so much faith in me." He got up abruptly, nearly tipping his glass of water over and stormed out of the house. He still hadn't answered my question.

After I'd cleaned up the kitchen, I retrieved the two halves of Lia Quinn's business card from my purse and laid them out on the kitchen counter, then proceeded to stare at the torn card until my eyes crossed. Mom had said Lia was doing a documentary on Brooke, and she was willing to pay me to participate. I wondered how much money she was talking about. I didn't know what Evan was willing to do to continue our journey to parenthood, but what was I willing to do? Could I dredge up all those horrible memories on cue for financial gain, to save my marriage and possibly become a mother? I guess it was time I found out.

Lia Quinn looked about my age, curvy with russet brown skin and a makeup free face. Her thick brown hair was slicked up into a high ponytail. She showed up to our meeting in a belted denim dress and red leather espadrilles laced around her ankles. Her black leather backpack purse reminded me of the one Dana Shields from Haver House had, and instantly reminded me of what I thought I'd seen on her shoulder. Could this be a sign that I needed to agree to participate in this woman's documentary?

"Thanks for agreeing to meet with me, Mrs. West."

We were sitting in the same diner I'd had lunch at with my mother just the other day. I remembered how annoyed I'd been when she brought up Lia Quinn approaching her, and now here I was meeting her.

"Well, I had a feeling if I didn't, you'd be cornering my mother on her driveway again."

Lia had the good grace to look embarrassed. "Sorry about that. Desperation fuels poor decisions and I was desperate to get ahold of you."

"That brings me to my first question."

"Which is?" she asked eagerly.

"Why me?"

"I beg your pardon?"

"Why are you so hot to talk to me? I have nothing new to add to this story that hasn't already been written about a million times. Why do you need to talk to me in particular?" I took a sip of my iced tea, not taking my eyes off her. She didn't flinch or fidget and didn't look away.

"You were Brooke Peters' best friend, Mrs. West. I know most parents think they know their kids, but everyone has two sides, the side they show their family, especially their parents, and the side reserved for friends. Since no one has seen Brooke's mom or brother in more than two decades, that leaves you, the best friend."

"Again, what new information do you think I might be able to give you?"

"None of those other stories told us who Brooke was, they concentrated on the details of her abduction. None of them focused on her as a person. You knew her better than anyone."

She wasn't wrong. Every article ever written about Brooke's abduction was laser focused on what happened the day she was taken. Maps of the park and playground were dissected ad nauseam, re-enactments were shown on every major true crime show, as were potential getaway routes used by her abductors. One show even had a cigarette butt, and a can of cherry cola, found near where the abductor's car had been parked, analyzed for DNA evidence at the show's expense. They both belonged to a park maintenance worker who'd had his lunch in his car the day before. He ended up suing the show when the court of public opinion put a target on his back, making his life hell, and he had to move out of state. The re-enactments even showed the two female child actors portraying me and Brooke entering the park and heading to the swings. Nothing about how I'd hung out at Brooke's house all morning before her mother shooed us out the door to go play so she could clean.

Brooke had wanted to go over to my house, but I knew my mother would be hungover on the couch. We only ended up in the park that day because I'd done something I'd only ever managed to do once that entire summer. Beat Brooke in a swing race. She needed payback and I needed ice cream. We decided on both. I'd asked myself a million times, would she still be here if I hadn't insisted we get ice cream first?

"Wouldn't you like the world to know that your friend was more than just a little girl who was in the wrong place at the wrong time? Wasn't she more than just a victim of circumstance?"

Of course, she was more than just a victim, but was I ready to share Brooke with the world after all this time? My memories of her were all I had left. She was frozen in time. Forever ten years old. If I shared my memories, I'd also have to acknowledge all the things Brooke would never be or experience. I couldn't worry about that when I was also dealing with some very real issues. Instead of answering her question, I asked one of my own.

"My mother mentioned there might be payment for my participation?" My face flushed and I was instantly ashamed and embarrassed for asking. Was I selling Brooke out?

"That's right, Mrs. West. I received a seventy-five k grant to make this documentary and your payment for participating would be about fifteen k."

Fifteen grand just to tell the story of my best friend. Brooke's story didn't have a price, but given the small portion our insurance would cover, fifteen k would cover at least one round of IVF.

"If you can pay me the money upfront, I'll tell you everything I know."

"Does that include confirming or dispelling any rumors about Brooke and her family?"

"What rumors?" I was instantly wary. What was she talking about?

"There was a rumor I heard that was never followed up by the police, that Brooke's brother Sam abducted her because he was mad at his mother, and Brooke was accidentally killed in the process."

My mouth fell open in shock as I stared at her. "That's complete bullshit. Sam was six years older than us and busy with school and his own friends. The little bit of time he spent with Brooke, he spent being a good big brother. The only reason that rumor got started was because their mother, Julia, let him use her car to practice for his driver's exam in the parking lot of the park. He used to pick us up there sometimes."

"What about the arguments with his mother?"

"He was a typical teenager. I argued so much with my mom when I was his age, I'm surprised she didn't knock me to the moon. Besides, what happened to you only wanting to share who Brooke was as a person?"

"That wasn't a lie, but people are going to expect this documentary to be about more than just her favorite cereal and what her stuffed bear's name was."

"She hated cereal and her stuffed turtle's name was Willa."

Lia smiled, then picked up her phone. "Do you prefer cash app or Venmo, Mrs. West?"

"Venmo and you can call me, Ava."

"Can I bring my goldfish, Herman?"

"Yes, you can. Just no cats or dogs or any other furry mammals, Mrs. Timmons."

It was my first full day in the trenches at Haver House and so far, it was a bit chaotic. The shelter had eleven spots open, and I was in charge of intake for all eleven of the women who'd showed up needing shelter. Mrs. Timmons was an elderly woman who needed temporary accommodation until a spot opened up at a local nursing home. Like so many of the women at Haver House, she had no family or friends to help her and would have ended up on the street.

I hadn't seen Dana all morning and didn't know what I'd say to her if I did. I couldn't exactly ask her to show me her shoulder so I could check if her birthmark matched the one my best friend, who was missing and presumed dead, had. I don't go looking for ways to sound crazy.

It only took me until lunch time to do the intake for all the women, with half moving in that day. The rest would filter in throughout the week as the women who were leaving the shelter said their goodbyes. Haver House wasn't a long-term facility. Residents could stay as briefly as a week and as long as ninety days. The staff worked diligently to find permanent housing for the residents and even if permanent housing couldn't be found, a referral to long-term shelter could always be arranged.

I was eating a bowl of Mrs. Brady's delicious vegetable soup and a slice of sourdough bread in the dining room when Dana finally made an appearance. She glanced my way as she fixed her food and then promptly went and sat down at the opposite end of the table despite me smiling and waving her over. Feeling a bit stung, I quickly finished my soup before emptying my tray and dumping my dirty dishes in the plastic tub on the table next to the kitchen. I had one more hour left on my shift before I could leave and that was to cover Adele's lunch hour.

"I'm just going to zip out to pick up my prescriptions. Don't worry. I won't be gone long."

"I'll be fine. Take your whole lunch hour," I assured her as she rushed out the door.

I sat behind her desk checking my phone every five minutes to see if I'd had a call back from the fertility clinic I'd been trying to make an appointment at since that money from Lia Quinn had hit my bank account.

I'd told Evan about it and although he'd been happy, he wasn't nearly as happy as I'd thought he'd be. I wondered if he'd gotten himself into something to get money for the IVF that he couldn't get out of. Either way, I wasn't going to let whatever was going on with him ruin this. I had another shot at conceiving, and I was going to take it.

The phone on Adele's desk rang and I was happy to have something else to focus on besides my personal life, and quickly answered it.

"Haver House. How may I help you?" My greeting was met by staticky silence. "Hello? This is Haver House. How may I help you?"

"Mother?" The voice was raspy, and I couldn't tell whether it was a man or a woman.

"I'm sorry, but you've reached Haver House women's shelter. Is your mother a resident here?"

"I need to speak to my mother."

"What is your mother's name?" My question was met by several more seconds of static. "Hello? Are you still there?"

"Moseby? Her name is Mrs. Moseby."

"Let me just check to see if she's a..." The call suddenly dropped, filling my ear with dial tone. I hung up and called back only to get a message that the number I had reached was not accepting calls. There wasn't even a prompt to leave a voicemail.

I put the phone back on the receiver and looked up just in time to see Dana standing in the doorway looking confused.

"Sorry. Didn't mean to bother you." She turned to go, and I jumped up.

"No. It's fine. Did you need something, Dana?"

She looked a bit taken aback that I remembered her name and took a tentative step inside the office. Today she was wearing the same jean shorts and flip-flops from yesterday but with a faded blue and white striped T-shirt. I stared at her, trying to find any trace of Brooke, though it had been twenty-five years. We were only ten back then and hadn't gone through puberty yet, and all the changes that brought with it. I didn't look a whole lot like I did when I was ten. Did anyone? And why was I looking anyway? Brooke was not the only kid with a star-shaped birthmark on the back of their shoulder. More importantly, wouldn't she remember me? Even if she didn't remember my face. Wouldn't the name Ava stir some kind of memory in her? Again, this was ridiculous on my part. This woman wasn't Brooke.

"I was looking for Adele."

"She's at lunch. Is there anything I can help you with?"

"Yeah, my room is hotter than the tenth circle of hell. She said she'd get me a fan last night, but by the time I remembered she never gave me one, she was gone for the day. It's hard to sleep in a pool of your own sweat."

"Sorry about that. I'll get you a fan from the supply closet." I rummaged around Adele's desk drawer until I found a ring of keys, one of them labeled supply closet #2.

I found out during my training that each floor in the house had a supply closet. The one that held the box fans was on the second floor. By the time I walked the flight of stairs to the second floor, trailed by Dana, a light sheen of sweat had broken out on my forehead and my shirt was starting to stick to my back. How in the world did they function in this heat, especially on the upper floors since heat traveled upwards. I inserted the key into the lock and was met with mild resistance before I was able to turn it and get the door open. Hot air wafted out of the small room. I reached around on the wall next to the door trying to find the light, but Dana reached past me to pull the string that was dangling from a naked lightbulb in the ceiling.

"Thanks." I gave her a sheepish grin before walking into the small claustrophobic space.

On one side were shelves with blankets, bedding, and towels. The top shelf held cleaning supplies and toiletries the residents most likely didn't have upon arrival such as soap, deodorant, lotion, as well as industrial-sized boxes of tampons and sanitary napkins. Four brand-new window fans, still in their boxes, were stacked on the bottom shelf. I grabbed one of the fans and noticed a clipboard hanging next to the door. It showed what supplies had been taken from the closet, the date and time and the residents' signature. The initials AM were by each signature, and I assumed Adele had been the one to sign off on everything that had gone out of this closet. I grabbed the clipboard and handed it to Dana. "I guess you need to fill this out, so we know who has what."

"No problem."

She took the clipboard from me and used the pen to fill out the next available space. Then I signed my initials next to her signature. She turned to walk away after a mumbled thank you, but for some inexplicable reason I called out to her.

"How is everything going so far? Do you like it here?"

She gave me an unreadable expression before replying, "It's better than being out on the streets or living in my car, but my goal is to not be here longer than I have to be."

"Well, that's the goal for everyone here." I wasn't sure what else to say because it had been a stupid question, to begin with.

What person in their right mind was going to say everything was fine and dandy and that they were enjoying living in a homeless shelter?

"You are such an idiot, Ava," I whispered under my breath before adding, "Let me know if there's anything else you need. I'm here for another twenty minutes."

"You can help me get my window open so I can put this fan in it. I can't believe I'm the only one in that room who's having problems with the heat."

"Sure. Lead the way." I'm not sure why I was so happy she was letting me help her. Maybe it was making me feel less guilty about everything I took for granted in my life.

Dana was staying on the third floor of the house. It had once been a ballroom and was now a dorm-style bedroom with ten sets of bunk beds with a row of five on either side of the room. Between each set of bunk beds was a narrow locker big enough to hang a minimal amount of clothing, and underneath were too large drawers, one for each occupant of the bunk. There were two large picture windows at either end of the room with two sets of three windows on either side of the room between the bunks.

The room wasn't nearly as big on the inside as it seemed from the outside, and I realized that part of the room had been turned into a large bathroom. I'd seen every area of the shelter during my tour except this space. I was told there were a few residents sleeping after getting off the night shift. There were four large bedrooms on the second floor. Private rooms that housed women with children, and three bedrooms on the first floor that housed elderly residents with mobility issues.

Dana's bunk was at the end on the right side of the room with a window between it and the set of bunk beds next to it. Hers was the top bunk, and I noticed she had yellow comforter with white polka dots and one large white fluffy pillow. Yellow. Not pink, which had been Brooke's favorite color. Mine was purple and still was. Once I got a look at what was resting against her pillow, I stopped and took an involuntary step forward to get a better look. It was a small stuffed animal, once green and yellow and now dingy, grayish and faded with age, a turtle.

"What's this?" I started to pick it up but stopped with my hand outstretched momentarily before falling back down to my side. I continued to stare at it like it was an ancient relic, because it was.

"That's Willa," she said, not bothering to look at me as she unboxed the fan. "I've had her forever. She goes everywhere with me."

If someone had punched me in the face, I wouldn't have been nearly as shocked as I was over that one little word. Willa. Brooke's late father had given her Willa on her third birthday a mere month before he was killed in a motorcycle accident. Except for when she played in the park with me, she did in fact take Willa the turtle with her everywhere, even to school and sleepovers at my house. Willa was always there and now here she is again.

"Brooke?" I whispered under my breath.

"What?" Dana looked slightly annoyed, and I realized I was supposed to be helping her with the window, which she was now standing next to.

"Nothing." It came out slightly breathless as I suddenly couldn't catch my breath. I was having a panic attack. Willa? How the hell did she have Willa?

"Sit down and put your head between your knees. I'll be right back." Dana shoved me down onto the bottom bunk, which was empty because the woman who'd been sleeping there all this week left this morning.

By the time Dana got back with a cold bottle of water, I had calmed down and was breathing normally again because clarity had finally dawned on me. There is no way Dana's stuffed animal could be Brooke's Willa. Willa was not with her when she was abducted, and I'd never known her to bring Willa to the park with us. There were not a lot of things from my past that I remembered every detail of, but I did remember that Brooke did not have Willa with her when she was abducted. In the days following the abduction, Brooke's mom Julia held a press conference begging for Brooke's safe return while holding Willa and crying. I couldn't deny that this stuffed animal would look just like Willa would look twenty-five well-worn and well-loved years later. The coincidence was just too much to be completely dismissed. I caught a glimpse of a birthmark that looked very similar to Brooke's on the back of Dana's right shoulder and now she had a stuffed animal similar to Brooke's. It couldn't be anything but a coincidence, but it still rattled me.

"You good?"

She handed me the bottle of water, and I took it, uncapping it and taking a long swig. "I think I just got overheated. It's really hot up here. I don't know how you guys stand it."

"We stand it because we don't have any other choice. It's either sweat to death in this hot box or be out on the streets." She didn't sound angry just very matter-of-fact, and I felt like an idiot once again.

"Are you from Elmhurst, Dana?" I should have just shut up and left before I kept on putting my foot in my mouth, but I couldn't. There was something about this woman that drew me to her. Damned if I knew why.

"Are you from Elmhurst?"

"Yep. Elmhurst born and raised. The only time I left was when I went away to Miami University for college and grad school. Then I moved right back."

"You have a master's degree, and you decided to come back to this place? Couldn't you find a job anywhere else?"

"Well," I began, wondering how much of my life I should share with this complete stranger. "I had every intention of leaving but then I met my husband, and his business is here so here I am." But for how long? I was seeing the side of Evan recently that I didn't much like, and I couldn't see dealing with his attitude long-term whether I got pregnant or not.

"So, your family is here then?"

Dana was looking at me like she was really interested in my answer, but I knew what she was doing. In keeping me busy answering her questions, it kept her from having to answer mine. And that was fine, she didn't owe me any answers. My job wasn't to befriend her and become her confidant. My job was to tend to her needs as a resident of Haver House.

"Enough about me. Let's get this window of yours open so we can put the fan in." I got up from the bed and was surprised to notice Dana looked a little disappointed I hadn't answered her question.

Once we got the window open, which wasn't easy since it was old and sticking, we put the fan in. I headed back down to the office just as Adele was arriving back from lunch.

"How was your first hour alone manning the office? I'm assuming since you haven't run away screaming or torn your hair out that things must've gone well?"

"It was fine," I assured her. "The only time I left the office was to get Dana Shields a fan from the supply closet on the second floor. I made sure she filled out the clipboard that was hanging beside the door."

"Darn it," she whispered under her breath. "She asked for one yesterday and I was so busy I forgot about it."

"No problem. She didn't seem mad at all."

"Good, because they won't have to be depending on fans for much longer. We got some grant money and even though it's not enough to get a new furnace and central air, we do have money in the budget to put window air conditioners in all the bedrooms."

"That's great for them, but what about us?" I picked up the small fan on Adele's desk so it blew directly into my face.

"Well, if there's money left over after buying air conditioners for the bedrooms, then we can absolutely get one for this office. I guess I'm just so used to it that it doesn't bother me as much anymore."

"My husband has his own construction company and there's always stuff left behind from jobs. What if I could snag a window air conditioner for the office?"

"Then I would love you forever."

"Oh, there was one weird thing that happened. Someone called looking for their mother. They said her name was Mrs. Moseby, but they hung up before I had a chance to look her up in the resident directory."

Adele froze and stared at me expressionless before letting out a nervous chuckle that felt forced. "We had a Mrs. Moseby here. She was one of our very first residents when we opened, but she went to live with her daughter and last I'd heard she died. Did they leave a number?"

"No. Just hung up and the number they called from isn't accepting calls."

"Well, that certainly wouldn't be the weirdest call we ever got. People call here all the time mistaking us for Haven House Dog Rescue."

We both laughed and I grabbed my purse from the bottom desk drawer. I was about to head out when Adele stopped me.

"Just a heads-up, Ava. Be careful around Dana Shields."

"Why? She seems perfectly nice. Did she do something?"

"I can't quite put a finger on it, but there's something off about her. I caught her in here when I got back from the restroom yesterday. It looked like she was looking for something, but when I asked her what it was, she asked me for the fan. It just felt like an excuse. Sure enough, when I looked in my drawer later, all the change was gone from the ashtray I keep in my drawer."

"You think she took it?"

"I'm not sure what I think. I used that change as petty cash and it was only a few dollars. But just be careful."

"Got it." I left, feeling an odd sense of disappointment. As I walked to my car, a sudden memory hit me: Brooke used to steal things, too.

SIX

AVA AND BROOKE

April 2000

"Where did you get all that?" Ava stared down in wonder at the big plastic bag of candy that Brooke had brought over to her house.

"I stole it from Sam," she said and then giggled so hard she made Ava giggle, too.

"Isn't he going to notice it's gone. It's a lot of candy."

"He won't notice it's gone until he gets the munchies after smoking weed with his boys."

"You are so bad." Ava reached inside the bag and pulled out a full-size Snickers bar, ripped off the paper and took a big bite.

Brooke pulled out a pack of Reese Cups and tore into them with equal excitement. The only time they were allowed candy like this was at Halloween, and since both girls had such big, sweet tooths, the candy was usually all gone a week later. Ava had finished her candy bar in three bites and was reaching inside the bag for some Hershey's Kisses when Brooke let her in on another secret.

"That's not all I got, either." She reached back into her back-pack, shoving aside Willa the turtle, and pulled out a tube of pink frosted lip gloss. She twisted the cap off and coated her lips with it, then blew Ava a kiss.

"Where did you get that from? I know your mom didn't buy that for you. We can't wear makeup until we're sixteen."

"I stole it from my babysitter, Brianna. She's got so much makeup she'll never even miss it, and if she does, I'll just tell my mom she lets her boyfriend Chris come over after mom told her she couldn't have boys over while she was babysitting. Instead of watching me, all they do is kiss and hug on the couch." Brooke leaned forward and, before Ava could stop her, she dabbed Ava's upper and lower lip with the gloss. "Just take your finger and rub it in all the way. It already looks great on you."

Ava did as she was told, but the gloss felt thick and unnatural on her lips. She didn't dare say anything because she knew it would make Brooke mad, and she didn't want her to stop being her friend. They spent the next hour gorging themselves on the candy to the point where Brooke nearly threw up. Both girls ran into the bathroom to wash the gloss off their lips as soon as they heard Ava's mom's key in the door.

"You better go. My mom is really grouchy until she gets her after-work wine." Ava was too embarrassed to tell Brooke that her mom had lost her job and her after-work wine had turned into her all-day-long wine. It wouldn't surprise her if her mom was half-drunk already.

While Ava's mom was putting away some groceries in the kitchen, Ava snuck Brooke out the front door. It wasn't until hours later, after she'd had her bath and was about to go to bed, that she realized her favorite pair of barrettes was missing from her dresser.

SEVEN

DANA

Dana left her car at the shelter and took a city bus to the Elmhurst Community College campus. With her shorts, tank top, flip-flops, and black backpack slung across her back, she looked just like a student. Maybe not one fresh out of high school, but with this being a community college that served students of all ages, she knew she fit right in. Classes had only been in session for a few days, so nobody batted an eye lid when she asked directions to the classroom she was looking for. Once she located the lecture hall where Calculus I was being taught, she was happy to see the class was already underway. She slipped inside the lecture hall, taking a seat in the back. The instructor, a white guy in his early forties, was teaching and Dana made just enough noise when she entered to cause the instructor, whose back was to the class, to turn to see who had just come in. She could tell by the tightness of his mouth that he was about to chastise her for being late.

Instead, when he looked at her, all the color drained from his face and he did a double take before quickly turning back to the chalkboard to finish whatever he was writing. She sat there for the entire forty-five-minute class with him occasionally looking up to where she sat to see if she was still there, and probably hoping she was a figment of his imagination, but she wasn't going anywhere.

At least not yet. When the lecture was mercifully over with, because the instructor's delivery had all the personality of wet paint, she waited until all the students had left before putting her backpack on and heading down the steps to talk to him. It had been a very long time since she'd last seen him, and close up, she couldn't help but notice how badly he was aging. He pretended not to notice her standing there as he quickly gathered his things to put inside a large leather briefcase that he probably thought made him look more important than he actually was. Finally, when he realized she wasn't about to leave, he looked up with an exasperated sigh.

"Can I help you? And make it quick because I have another class I'm running late for. It'll probably be best if you catch me during my office hours."

"Now, Joshy, you're just being rude. It's been a long time, but I know you remember me. I'm probably the one person in your entire miserable life that you can't forget."

That got his full attention. He looked up at her, and then to the doors of the lecture hall where students for the next class were waiting in the hallway to enter.

"What do you want?"

"I want a lot of things and none of them would be very beneficial to you. I just came here to warn you."

"About what in particular?" He looked at her again, with the same disdain he always had for people like her – people with brown skin.

It was a look that reminded her that, had things been different, he wouldn't be associating with her at all. Back in the day their circumstances made them equals in the eyes of society and she wasn't going to let him forget it.

"I came to tell you to get your affairs in order, Joshy. Justice is coming."

She turned to go when he stopped her, a frantic edge to his voice.

"What do you mean?"

"The *mother* of our big secret is about to sing like a bird. The twenty-fifth anniversary is coming up next month and she wants to clear her conscience, and she's got all of the receipts. All of them."

"Well, if she's got my receipts, then she's got yours, too!" He called out after her as she climbed the steps.

Once she got to the top, she turned and gave him a smile. "Yeah, but I was an innocent victim, and my receipts won't land me in jail."

"Get the hell out of my classroom," he hissed.

Dana exited the classroom quickly, heading out the nearest exit to catch the next bus back into town, satisfied that her plan to be free of her past was in motion.

EIGHT

LIA

Now that I had Ava West on board, I could breathe a little, just a little. Ray was certainly happy, but for the first time I wondered if she'd be able to give me enough information to carry this documentary. So far, I had scheduled interviews with Brooke's teachers and a few of her former neighbors, and now her best friend was willing to participate. I was surprised she'd been so willing, but I guess it was true that everybody had a price. Even me. Though, something was still missing. I still needed that big plot twist. I needed information that nobody else had, and as much as I didn't want to, I pulled the phone number up on my phone that had been given to me by someone who had gone to church with Brooke's family every Sunday. A woman named Mavis Brady. I took a deep breath and dialed the number hoping that this wouldn't be like pulling teeth. Getting people to talk about this poor girl who disappeared twenty-five years ago was proving harder than I ever imagined. It wasn't just that their memories were foggy, since it had been more than two decades, there was something else going on here. There was a reason these people were so reluctant to talk about Brooke Peters. Maybe when I found out why that was, I'd find my big plot twist.

NINE

AVA

For once Evan and I had a good day. We spent the morning at Asher Clinic with a fertility specialist named Dr. Regina Glenn. Dr. Glenn thought we were the perfect candidates for IVF. She told us to have realistic expectations as it may take more than one round, and I needed to have one normal menstrual cycle before we even started the process. I was paying for this first round, and Evan promised that if we needed to do a second round, he'd pay for it. Beyond that I didn't know what would happen or where the money would come from if two rounds didn't work.

"Thanks, babe." Evan reached over and squeezed my thigh while we were in the car on the way home.

"For what?" It had been so long since my husband had touched me in an intimate way, I was shocked at my response. A couple of months had passed since we'd made love and now, I was feeling shy and awkward at his touch.

"For putting up with my ass. I know I haven't been the easiest person to live with. There's just a lot going on."

"Like what?" I knew he'd been disappointed when I told him I wanted to put having a baby on hold for a while, but he never let on that there was anything else bothering him.

"I had to let a couple of my guys go. I hate that shit. I've never had to let anybody who worked for me go for reasons other than doing a shitty job. Now, instead of managing the day-to-day business, I've had to take their places on the construction site."

"Why didn't you tell me this sooner? IVF is going to cost a lot of money. We could've waited for a while. Possibly even next year, until your business is more stable again."

"Neither one of us is getting any younger and if it's not now, then something else may come up next year to push us back even further."

We were silent for a while with Evan still massaging my thigh. Suddenly, the flame his touch had ignited was snuffed out. I knew I needed to get over these feelings. I squeezed his hand instead and said, "Why don't I make us a special dinner tonight to celebrate?"

He gave me a big grateful smile, which I knew was because I'd stopped asking questions he didn't want to answer. At the next red light, he leaned over and gave me a soft kiss. As my lips parted and the kiss deepened, my mind couldn't shake the fact that something still felt off with him.

Later that night, as we lay curled naked in bed, I was falling to sleep with Evan's soft snoring in my ear, when my phone beeped with a message. It was after midnight. Who in the world would be texting me at this time of night? Fearing it might be my mother or some other kind of emergency, I reached out and grabbed my phone from the bedside table. I'd been wrong. It wasn't a text message, it was an alert from our doorbell camera that someone was on the front porch. I pulled up the camera feed and let out a loud gasp. Standing on our front porch looking dead into the camera was a figure in a black baggy suit, a baseball cap pulled low over their face. I sat bolt upright and screamed, waking Evan.

"What's wrong?"

I went to show him my phone, but there was nothing in my hands. I looked over and saw my phone on my bedside table where I'd put it before I climbed into bed. That's when I realized it had just been a dream. I couldn't stop trembling, and Evan pulled me into his arms.

"It was a nightmare," I said, still trembling as he stroked my hair and back. "It was just a nightmare. I'm sorry. I didn't mean to wake you up." I tried to pull out of his arms, but he held on fast. That small act of kindness from my husband after weeks of being frozen out and made to feel wrong, made me cry.

"It's okay, babe. I got you. I've always got you," he whispered into my hair, making me instantly tense up. What had he just said?

"Well, where the hell have you been for the past two months? Why didn't you have me then when I needed you the most?" I pulled out of his embrace, got out of bed and grabbed my robe from a nearby chair as I headed downstairs to the kitchen.

I poured myself a glass of water and was half finished with it by the time Evan came down the stairs, giving me a contrite look.

"I am so sorry. I'll do anything to make it up to you. Just tell me what you need. I know it won't make up for the last couple of months, but I'm here now."

For some reason his calm, reassuring tone, like he was trying to calm an angry dog, made me even more annoyed. "For how long? What happens if the IVF doesn't work? Are you going to go back to treating me like I don't exist? And heaven forbid I want to take a break again."

"Babe, I..."

"Babe my ass. What the hell is going on with you, Evan? Why are you so against adoption? What does it matter how we get to be parents as long as we get to be parents? I thought you of all people would understand that."

My husband sighed heavily and leaned against the kitchen island. I could see the indecision flitting across his face and was suddenly terrified of what he was about to say. He gently took my hand, and I resisted the urge to yank it out of his grasp. I allowed myself to be led over to the kitchen table and sat down. He sat across from me, but seemed hesitant to explain himself.

"Evan? What is it?" I said, reaching out to touch his hand, causing him to finally look at me.

"Something happened six months ago."

"What?"

"I got a letter from a lawyer claiming to represent my mother's estate."

"Your mother?"

Evan had been raised by his paternal grandmother until he was six, having been the product of an affair between his mother, a married white woman, and his father, a local black handyman. Not wanting her husband to find out, she hid her pregnancy, gave birth in secret, and signed away her parental rights. She turned baby Evan over to his father who gave him to his own mother to raise. After Evan's grandmother died, he went to live with his father, an abusive alcoholic. When his dad died five years later, he was placed in foster care until he aged out at eighteen, already on a path to prison.

"What did the letter say?"

"That she left me some money. A lot of money."

"How much money are we talking?"

"Two hundred and fifty thousand dollars."

"What!" I stood straight up, almost sending my chair toppling backwards. That's when it hit me and I sat back down, hard. "This is what you meant when you said you'd get the money for the IVF treatments, wasn't it?"

He merely nodded and I felt horrible for not trusting him, but what else was I supposed to think? "Why didn't you tell me? Why keep this from me?" I felt myself starting to get angry again.

"Because I'm not sure I want her damned guilt money. I needed a mother. I wanted *her*, and that's not anything she can make up for by giving me a check after the fact. It feels like bonus pay for staying away from her so she could pretend I didn't exist."

"You knew who she was? How did you find out?"

"I've always known. My dad told me during one of his drunken rages. He loved reminding me how unwanted I'd been by the both of them, a shitty little consequence that ruined the good thing he had going with her. That's what he used to call me. His shitty little consequence. I was only a kid." Evan buried his head in his hands. I got up and went to him, wrapping my arms around him from behind. He turned and buried his face against me.

We stayed like that for a few minutes before he pulled away and I sat down next to him.

"I'm so sorry, Evan. I had no idea you went through all of that." I knew he'd had it rough growing up, but had no idea it had been that bad.

"It wasn't all bad. After my grandma died, I went to live with this amazing couple, the Davises, Jeff and Lori. The eight months I was with them was the happiest time of my life. They tried to adopt me."

"What happened?" As a social worker I already knew. Children can't be adopted unless their parents agree to it. In Evan's case, his father.

"My dad found out and decided he wanted me, especially after he realized he could get public assistance by having a kid. One minute I was a happy six-year-old in a loving home with two people who chose me, the next I was back with my piece of shit father who couldn't hold a job and disappeared on benders as soon as he got that check on the first of the month. By the time I was removed from his custody, the Davises had moved overseas."

Understanding finally dawned on me, and I reached out and wiped my husband's angry tears away with my fingers. "That's why you don't want to adopt, isn't it? You're afraid that what happened with the Davises could happen to us."

"I couldn't deal with that, Ava, and I damned sure couldn't put a little kid through that. Giving them hope only to have it snatched away."

Now wasn't the time to convince him he had nothing to worry about. Instead, I put my arms around him hoping his admission could finally propel us forward, whether I got pregnant or not.

· · ·

The shelter was at capacity, so there were no more new residents to go through intake. I went in any way to see if there was anything I could help Adele with. It was a good thing I did because Adele had called off sick and when I got there, Kerri was trying to break up a dispute in the dining room between two women playing cards.

"She's a cheater. I don't want anything to do with cheaters," said a woman named Wilma, a middle-aged woman who, according to Adele, had bipolar disorder and wasn't good about taking her meds.

"And she's crazy," said the other woman. I recognized her as Mrs. Timmons, the elderly woman with the goldfish who was only there for a short time while waiting for a nursing home placement.

I started to go over to see if Kerri needed help when she turned to me and shook her head, indicating she had it under control. So I headed back to Adele's office and started sorting the mail, most of which were bills. I arranged them into piles and noticed one of them was from a security company I recognized from working for Children's Services. If I was correct, in the envelope were background checks on all the residents. Every resident had to submit to a background check before they were allowed to stay at Haver House.

In light of what Adele had told me about Dana's possible stealing, I was hot to open the envelope to see if she had a criminal background. Indecision ping-ponged around my brain and my fingers twitched, itching to rip open the envelope and read the reports. After all, even though I wasn't getting paid, I was technically working here. Shouldn't I be privy to the information about the residents I was working with? Thankfully, the decision was taken out of my hands when Kerri finally arrived back in the office, having escorted Mrs. Timmons back to her room and determining that Wilma had indeed not taken her meds for two days.

"That looked pretty intense back there."

"That's the third time in two days that Wilma has flared up like that. If she keeps up this behavior and refuses to take her meds, we may have to find her another place to stay. We take the safety of our residents very seriously. We want them to feel safe here."

"The heat also doesn't help. I'm cranky too when I'm too hot."

"Me too," Kerri conceded. "But I'm not violent when I'm cranky, just annoying. Wilma swung on poor Mrs. Timmons. She's eighty-two. Wilma could have knocked her down and she could have broken a hip or something."

"I'm not sure we can force Wilma to take her meds. Do you think we can make it a requirement for her continued stay here?"

"Maybe. I'll have to talk to Selma. At any rate I'll have to write this up in my report."

When I had my tour of the facility, I was supposed to meet Selma Ross, the director, but she'd been called away to an impromptu meeting.

"Maybe I'll finally get to meet her today. Is she around?"

"Should be. She's got an open-door policy, so just go knock on her door. I'd introduce you, but I need to write this up before I go." I got up to give Kerri access to Adele's computer and headed out into the foyer.

By now, everything had quieted down. Wilma was outside taking a cigarette break. When I got to the director's office, I noticed her door was slightly ajar and I could hear her talking on the phone. I should have waited and came back later. Instead, I listened.

"Tell her to take all the time she needs, James. We can hold down the fort in her absence."

I wondered if she was talking about Adele, only because she was the only person who wasn't around today. When Selma ended her call, I waited another sixty seconds before knocking on her door.

"Come in."

I walked into a surprisingly large and spacious office with a large picture window that looked out over the backyard. I was also surprised to see a window air conditioner cranking out cool air from a side window. I guess being the director earned her some perks, but her sitting in a cool office while the rest of us were sweating it out in the heat made me more than a little annoyed. It must've shown on my face, judging by the way Selma Ross laughed.

"You must be Ava West, right? I wondered when I'd finally get to meet you. I'm Selma." She stood up and held out her hand, which I shook.

Her engaging smile caught me off guard, making me instantly like her despite what I thought when I walked into the office. It still sucked that the rest of us weren't able to work in such comfort, but the woman's palpable charm suddenly took the sting out of my anger.

Selma Ross was an attractive older black woman. I guessed she was around my mom's age; late fifties. Selma wore a black T-shirt with a floral print wrap skirt. Her dark brown hair, liberally sprinkled with streaks of gray, was pulled back into a messy bun at the back of her head and large gold hoop hung from her earrings. Her perfume was subtle. Although there was nothing fancy about what she was wearing, I could tell that everything was well-made and expensive.

"It's so nice to meet you, Selma. I figured I better come and finally introduce myself since you were at a meeting on my first day."

"I'm so glad you did. I was planning to come introduce myself today but haven't been able to pull myself away from the phone all morning. Welcome. We are so glad you're here. I hear you've already been through your first intake. How did that go?"

"It was fine. I'm happy to be of service to these women."

"Kerri tells me you guys are former coworkers at Children's Services?"

"That's right. I'm on a leave of absence right now, but I go back to work full time next month."

"Are you planning to stay on here in some capacity after you return to work?"

"That's the plan." Truthfully, I hadn't given what happens

after I went back to work much thought. I liked it here and hoped I could continue.

Then I remembered how fried I felt at the end of most of my days working for Children's Services. I would go to work so full of hope and ready to help every morning, and come home completely heartbroken over the situations where my hands were tied. Here it felt like I was making a difference in a way that I couldn't at my regular job. The realization of that brought unexpected tears to my eyes. If Selma noticed, she didn't let on.

"I'm glad to hear that. Whatever time you can give us is greatly appreciated."

"Thank you. I can see that you're busy. So, I'll let you get back to work." I turned to go when she stopped me.

"Ava. There's a window air conditioner for Adele's office in the supply closet down the hall. Adele is the one who pays all the shelter's bills, and she can be very frugal when it comes to saving us money. She's the reason why none of the window units have been installed yet. Running them raises the electricity bill. She's trying to come up with rules for everyone, so they aren't running all day, but she's just stalling. So please don't think I'm in here living it up in comfort while the rest of you are suffering. Maybe you can talk her into finally putting these window units in. Kerri tried and failed, but maybe she'll listen to you."

"I most certainly will and thanks for letting me know."

When I left the director's office, I wasted no time pulling one of the window units out of the supply closet wondering why Adele hadn't mentioned they'd already been purchased when she'd told me about the grant. I dragged it into the hot stuffy office and proceeded to unbox it. If Adele got mad, so be it. She could always turn the air conditioner off when she was working here. Making the rest of us toil in this humid environment meant a hostile work setting as far as I was concerned.

To get to the window that I would have to install the unit in, I had to pull a short filing cabinet away from in front of the window. On top was an aloe plant and a picture of Adele and her husband. It looked a good twenty years old, with a much slimmer Adele smiling from underneath a veil, standing next to a tall, handsome black man. Both were beaming like they'd just won the lottery. I remembered that feeling; my own wedding day and how magical it felt. I had no idea that eight years later I'd be married to a man I could barely stand some days. Yet here I was trying to have a baby with him.

The other side of the frame held another picture, a more recent one of her and her husband, still looking like they'd won the lottery. I removed the picture and the plant and pulled the low filing cabinet out of the way, and heard something fall behind it. I reached down to pick it up. It was a framed degree for Dr. Adele Mackie, a psychiatrist.

Adele was a doctor. Was she retired from her field? Granted she only looked like she was in her mid-to-late fifties but that didn't mean she couldn't have retired early. Was that why she was working here as an admin assistant? I sat the framed degree on top of the desk and then got busy installing the air conditioner. By the time I left two hours later, the room was nice and cool, but I made sure to turn it off before I left.

I stopped at the grocery store on the way home. Now that things had gotten better with Evan, dinners were more tolerable, and we were actually spending time together instead of him disappearing down to the lower level to park himself in front of the TV with a beer. I was headed home through downtown when I saw something at a traffic light that almost made me stop, and nearly miss being rear ended. The car behind swerved around me and the driver laid on his horn, flashing me the finger as he passed, but I was too busy staring at the two women arguing on the corner across the street to my left. It was Dana Shields and Adele, who hardly looked sick to me. Although her face was red. It was red from anger as she and Dana went back and forth with Dana gesticulating wildly and Adele looking like she was ready to explode.

I had no choice but to go through the intersection because another car was laying on their horn behind me. I hadn't moved when the light turned green, so I drove through the intersection and then round at the corner to see what was going on and if either woman needed help. It looked like whatever was going on was escalating to the point where the two seemed like they were about to come to blows. Once I'd rounded the corner to park and get out, they were gone. I looked around to see if I could see either woman walking down the street or driving off, but they were gone. I even walked up one side of the block, then across the street and down the other side to see if they were sitting inside one of the restaurants or cafés, but they were nowhere to be found.

TEN

LIA

"Thank you so much for meeting with me, Mrs. Brady. I appreciate you taking the time to answer a few questions for me."

We were at a diner a few blocks from Mrs. Brady's church, Mount Hope. I needed to be quick because she didn't have much time before she had to be at church to teach adult Sunday school. That was the only thing that got me out of bed practically at the crack of dawn. Granted it was almost 9 o'clock, but the night owl in me cringed when she told me what time she wanted to meet. It had meant going to bed at a decent hour, to be up and functional at that early hour.

"When you said you were making a documentary about that poor Peters girl, I could hardly not agree, now, could I?"

"A lot of the people in this town don't seem to want to talk about Brooke Peters. Would you happen to know why that is?"

"Are you gonna record me?" she asked as she eyed my recorder which I'd placed in the center of the table.

"Yes, ma'am. That's the way it works. You tell your story, and I go over it to see if it's something that we can use for the documentary. Do I have your permission to do that?"

"Shouldn't you have asked me that before you brought that recorder out?"

My face burned with embarrassment, but she threw her head back and laughed.

"I don't care if you record me. What I'm gonna tell you is nothing but pure facts and everybody in this town knows it. All I ask is that, if you put me in front of a camera, make sure you get my left side because that's my best side. You got that?"

"Absolutely." I liked this woman already and had a good feeling about this interview.

"What is it you wanna know?"

"What were the Peters like? And I'm not just talking about Brooke. I'm talking about her mom and her older brother Sam, too?"

"You need to be asking me about that deadbeat daddy of hers?"

Despite the time I'd spent doing research on Brooke Peters and her family, her father was someone I had very little information on.

"And what about her father? I was under the impression that he was deceased?"

Mavis Brady let out a snort of laughter before taking a sip of her black coffee. "And how did you come to that conclusion? Did you find an obit on him?"

"No." That was because I hadn't bothered to look for Brooke's father's obit. When everyone I talked to just said he was gone, by gone I thought they meant dead. Now, I felt stupid for not having done my due diligence.

"Well, what does that tell you, young lady? That man is alive as you and me, although Julia told Brooke he was dead because he may as well have been."

"What about Sam? Was he also told his father was dead?"

"Brooke and Sam didn't have the same daddy. Julia was actually married to Sam's daddy. They split up when he was seven, when she found out she and her husband had a little bit too much in common, if you know what I mean."

It took me a few seconds to realize exactly what she was talking about.

"You mean he's gay?"

"Yep. He's gay. Last I heard he's living in Florida with his partner, and they've been together twice as long as he was with Julia. I don't think he's in Sam's life, but who knows about now. I haven't seen them in years."

"What about Brooke's father? Was he ever in her life?"

"Every once in a while, he'd turn up with some gift for Brooke and spend a little time with her. Just long enough for Julia to think he'd straightened himself out and was home for good to be the man she'd always dreamed of. Never happened and was never gonna happen."

"Why was that?"

"Coz he was an addict. That's why. Strung out on that crack mess. He used to be such a good-looking young man, too, but then them drugs got a hold of him. Last time I saw him he looked like he could've been on that show that was popular a while back. What was it called? Walking and dead?"

"You mean *The Walking Dead*?" I had to bite my lip to keep from laughing in this woman's face.

"Whatever. All I know is he left Julia when Brooke was about three."

"You never saw him again?"

"Actually, I did see him. A few years later, I saw him in town. It looked like he had gotten his life together although he wasn't back to his old fine self, but he looked a hell of a lot better."

"Where did you see him? Did you speak to him?"

"He was across the street when I was coming out of the dry cleaners. Back when we still had a dry cleaner. He looked at me. I looked at him. We nodded at each other and that was that. By the time I got my clothes settled across my backseat, I looked back and he was gone."

"What's his name?"

"You really aren't very good at this research stuff, are you? How are you gonna make a documentary when you don't know half of what was going on in that girl's life?"

"That's why I'm talking to you. I was told you knew everything that went on in this town. Is that true?"

Mrs. Brady had a smug, satisfied look on her face and took a long, drawn-out sip of her coffee purposefully making me wait for whatever juicy tidbits she was about to drop onto my lap. It took everything in me not to reach out and pull the words out of her mouth.

"His name is Nathaniel Peters. Born and raised right here in Elmhurst. Ran off to New York City right out of high school trying to be a rapper and no one saw him for about twelve years. Then he turned up back here in town and started dating Julia Dodson, and knocked her up without the benefit of marriage. Only thing he had to give that child was his name and that was of questionable worth."

"Was he already an addict when he came back to town?"

"If I was a betting woman, and except for church bingo, I am not, I'd say he probably was, but when he got home and couldn't find work, he hooked up with his old bad crowd of friends. It probably made a small problem a bigger one."

"Do you know why he was back in town a few years after he left?"

"His mama died. He was back for the funeral. I think he tried and succeeded in getting back together with Julia for a hot minute. The next thing I knew Julia was looking like her dog had just died at church and someone told me she'd kicked him out because he did something to Brooke."

That made me sit up straight and stare at her in shock. "I never heard this story. Do you know what he did to Brooke?"

"No one would really say. All I know is it didn't have anything to do with him molesting her or anything like that. Though it was bad enough for Julia to slash his face with a knife and threatened to kill him if she saw his miserable butt again."

Was this the reason why no one ever wanted to talk about Brooke? And why didn't Nathaniel Peters go to jail if what he had done was so bad that Julia had cut him with a knife? And where was Nathaniel now?

"Why didn't she report him to the police?"

"Because she knew if she did, she could get arrested, too, for cutting him, and then Sam and Brooke would be handed over to their fathers. Sam would have been fine. It was Brooke she was worried about. Nate wasn't a good father."

"Mrs. Brady, what do you think happened to Brooke Peters?"

The elderly woman's face instantly went slack before her eyes filled with tears. She shook her head and looked away. "Isn't it obvious? That baby is dead."

"You think her abductor killed her?" Of course that's what everyone thought. That Brooke Peters had been abducted by a child molester and killed, and her remains were yet to be found. Instead of answering my question, Mavis Brady reached out and switched off the recorder.

"I can't have this being recorded." She sat up straight in the booth with her shoulders back, her head jutted forward. Her eyes were wide.

"You can't have what being recorded?" What was this woman about to tell me and why was she suddenly looking so scared.

I slid my hand inside my purse, which was next to me in the booth, and grabbed my backup recorder and pressed the record button. Ohio was a one-party state, meaning only one person taking part in a conversation had to consent to it being recorded. As far as this conversation was concerned, that one person was me.

"Mrs. Brady? Are you okay? Do you want to stop?"

"No, but this isn't for your documentary, and I mean it. Enough people have been hurt by what happened to Brooke, and I don't want Natalie and Ava suffering any more than they already have."

"What do you mean?" I knew what she was talking about, but I wanted to hear her say it.

"What happened to Brooke traumatized Ava. She had to see a therapist for years afterwards because she kept having nightmares, and for a long time she wouldn't even talk. I ran into her recently and she seems to be doing just fine. No need to dredge up information that'll make her feel bad all over again, and probably even cause a problem between her and her mama."

"What would cause Ava West to have an issue with her mother over what happened to Brooke?"

Mrs. Brady drained the last of her coffee and held up a hand to the girl behind the counter to bring her more. Once her coffee cup was filled to the brim again, Mrs. Brady turned her attention back to me and let out a weary sigh.

"Natalie, her mama, lost her mind when her husband Clay left her for a woman he'd met up in Seattle. She wanted to blame everything on the other woman, but it was hardly Clay's first rodeo. Everybody knew he was always running around on her. There was only one way that marriage was going to end up, with Natalie left in the lurch and broken-hearted."

"But how does this..." I began before she held up a hand.

"I'm getting there. Don't rush me, young lady. It's rude."

"Sorry. Please continue." I was not a patient person, and it was killing me waiting to hear what she was about to tell me.

"Now, like I said, Natalie completely fell apart when Clay left. Usually, he was content just to run around on her. I honestly don't think she cared as long as he kept coming back to her every night. Once he made it clear he wasn't coming back, and she and Ava weren't welcome in Seattle, she had a breakdown. Started drinking. She was about to lose the house, too, because Clay refused to send her any money, he was too busy spending it on that other gal. Instead of letting the house go and getting an apartment she could afford, she did something truly stupid and borrowed money from some people she had no business borrowing money from. Then she couldn't keep up with the payments. These are people you do not wanna leave hanging. They want their money, and they get it by any means necessary."

I stared at her, and she fixed me with her steely gaze, willing me to understand what she was trying to say. It took a minute, but I finally got it, and the bottom dropped out of my stomach and adrenaline rushed through my veins.

"You think they got the wrong girl, don't you? You think the plan had been to kidnap Ava because of Natalie not paying her debt, but the kidnappers made a mistake and got Brooke instead?"

She nodded as a single tear trickled out of the corner of her eye, and she angrily wiped it away with the back of her hand. "I think Brooke saw those men's faces and when they realized they had the wrong girl, they got rid of her."

More tears followed and I knew I should have handed this woman a tissue, but I was too excited to think about anything other than the two words that instantly popped into my head. Plot twist. I had my plot twist.

"Did you ever share this theory with the police?"

Mavis Brady vigorously shook her head and then, after wiping her eyes, grabbed her giant purse and slung it over her arm and exited the booth. "I already told you I won't be sharing that theory because it won't bring that little girl back. It will cause even more damage if I'm right, and I hope to God I'm not right. Now, you have a blessed day, young lady, and don't forget what I told you about my left side."

I watched her leave and once she was gone, I looked inside my purse, only to discover my recorder's battery died exactly a minute and twelve seconds into the older woman's story. I sat back against the vinyl booth and almost started crying myself.

ELEVEN

AVA

When I went back to the shelter the following week, I was happy to see Adele back at work. I was unsure what kind of reception I would get after I'd put the window air conditioners in not only in her office but two in the large dorm Dana stayed, and one in each of the bedrooms on the second and first floors. When I walked into Adele's office, I was surprised the air conditioner was on. However, it was on its lowest setting and while the room was cooler, it was just cool enough to be comfortable.

"Hey, Adele. How are you feeling?"

"Better. Thanks so much for holding down the fort. I see you got a lot done while I was gone." She nodded towards the window and at first, I thought she might be mad I had infringed on her territory.

"Yeah, it was getting pretty bad in here. Selma told me the window units were in the supply closet down the hall, and just so you know everyone is so much happier and cooler. I hope you don't mind?" I really didn't care whether she minded or not. It was ridiculous to work in that kind of heat when we didn't have to.

"Thanks, Ava. If you knew how I grew up, then you'd under-stand that being frugal and saving money was ground into me by my parents. It's a hard mindset to shake and spills over into every area of my life. I don't know how my husband puts up with me."

"How long have you been married?"

"James and I have been married for twenty-seven years." She smiled and glanced over at the framed wedding pictures on the filing cabinet that sat under the window with the air-conditioning unit in it. Then she got a glimpse of what was next to it and a frown instantly popped up on her face. She was staring at the framed degree which had fallen behind the filing cabinet. Why did she look annoyed? She had to have been the one to bring it to the office. How else would it have gotten here otherwise?

"Is something wrong?"

She got up and snatched the framed degree and shoved it into her desk drawer.

"No. I'm good. Just someone's idea of a stupid joke that I didn't find funny."

She was so agitated that I didn't bother pressing her further, but there was something I wanted to know.

"Hey, I don't mean to pry, but I could've sworn I saw you downtown last week having a very intense-looking conversation with Dana Shields. Was it about your stolen change?"

She gave me a completely blank look and then shrugged. "I honestly have no idea what you're talking about. I've been sick with a sinus infection, and I didn't leave the house for days."

"Oh, I'm sorry. I must've been mistaken." I hadn't been mistaken. I had definitely seen Adele arguing with Dana downtown. So, why was she lying?

"We've got about six new residents going through intake this morning. You can go ahead and use this office while I get the paperwork and help the six women who are leaving today."

She left the office so quickly it didn't take a genius to figure out she wanted to get away from me.

· · ·

Adele managed to find an excuse not to come back to the office while I was there even after intake was over. I took a short break on the back porch and was stopped by Mrs. Brady on my way back in.

"If you're hungry, I made up some box lunches. You can just grab one out of the fridge. You got your choice of turkey, roast beef, and tuna salad sandwiches. Even got one with just cheese and veggies for the non-meat eaters. Got some of my potato salad in there, too, and some snickerdoodles."

"That sounds delicious, Mrs. Brady. Thanks for letting me know." I headed past her into the kitchen to snag a box of lunch even though my shift would be over in an hour. I could easily grab something for lunch on my way home, but I wasn't about to turn down any of Mrs. Brady's food."

"Just make sure you get one before they're gone. Adele even grabbed one before she took off."

"She left? When? Has she gone for the day?"

"Yep. About twenty minutes ago. I don't think she's coming back because she said she was starting to feel bad again. Apparently not bad enough to not eat because that's a big lunch in that box. I need to get out of here. I've got a doctor's appointment, so you have a blessed day, young lady."

I watched her go as annoyance clouded my otherwise good morning. Adele wasn't coming back, and Kerri was meeting with wedding vendors today and wouldn't be in. Did that mean I was stuck here all afternoon working Adele's shift? It's not like I had anything else to do. But why would Adele be so rude as to not tell me she wasn't feeling well and wouldn't be back? Why was she avoiding me and lying about her confrontation with Dana downtown? Speaking of Dana, where the hell was she? I hadn't seen her all day, and a brief check of the parking lot showed that her car was in the lot. Was she avoiding me, too? That made no sense because she didn't even know I'd seen them arguing, unless Adele had told her. Then another thought struck me. If Adele and Kerri weren't going to be in the office for the rest of the afternoon, that meant I had access to the office and everything in it, including all of the residents' files.

I snagged a box lunch with a roast beef sandwich and headed into the office. I powered through the sandwich and potato salad and was munching on a snickerdoodle as I perused the files. Most of them I avoided because I already knew what was in them, since I had done their intake. There was really only one file I wanted to see, Dana's. Except, when I pulled her file from the back of the drawer, I was sorely disappointed to see a mostly blank form. Dana Shields, age thirty-five and that was basically it, aside from the registration for her late model Hyundai. There was a note attached to her file in Adele's handwriting reminding her to ask for Dana's driver's license, which she hadn't had with her at the time of her intake.

One of the things that Adele had drilled into me during my training was that all the shelter's residents must have at least one form of picture ID, either a state ID, driver's license, or passport. That was non-negotiable, and if they didn't have it, they would lose their spot in the shelter and have to be added back to the queue. So, why had she let Dana slide? Was that what they were arguing about downtown? Had Dana still not provided her ID? Should I ask Adele the next time I saw her, whenever the hell that was, since she seemed to be purposefully making herself scarce? I put Dana's file back in its spot, careful not to get cookie crumbs on it when I spied another folder that I was desperate to look through. It was the folder with the residents' background checks. Then another thought hit me. Dana's file should have had her completed background check in it like everyone else's file, but it didn't. How could she have had her background checked when she hadn't provided a photo ID?

The envelope with the most recent background check was still sealed. Why hadn't Adele opened it? Knowing she probably wasn't going to be happy but realizing it was not addressed to a specific person, such as Selma Ross, I figured I may as well open the envelope and sort them into the proper files since it seemed I was going to be stuck here all afternoon. I opened the envelope which contained twelve background checks and put them in alphabetical order.

I quickly scanned each of them, looking for felony arrests or violent offenses that would need to be brought to Director Ross's attention, but only found minor charges like traffic tickets, shoplifting, and trespassing. I wasn't surprised to not find one for Dana. Who was this woman and where had she come from? Why did she have a birthmark similar to Brooke's on the back of her right shoulder and why did she have a stuffed turtle precisely like Brooke's beloved Willa?

I was so caught up with all these thoughts whirling around my brain, I nearly jumped out of my skin when I looked up to see elderly Mrs. Timmons smiling at me.

"You must be having a really nice daydream. I've been standing here for almost a full minute."

"I am so sorry, Mrs. Timmons. Was there something you needed?"

"Well," she said, taking a step forward and glancing over her shoulder before lowering her voice. "That air conditioner you put in my room stopped working. I hope I didn't break it. I don't have any money to fix it if I did." She sounded close to tears, and I instantly got up and put an arm around her.

"Don't worry, Mrs. Timmons. Let me take a look and see if I can I figure out what's going on." I highly doubted she'd broken a brand-new air-conditioning unit, but I needed to see what she was talking about.

I followed Mrs. Timmons out of the office and around the corner to her small, single room which consisted of a twin bed, a dresser, a rocking chair and a window overlooking the playground in which sat a window air-conditioning unit. It had only been a week since I'd put the air-conditioning unit in the window of her muggy bedroom, and it had worked just fine. I walked over to the unit and saw that it was indeed plugged in and set on the very lowest setting. Mrs. Timmons had commented that she only needed to turn it on at night because by the end of the day the heat in her room had gotten unbearable and the fan she was using wasn't cutting it.

"I swear I haven't touched it at all, except to turn it on and off."

"It's fine, Mrs. Timmons," I said to reassure her. "You didn't do anything wrong."

I wasn't quite sure what I thought I could do by looking at the air conditioner, other than ease the elderly woman's mind. I unplugged and re-plugged it and actually pulled the unit out of the window to make sure the cord hadn't come loose from the back. It had. I pushed buttons and did everything I could, but the air conditioner was very obviously dead, which confused me since it was brand-new out of the box. Or was it? I set it on the floor and noticed something that I hadn't when I installed it. The words property of ECC was written on the back of the unit with what look like a black sharpie. This air-conditioning unit was used.

"I'll be right back. I just need to check on something," I told the elderly woman.

I left her room and headed back to the office where I pulled the air-conditioning unit that was in Adele's office window slightly out of the window to check the back and sure enough, there were the words property of ECC written on the back. I spent the next twenty minutes running around to all the bedrooms, which were thankfully empty at that time of the day, and checked all of the window air-conditioning units to find the same thing on all of them. The only one that didn't have writing was the unit in Selma Ross's office. The rest of them were all used units. I was so confused because I had taken them out of brand-new boxes. I even went out to the dumpster area next to the playground where the boxes were stacked waiting to be broken down by the handyman and put into the dumpster.

I must've been so excited to stick these units in all the windows that I'd failed to notice that, while similar, they did not look like the pictures on the boxes. *What the hell is going on?* Had Adele cheaped out and bought used units to save money? I wasn't sure what annoyed me more, the fact that she was gone for the day and I couldn't ask her about this, or the knowledge that one by one these units were going to break down and more money would have to be spent replacing them. In the meantime, I took the window air-conditioning unit from Adele's office and put it in Mrs. Timmons' room, for which she was very grateful.

A few hours later, as I was gathering my things and heading to my car to leave for the day, I ran into Selma Ross who was arriving for her evening shift.

"Ava? It's kind of late for you to be here, isn't it?"

"Kerri had meetings with vendors for her wedding and Adele was here but left because she wasn't feeling well. I guess she's not one hundred percent yet."

"Really? I hadn't heard anything about her leaving. Normally, she's very good about keeping me informed about things like that."

"She didn't tell me, either. I heard it from Mrs. Brady."

Yes, I snitched on her because I was still annoyed and very confused. I hadn't known Adele for that long, but she exuded professionalism through her pores, so what was up with her now? She should be very glad that I wasn't about to tell the director that she had allowed a woman with no ID or background check a spot at the shelter. I was annoyed, but I wasn't that mad. That could be a firing offense.

"Well, thanks for letting me know. Let me give her a call and make sure everything's okay. You have a nice evening."

We parted ways and I suddenly remembered the air-conditioning units. Selma needed to know that every one of those units, except for the one in her office, was used. Before I could turn to head back inside, I saw Dana talking to Wilma. Dana put her hand on Wilma's shoulder, at which point Wilma reached her hand all the way back and swung it forward, cracking Dana hard across the face. Dana's hands instantly shot out, shoving Wilma to the ground, before she took off walking down the street. I ran over to Wilma who was looking bewildered as she sat on her ass in the hard packed dirt near the swing set. I hadn't been on a swing set in twenty-five years and the sight of them still had a visceral reaction on me. I turned my back on it and squatted down next to Wilma.

"Are you okay? Why did you hit Dana?" I helped her to her feet and noticed the blank, confused look on her face as she shrugged out of my grasp.

"I didn't do anything," she muttered under her breath before spitting on the grass and turning to walk back into the house.

She seemed fine, so I decided to go after Dana. I hopped in my car and drove around the block, spotting her sitting at a bus stop. I parked and got out and approached her. Her legs were drawn up to her chest and she was rocking back and forth as tears streamed from her eyes and blood trickled from her nose.

"Dana? I saw what happened. Are you okay?" I pulled a napkin from my pocket and handed it to her, but she continued to stare straight ahead and rock back and forth. So, I took it upon myself to wipe her streaming eyes, then gave her the napkin to press against her still bleeding nose.

"I thought I was safe there. I'm not safe anywhere." Her voice was so low I almost didn't catch what she said, and it made me freeze.

"What do you mean? Of course you're safe. Wilma is off her meds, and after what just happened, I'm not sure we're going to be allowing her to stay at Haver House."

Dana abruptly pulled the tissue away from her nose and threw it onto the ground.

"Please don't say anything. It was all my fault she acted like that. She doesn't have any place else to go. I think she's worn out her welcome at just about every shelter in town according to the other women."

"What in the world did you say to her to make her slap you like that?"

"I shouldn't have touched her. I invaded her space and that's not cool. I just wanted her to push me on the swings. I used to love the swings. I was always so happy when I was flying so high I almost wrapped the chain around the top. I had a friend once and we used to love to swing."

What had she just said? I stared at her with my mouth hanging open as tears filled my eyes. It couldn't be. This woman couldn't be Brooke. Yet all of the signs were there. The birthmark. Willa the stuffed turtle. And now she had just told me how much she loved to swing and how she had a friend who used to swing with her. Me? Was she talking about me? It was all too much, and I stood up and walked away from her and discreetly wiped my eyes, but I hadn't been quick enough, and she'd seen me.

"Hey, I'm the one that got their face slapped. Why are you crying?"

"Your friend," I said as I turned to face her, no longer trying to disguise the tears streaming down my face. "What was your friend's name? The one you used to like to play on the swings with. What was her name?"

Dana stared at me much the same way she'd probably looked at Wilma right before she smacked her. She shrugged and then looked down at her feet before replying.

"That was a million years ago. I was just a little girl. I had lots of friends back then."

It wasn't a lie. Brooke had been very popular and had lots of friends when we were in elementary school. Everyone wanted to be her friend, but I was the lucky one who got to be her very best friend, which also meant I got to be the one to witness her ripped away from her life in an instant. Could everyone have been wrong and whoever took her didn't do horrible things to her before killing her? All of the evidence was pointing away from a truth that I had accepted a long time ago. My best friend was gone, but here I was talking to a woman who seemed to have come from nowhere. Her memory loss and homelessness could easily be explained by having lived through trauma that had left her unable to participate in normal society. Who was this woman? How could I find out? If by some miracle this *was* Brooke, where had she been for the last twenty-five years?

"Thanks for helping me. It's Ava, right?"

I merely nodded and watched as she started heading back towards the shelter.

"Where are you going?" I asked, trailing behind her.

"Back to the shelter to take a shower."

"I've got my car. Let me drive you back."

"No, thanks. I'm good. Promise me you won't tell them what Wilma did. They'll put her out and I can't have that on my conscience."

"I have to file a report on this. I'm sorry, Dana, but my hands are tied, and I thought you said you felt unsafe."

She rolled her eyes and wiped away a thin trickle of blood that ran from her nose as indecision flitted across her face. She finally sighed. "I never said it was Wilma that was making me feel unsafe."

"Who then? Tell me and I'm sure we can get it all sorted out."

Dana let out a mirthless chuckle and shook her head. "It's that admin assistant, Adele. Can you sort that out?"

She didn't wait for my reply and took off running back towards the shelter, leaving me standing open-mouthed on the sidewalk in shock. A couple of minutes passed before I finally got into my car and headed back to the shelter. I went to check on Wilma and found her in the dining room playing cards with two other women, laughing and joking as if nothing had happened. Then I went to write up the report of Wilma's attack on Dana. I felt horrible because I knew this was probably the final straw for her and we would have to find someplace else for her to go. She was clearly a danger to the other residents.

When I was done, I went up to check on Dana and was stunned to see her stuff was gone, including Willa the stuffed turtle. I knew she was not coming back. What had she been talking about when she'd said it was Adele who was making her feel unsafe? She certainly looked very angry when I saw them arguing downtown. Did this have something to do with her not being able to provide ID? And did it really matter now that Dana had taken off?

TWELVE

ADELE

Adele lied to her husband James when she told him she was going to zip out to the store to get some things that she needed to finish dinner. He'd been busy in the garage working on the Camaro he'd been restoring for the better part of three years and barely looked at her. Good, because she wasn't really going to the store. She pulled into the parking lot of Pleasant Street Park near the older, rarely used section near a playground with a rusted-out slide and a broken swing set. The note slipped under her windshield that morning had simply instructed her to meet them at the park near the old playground swings at six o'clock.

She decided not to turn her car off, hoping this would be a brief interaction, and she could go home and finish the beef stew they were having that night. She waited for twenty minutes, and no one showed up. She was just about to leave, figuring it had been a big joke, when a loud rap on her side window made her jump. She looked at the face staring at her through her window and her heart continued to beat crazily. They stood outside her car waiting for her to get out. She reached for her door handle while her right hand slid inside her purse and pulled out the envelope of cash she had brought with her. She got out of the car, looking around briefly before holding out the envelope. The person just stared at it with mild amusement.

"It's...it's all I've got. Now, please leave me alone."

"You think that's going to make up for everything you've done?" Their voice was low and raspy, the way a person who needed to clear their throat sounded.

"Who are you? What do you..." she began before it finally hit her and she took an involuntary step backwards, not taking her eyes off the person in front of her. Then she looked around wildly taking in the abandoned playground fifty yards from where she was parked with its rusty broken swing set. "Is this...? Is this where it happened?" The person continued to stare at her without answering. "It wasn't my fault. I had no idea what they were planning to do that day."

Instead of replying or taking the money, the figure rushed at her, pinning her against the side of the car. The knife they'd stabbed her with slid into her like a hot knife through butter. She didn't even realize she'd been stabbed until the person pulled back, revealing the knife covered in streaks of blood. Her blood, which seeped through a wound near her heart, staining her blue T-shirt. She looked down at the growing stain in bewilderment. She started to open her mouth to ask why, but she knew why. Instead, she slid wordlessly down the side of the car into a heap on the ground as blood quickly pooled beneath her, the money envelope still clutched in a death grip as her life bled away.

THIRTEEN

AVA

I was startled awake by my phone ringing. I'd fallen asleep on the couch after a dinner of pizza eaten alone because Evan was still in Columbus. Still groggy, I grabbed my phone from the coffee table. It was Selma Ross from Haver House. It was also after eleven. Why in the world was she calling me so late?

"Hello?" My voice was thick with sleep, and I quickly sat up and took a sip from my glass of water sitting on the coffee table, noticing the condensation from the glass had left a large water ring on the table.

"Ava?" Her voice was so low and muffled that, at first, I wasn't sure it was her.

"Selma?" I said uncertainly. "Is everything okay?" I added when she didn't answer right away and all I heard was heavy breathing.

"Ava...I am so sorry to be calling you so late, but I have some terrible news."

Before I could even respond, Selma told me something that made absolutely no sense. Adele was dead.

"Oh my god," I said. Suddenly, it was like all the breath had been squeezed from my lungs and I could barely get the words out.

"She...went home sick...this morning. Was...was it a heart attack? A stroke?"

"Ava, she was stabbed. Someone killed her. They found her in the park."

Murdered? Had I just heard her right? But that couldn't be true. How did she go from leaving work early to being found dead...where?

"What did you just say?" It came out in a whisper, and I thought I'd have to repeat myself, but Selma had heard me.

"I said Adele is dead. She was stabbed."

"I heard that part. Where did you say she was found?"

"Her husband James said she was found in Pleasant Street Park near some old playground."

There was only one old playground in that park and that was the playground Brooke had disappeared from. A newer, nicer playground was built the year after her abduction, but I never played there. I'd never gone back to Pleasant Street Park again. I was suddenly light-headed, and tears blurred my eyes at the thought of poor Adele lying dead in that park near that playground of all places.

"Ava? Are you still there?"

Now, it was me not responding. I couldn't because my phone had slipped from my fingers.

Everyone at Haver House floated through the days after Adele's murder like we were wading through syrup. The police had initially thought it was a robbery gone wrong, but I'd since read in the papers that robbery hadn't been the motive because her purse, cell phone, and jewelry were with her when she was found in the park by a woman walking her dog. The news had shown crime scene tape around Adele's car which was parked fifty feet from the playground and the set of swings that Brooke and I had been on when she'd been abducted. In fact, her car was parked very near where Brooke's abductor's car had been parked. Could this be a coincidence?

The shelter held a memorial service for Adele a few days after she died. Everyone was shell-shocked, especially her husband James who was sitting in a chair in the corner of the living room as people walked up to him one by one telling him how sorry they were for his loss. I knew from experience that once someone was dead, there wasn't anything anybody could say that would make it better. I didn't quite know what to say to him and instead went into the kitchen to see if Mrs. Brady needed any help with the food. The only person in the kitchen was Kerri. Her face was red and blotchy, her eyes swollen with tears, and she was clutching the gold pendant that always hung on a thin chain around her neck, rubbing it between her right thumb and index finger like the act gave her comfort. Of all the people at Haver House, both staff and residents, Kerri was taking Adele's death the hardest.

"I just can't believe it. Who would want to hurt Adele? She was the sweetest person ever." She wiped her tears away with the back of her hand. I pulled a tissue from my purse, handed it to her and rubbed her back as she wiped her eyes again and blew her nose. "Did you know she introduced me to Josh?"

"She did?" I said, confused. "I thought you guys met at work. Speaking of Josh, is he here tonight? I was hoping to finally meet him."

"He had a class to teach tonight, and he couldn't find anyone to fill in for him, or he'd be here. Technically, we did meet in passing at work, but Adele knew him and thought we'd hit it off and personally introduced us."

"I'm so sorry I didn't get the chance to know her better."

And it was the truth. Maybe if I'd known Adele better, I'd have answers to so many of my questions, like why did Dana Shields tell me she was making her feel unsafe? Where the hell had Dana gone? Why had she left? What had she and Adele been arguing about downtown?

"I hadn't really known her that long, either, but she quickly became a good friend, especially after my grandma died. I was having a hard time with her death and everything that came with it. That's why she introduced me to Josh. His mom had also recently died, and we bonded over our grief."

Kerri dissolved into tears again and I couldn't help but notice the contrast in how Kerri felt about Adele and how Dana had felt about her. She was one woman's good friend and another woman's reason to leave what should have been a safe haven.

I handed Kerri another tissue, and she straightened up, wiped her eyes, and cleared her throat. "Thanks, Ava. I think I'll be okay. I just need a couple of minutes."

I took that as my cue that she needed to be alone. I gave her a smile and left her in the kitchen. As I was heading down the hall, I spotted James Mackie standing in front of Adele's closed office door. I was one of only a few people who had yet to approach him with my condolences. I was about to walk up to him when he opened the office door and slipped inside, leaving the door ajar behind him. Uncertain whether I should disturb him or not, I hesitated several long seconds before pulling the door all the way open and walking inside.

"Mr. Mackie?" I said softly so as not to startle him.

He turned around and I could see how red-rimmed and tired his eyes were. He held their framed wedding picture in his hands and set it down when he spotted me. He was even more handsome in person.

"Yes?" His voice was surprisingly deep.

"I know there is nothing I can say to make any of this better, but I just wanted you to know that even though I only knew Adele for a brief time, I really enjoyed working with her. She was a very special person."

He nodded and then walked over to her chair behind her desk where her sweater was still draped over the back and stroked it as a tear streamed out of the corner of his eye.

"I'm happy to box up all of her things for you if you'd like."

"I'd really appreciate that...Uh, I'm sorry. I don't know your name."

"Ava West. I've only been working here for about two weeks as a volunteer."

"I think I remember Adele mentioning you and what a nice person you are. And thank you for the offer, I can barely look at her stuff right now. I still can't wrap my head around all of this. It's like a nightmare I can't wake up from. She just told me she was slipping out to go to the store. I have no idea what she was doing in that park. Whoever killed her must've forced her to go there."

I didn't dare bring up the fact that the papers said it wasn't a robbery because nothing was taken. Now was not the time. A robbery gone wrong was what James Mackie needed to believe, and I wasn't going to take that away from him. Instead, I offered him a tissue from the packet in my purse, and he gladly accepted it. Though, there was one thing I needed to know, and I knew I might not get another chance to ask him.

"Mr. Mackie, why did Adele stop being a psychiatrist?"

His right eyebrow lifted in surprise. "You knew about that? That's not something she shared with a lot of people."

"No, she didn't tell me herself. I found her framed degree. It had fallen down behind a filing cabinet. She didn't seem happy that I'd found it."

He gave me a small sad smile and shook his head. "My wife practiced psychiatry for almost three decades. She had a particular specialty that she had a high rate of success with, but then something went wrong and she walked away and never looked back."

"If you don't mind me asking, what happened?"

James Mackie hesitated only for a moment before leaning against the edge of his wife's desk and clearing his throat. "My wife worked with people struggling with addiction. She worked to free them of the mental and emotional hold their addictions had on them. Like I said, she had a very high rate of success, but she couldn't get through to everyone. Every addict that turned their back on their families, friends and old lives to go back to whatever drug had gotten its hooks into them was a knife in my wife's heart. There was one particular patient who was the final straw for my wife. No matter how hard my wife tried, she couldn't get through to this patient and they ended up taking their life. My wife soured on psychiatry and her love of the profession died with that patient."

Now, I understood why Adele had seemed so angry and dismissive when I found the framed photo of her degree, but why display it at all if she felt that way? Then I remembered she said it had been somebody's idea of a sick joke. Did that mean she wasn't the one who'd put the framed degree in her office? If that was true, could it have something to do with whoever killed her?

"She seemed angry when I asked her about it. If I had known, I wouldn't have said anything."

"There was absolutely no way for you to know about this. It happened over a decade ago. She never went back to her private practice."

It was on the tip of my tongue to tell him what his wife had said about the framed degree in her office when Selma Ross turned up in the doorway.

"James, could you please come see me in my office before you leave?"

"I was just leaving. I'll give you two some privacy."

I quickly left, pulling the office door shut behind me before remembering I'd left my purse behind and shoved the door open just a crack, fully intending to knock when I saw something that made me snatch the door shut quietly. I'd nearly walked in on James Mackie and Selma Ross in a passionate embrace.

Half an hour later, after Selma went back to her office, James rejoined the gathering in the dining room where Mrs. Brady had laid out a spread of food. I snuck back into Adele's office and grabbed my purse, then made my getaway still reeling from what I had witnessed. What had I seen? Was it a grieving man being comforted by his wife's very attractive boss or was it something else? I sat behind the wheel of my car and thought hard, remembering how James Mackie's hand was on Selma's lower back, pressing her close to him, and how I'd seen Selma's glossy red lips pressed against the side of James's neck. That was not the kind of embrace you gave a man grieving his wife's death. I wonder how long it had been going on.

Was James Mackie so hot to be with Selma Ross he'd gotten rid of his wife? His grief had seemed so genuine, or maybe that was guilt. However, it was entirely possible my own father's affair had clouded my judgment. All I knew was that it was time for me to get home. I was about to start my car when a loud rap on the passenger side window nearly made me jump out of my skin. What shocked me more was who it was. It was Dana Shields. I was about to press the button to lower my window when Dana impatiently jerked the door open and got into my car, uninvited. She tossed her backpack onto my backseat.

"Where have you been? Do you know what happened to Adele?"

"Of course, I know what happened to her!" she snapped at me before giving me a contrite look. "Sorry."

"Dana? What is going on? I saw you and Adele arguing downtown last week. What was that about? And why was Adele even letting you stay at Haver House when you didn't have ID?"

"Are you going to let me talk or are you just going to keep asking me questions? And I don't want to talk about this here. Anywhere but here."

"Wait a minute," I said, looking around. "Where's your car and the rest of your stuff?"

She let out an exaggerated sigh. "I had to leave my clothes and stuff in a locker at the bus station, and I sold my car because I needed the money. Plus, I couldn't afford gas and car insurance anymore anyway. Now, can we please go?"

I started the car, wondering why she was in such a hurry when I noticed the strong stench of body odor that had filled my car.

Dana must not have bathed since the last time I saw her. That and the overall aura of desperation rolling off her just as strongly as her body odor caused me to make a snap decision I hoped I wouldn't regret. I pulled out of the shelter's parking lot and made a right once I'd driven to the end of the drive.

"Where are we going?" Dana asked with a slight edge of panic to her voice.

"Someplace where you'll be safe. I promise. You'll even be able to shower and get some clean clothes and some food to eat."

"And where would that be? I only got a few hundred dollars for my car and..."

"You won't need any money," I said, cutting her off. "I'm offering you something that doesn't cost money."

"What would that be? Because everything has a price."

The suspicion in her voice cut me to the core. How long had it been since this woman had been able to trust anyone? Then again, if she was Brooke, I already knew the answer to that question.

"Hospitality and human kindness."

Five minutes later, we were turning into the narrow alleyway that led to the garage of my town house. Evan had been in Columbus for the week and probably wouldn't be home until late the next day. I didn't want to think about what his response would be when he found out I'd brought work home with me. I love my husband, but I was always surprised by his mistrust of strangers. It's not that I didn't think a healthy dose of mistrust was a bad idea, but my husband and I lived our lives with differing degrees of empathy that had caused more than a few arguments during our time together.

"Who lives here?"

"Who do you think?" I gave her a bright smile and then got out of the car and gestured for her to do the same.

She followed me to the side door, and we entered the town house through the spacious kitchen, which was my favorite room in the entire house. I turned to see Dana still lingering in the doorway looking around, unsure about whether she should come in.

"Close the door behind or you're going to let flies in."

Dana did as she was told but still lingered a few steps away from the door, still looking around suspiciously.

"Are you sure about this? What will your husband think?"

"This is just a temporary situation and my husband's not home right now. Now, what would you like to eat? I've got leftover spaghetti or leftover pizza. Pick your poison."

Dana took a tentative step towards the refrigerator and gave me a small smile just as I heard the loud rumble of her stomach. When did she eat last?

"How about both? I'm starved."

I quickly left the kitchen and returned with a towel and a washcloth and handed them to her.

"While I get dinner together, the bathroom is up the stairs, second door to your left. When you're done, I have some pajamas you can wear, and then we can eat. How's that sound?"

"Like heaven."

She took the towel and washcloth, and I watched her disappear up the steps. A few minutes later, I heard the shower running and pulled food from the fridge to heat up.

Later, as we were settled on the couch in the TV room with a glass of white wine for me and one of Evan's beers for Dana, I asked her again what I needed to know.

"Alright, now I need to know what happened with you and Adele and where did you run off to?"

It took her almost a full minute to answer and by then she'd drained half her beer and set it down on the table wiping her mouth on the sleeve of the pajama shirt that I'd lent her.

"I had to get out of there. I felt like the walls were closing in on me."

"Why? Was it because of Adele? You made it sound like she was the reason you didn't feel safe at Haver House."

"She was the reason, but it's not because of what you think.

She never did anything bad to me. She was trying to be my therapist, and I didn't need that shit. I just needed a nice warm place to lay my head and food in my stomach. She was trying to save my soul even though I told her to leave me the hell alone. She just wouldn't, and was always at me talking about my feelings and shit."

I was so relieved to hear that. I was worried she had done something to Adele in the park and relief washed over me, instantly relaxing me as I drained my glass of wine.

"Okay. That explains why you left, but why were you arguing with Adele downtown?"

"How do you even know about that? Were you following me or did she tell you?"

Dana's obvious paranoia concerned me. Was this why Adele had been so adamant about trying to administer some kind of therapy to her? According to her husband she'd left all that behind, but after what I'd witnessed at the memorial service, I wasn't so sure about anything James Mackie had told me.

"Why would I be following you? I was on my way home and saw the two of you going at it. I was concerned."

"Look," she said with a weary sigh. "My driver's license expired and I was in the process of getting it renewed. You know they just don't issue the physical license at the DMV anymore, right? They give you a license receipt to use until they send the card to you in the mail. Only I didn't have an address for them to send it to, and it was just a big mess. She was constantly on my ass about it because she said she could get fired from her job for letting me stay there with no ID."

"What happened to the receipt? You could have just used that for your identification."

"I lost it between moves and every time I go back to get a replacement, they're crowded, and crowds make me nervous."

"It's okay, Dana." I reached out and gave her hand a quick squeeze to calm her down. I could tell she was getting anxious.

What she'd just said made perfect sense, but there was something about how her eyes wouldn't meet mine that made me realize there was more to the story she wasn't telling me. I looked over at her to see her head laid back against the couch and her eyes starting to droop. She must be exhausted.

"I was camping out in the woods," she continued with her eyes now closed. "But I had to leave because the woods aren't like they are in Disney movies with cute little animals frolicking around just waiting to braid your hair. A lot of creepy shit goes on in the woods, especially at night, and I had to leave. I headed back to the shelter to see if my spot was still open. I didn't even know about what happened to Adele until I got there and talked to Wilma, and then I knew I really couldn't go back. That's when I saw you sitting in your car. You looked really freaked out. What happened?"

I wasn't about to tell her what I'd seen in Adele's office. Instead, I stared at my empty wine glass and yawned before replying.

"Everything that happened just caught up with me. I still can't believe Adele is gone. I hadn't known her for very long, but I really liked her. I just can't wrap my head around the fact that someone killed her in the same park that..." I stopped abruptly because I'd been about to say in the same park near where she'd been abducted.

"Same park that what?" She glanced over at me with a look of mild curiosity.

Of course, she had no idea what I was about to say and even if I'd said it, I got the distinct impression she still wouldn't know what the hell I was talking about because this woman couldn't possibly be Brooke. Maybe, if I kept telling myself that, I would actually believe it.

"Nothing. I'm just really tired and it's getting late. We should probably turn in. We've got a nice guest bedroom upstairs, or you can sleep here on the couch if you're more comfortable. I'll leave it up to you." I gathered up our glasses and headed into the kitchen.

"Guest bedroom will be cool. Your couch is nice, but I never turn down an opportunity to sleep in a bed."

She followed me up to the second floor where the door to the guest bedroom, which was next to the bathroom, was already open. I flipped on the lights, glancing at the bedroom across the hall and noticing the door was slightly ajar. Dana noticed me looking and gave me a sheepish look.

"Sorry. I got turned around when I got up here and thought that was the bathroom. I didn't know you had a baby."

Her words were like a punch to the gut, and I kicked myself for not going ahead and locking that room up until it was actually in use. It was a nursery decorated for a baby that may not ever come despite the fact we'd been approved for IVF treatments and had the money for at least two rounds.

"Not yet, but we're all ready to go just as soon as I get pregnant."

Dana opened her mouth to say something else, but what she was about to say, I'll never know because the hard set of my jaw and the tightness of my smile prevented her from saying another word.

"I hope you'll be comfortable here. Are you an early bird or a late sleeper?"

"Depends on my situation at any given time." She sat down on the edge of the queen size bed. "A lot of food banks you have to get there early if you want anything that hasn't been picked over, same way with churches and schools that give away free meals. So, I guess I'm an early bird out of necessity. Why are you asking?"

"I'm not much of an early bird. So, if you get up and I'm still in bed, help yourself to any food in the kitchen. There's fruit in the basket on the counter. There's a coffee maker if you want coffee and there's also teabags, and bagels and cream cheese in the fridge. If you're feeling really adventurous, there's eggs and bacon in the fridge. Now, I'll let you get some sleep. Good night."

"Ava," Dana called out before I could close the door. I turned. "Thanks. I really appreciate you letting me crash here. And don't worry I won't be the guest that wears out their welcome."

"You're very welcome, Dana. And why don't we just take it one day at a time?"

I headed into the master suite, changed into my bed clothes, then slid under the cool covers and lay there staring at the ceiling. What had I done bringing her here and what did I hope to accomplish by helping her? But I knew the answer to that question. I knew it the minute I laid eyes on the raised birthmark on the back of her shoulder and the stuffed turtle on her bed at the shelter. As much as I tried to deny it and pretend otherwise, I was helping Dana Shields because in my heart I knew she was Brooke.

I didn't think I'd be able to sleep, but I was out in less than ten minutes. When I rolled over and looked at my bedside clock the next morning, it was nearly 9:30. I grabbed my robe and quickly headed out of the bedroom towards the steps and the smell of coffee. The sounds of conversation floated up from the kitchen. My heart dropped into my stomach. Evan was home. He wasn't supposed to be home until later tonight and I hadn't figured out what I was going to tell him about our guest. When I arrived in the kitchen, both he and Dana were sitting at the kitchen island drinking coffee. Dana had a half-eaten banana lying on a napkin in front of her and the tension in the room was so thick I could've carved it up and cooked it.

"Good morning," I said to Dana. "And welcome home, babe," I said to my husband who gave me a tight smile as I planted a kiss on his cheek.

I hadn't been with this man for eight years not to know that he was annoyed right now. I wasn't about to catch his mood and make our guest feel unwelcome, and I couldn't help but notice that Dana was looking very uncomfortable.

"Morning," they both said in unison.

"I see you guys have met?" I looked from my husband to Dana who nodded slowly while my husband said nothing at all, causing anger to flare up in me at his rudeness.

"I should get going." Dana shoved the last of her banana in her mouth and darted out of the kitchen before I could say a word.

"What the hell is wrong with you?" I said, rounding on my husband. "What did you say to her?"

"What the hell is wrong with me? Who the hell is that, Ava? I walked in here this morning expecting to see my wife and I find some strange woman sitting in my kitchen, eating my food, and wearing your clothes. She said she met you at that homeless shelter. You brought a homeless stranger into our house?"

"She is a human being, who happens to be homeless, yes. You act like I brought an ax murderer home."

"How do I know that you haven't? Do you even know this woman?"

"Hold up. How is this any different to when you brought Joey home from work with you when his wife kicked him out, then let him stay in our basement. He refused to leave for a month. We almost had to get the police involved to get him the hell out of our house. How is this any different to that? And it's just a few days until I can find a new placement for her."

"It's different because I asked you before I brought Joey home. I didn't just bring a stranger home like a stray cat without saying anything to you first. That's what's different."

I glared at him because he did have a point. Asking Evan had been the last thing on my mind when I decided to bring Dana home with me. Probably because I already knew he wouldn't be happy with it, and I knew I was going to do it anyway.

"Look." I took a step closer to him, putting a hand on his arm, surprised he didn't pull away from me. "I'm sorry. I really am, but you have no idea what happened this week." I proceeded to tell him about Adele and his face softened just a bit before something else made him angry.

"Why am I just now hearing about this? A woman you work with was murdered and you didn't even call and tell me about it?"

I let out a frustrated sigh. "We can talk about this later. I'll be right back to cook you a nice breakfast."

Before he could protest, I was back up on the second floor and had knocked on the guest bedroom door, only to have Dana answer it fully dressed in the clothes she'd arrived in, that I'd washed last night. Her backpack was slung on her back.

"Where are you going? You haven't had breakfast yet."

"I had a banana, and I can tell your man doesn't want me here. I don't want to be any place where I'm not wanted. So, I'm out."

"He's not mad at you. He's mad at me for not telling him about anything that's happened this week. It's okay. I promise. Please come down and let me cook you both breakfast and, besides, where are you going to go? Especially since you sold your car. It's way too hot out there right now to be wandering around not knowing where you're going to sleep."

I wasn't sure if Dana was just tired of hustling and grinding to try to find her next meal and place to sleep, but she nodded and mutely followed me back down to the kitchen. I'd assumed Evan would be in his man cave sulking, but to my surprise he was whipping up eggs and had laid out strips of bacon on our stovetop griddle. It was either a genuine apology for being a heartless ass, although he did have every right to be concerned about who I was bringing into the house, or he didn't want me to be mad at him and change my mind about starting IVF. Either way, twenty minutes later, we were all sitting at the kitchen table chowing down on Evan's big breakfast. I had forgotten what a good cook my husband was, and I was feeling so much more hopeful that we could get our marriage back on track.

While we ate, Evan grilled Dana with questions that she answered in a forthcoming way, which she hadn't been with me. I pride myself on being the more empathetic of the two of us, but Evan had a way with people that I just didn't. Before I knew it, I found out that Dana had last been living in the Dayton area and had become homeless when she abruptly lost her job a few months ago. She had just enough gas in her tank to get her to Elmhurst where she decided she would try and put down new roots. I'm not sure what I thought she was going to say, but it didn't sound like she had any past connection to Elmhurst, making my heart deflate a little.

"How do you like it here in Elmhurst?" I asked around a mouthful of scrambled eggs.

"It's nice enough," she conceded. "The homeless part kind of sucks, but it's alright." The deadpan way in which she had delivered that last line made Evan snort with laughter. Before we knew it, all three of us were laughing.

Once we'd eaten, Evan disappeared upstairs to take a shower. Dana helped me clear the table and insisted on cleaning up the kitchen.

"No. You're our guest and guests don't clean up the kitchen."

"It would make me feel a whole lot better and like I'm not leeching off of you."

"I don't think..." I began, but I didn't get far.

"Just let me clean up the damn kitchen. It's not that serious. I promise." She looked mildly annoyed and stared at me until I relented.

"Fine. And thank you. Dishwasher detergent is in the cabinet under the sink and..."

"I think I can figure it out." She got busy scraping the breakfast dishes.

I gave her a smile and headed straight for the bathroom. I stripped off my clothes and slipped inside the shower with Evan. He gave me a look of surprise that gave way to a smile as I pressed myself against his soap slicked body. I looked up at him and he pressed his lips against mine.

"What about our guest?"

"She's busy cleaning up the kitchen."

He picked me up and my legs wrapped around his waist. We made love with an intensity I hadn't felt towards him in a very long time.

Afterwards, once Evan was in bed asleep and snoring, I headed back down to the kitchen hoping Dana hadn't heard us. The kitchen was empty and there was a note on the kitchen island. The sight of it made my heart sink. It read:

Gone to the library. Back later. D.

I instantly relaxed because I realized in that moment that I was going to prove Dana was Brooke, and nothing could stand in my way.

My plan had been to spend the day at home with my husband, but I should've known that whenever I made plans, God would laugh at me. A little past noon I got a phone call from Selma asking if I was available to come in to work the afternoon shift. Her voice sounded casual enough, but there was an edge to it that made me realize that saying no was not going to make her very happy. So, I agreed and hoped I didn't have to see the woman after what I had witnessed at Adele's memorial service. The sight of her lips pressed against James Mackie's neck was burned into my memory forever. When I arrived at Haver House, I realized I was being asked to come in for more than just coverage.

The police were there packing up things from Adele's office into boxes under the watchful eye of my boss.

Annoyance flared up in me because Selma could've warned me about it over the phone but didn't. Why? Then I realized something else with dread. When I'd talked to the police the day after Adele's murder, it had just been uniformed officers getting details of her last morning at work to retrace her steps. If they were back, it meant they were probably going to ask me if I knew anyone who would want to hurt Adele.

The only person I knew she'd had an altercation with was Dana. There was no way I could tell them about that. Even though I didn't think she was involved in any way in Adele's murder, I didn't want Dana added to some short list of suspects. As far as I was concerned, the only people who probably wanted her gone were her boss and her husband.

"What's going on?" I tried to keep the contempt out of my

voice when I looked at Selma but must not have completely succeeded as she couldn't look me in the eye.

"They're confiscating anything from the office they think might provide a motive, and lead them to a suspect." Her voice was flat and her eyes red-rimmed. Was it from guilt, sadness, or both?

"Why would they think there was evidence here of all places?"

"I have no idea what they're thinking, but I'm glad they're being thorough. James called this morning and said they've been at his house all morning as well."

James called this morning, huh? I wonder if he called her this morning after he'd arrived home from her house and found the police on his doorstep. I had to stop thinking like this, basing it on a glimpse of something I'd seen for mere seconds and may have misinterpreted, but I just couldn't help myself.

"Whoever ripped Adele away from her husband deserves whatever they get." I gave Selma a hard look and instantly felt bad when she burst into tears and rushed back to her office.

I'm not normally this bitchy and who knows maybe Adele knew what was going on between her husband and boss, although I doubted it.

"Mrs. West?" A short heavyset black man of about sixty wearing a tight navy suit with close cropped graying hair and a thick salt and pepper beard and mustache stood behind me.

"Yes."

"I'm Detective Michael Avery and I just wanted to ask you some questions about Adele Mackie."

"Of course, Detective. Why don't we go across the hall into the living room?"

He followed me into the living room and pulled the double doors closed behind him. I put my hands in my pockets so he wouldn't see them shaking and then took a seat on the hard floral printed sofa as he sat in a leather chair opposite me.

"I understand you're volunteering here, Mrs. West." He was looking down at a notepad.

"That's right, but I've only been volunteering here for a few weeks."

"Then you didn't know Adele Mackie very well, correct?"

"No, but I really liked her. She was very kind to me, professional, and good at her job."

Although, I wondered how well they would think she was doing her job when they looked through the files and found Dana's nearly empty folder. Would it matter that Dana had left and given up her spot, or would they think that was grounds for murder?

"Given the nature of this environment and the clients that you come in contact with on a regular basis. Do you think any of them could have done Mrs. Mackie harm?"

"Honestly, no. The shelter requires background checks on all the residents that are offered spots here. It was my understanding that anyone with violent records on their background checks wouldn't have been offered a spot here."

"You never witnessed any threats towards Mrs. Mackie by any of the residents here?"

"Not at all."

"She never mentioned having had any violent encounters with any of the residents here, maybe someone who is no longer here?"

"I never witnessed, or was made aware of, any violent confrontations or physical threats towards Mrs. Mackie while I was here. Like I said, I've only been here for a couple of weeks. I'm sure the people who've been here longer would know better."

"What about you, Mrs. West? Have you experienced any threats or violence from any of the residents here during your short time here?"

"No, not at all. All the women have been very sweet and easy to work with."

He jotted down something in his notebook, then began flipping through it for almost a full minute like he'd forgotten I was there before I finally cleared my throat.

"Will that be all, Detective Avery?"

"Uh, sorry about that. Yes. You're free to go for now. Just know that we may need to question you again further."

About what? I had wanted to say but didn't, I wanted to get as far away from this man as fast as possible. I headed out of the living room and made a beeline for the kitchen where Mrs. Brady was cleaning up.

"Do you need some help? I need something to do."

"You can empty the trash in here as well as in the dining room, and take both bags out to the dumpster."

"Did the police talk to you, too?" I asked as I started lifting the large trash bag out of the overly full kitchen trash can.

"They did and a fat lot of good it did 'em, too. I'm mostly in this kitchen when I'm here and I don't see a lot of stuff. I can't think of a single person who would have wanted Adele gone, except maybe..."

She didn't have to say another word. We both looked at each other and knew exactly what the other was thinking. She knew about James and Selma, too. I looked at her and shook my head, indicating I knew exactly what she was talking about. She sucked her teeth in disgust and looked away.

"Did you tell that detective about them?"

"Did you?"

I quickly shook my head.

"Good. Coz no telling what was going on in that marriage. People with these open marriages and swinging and nonsense. Ain't nothing good ever come of that. Of course, a lot of women are in open marriages and don't even know it."

"Do you think she knew?"

"Hard to tell. All I know is it was none of my business and I'm gonna sit on that information a little longer until we get more details about what happened to poor Adele. I am so happy they don't have children who would have been robbed of their mother and left with a cheating ass daddy."

If anyone could relate to that, it was me.

FOURTEEN

AVA AND BROOKE

May 2000

In her room, Ava turned the TV up a little louder to drown out the noise coming from downstairs. She wished she hadn't asked Brooke to spend the night. She thought she was being slick by asking her mom when she was hungover on the couch, knowing her mom would tell her yes just to get rid of her so she could go back to sleep. But now she was wide awake, drunk, and screaming into the phone at her father, alternating between shouting and sobbing and begging him to come home. She'd even stooped so low as to tell him that Ava was having nightmares because of what was going on between them. It was a big lie. She wasn't having nightmares at all, and she hated listening to her mother's desperate lies. She wanted him home, too, in the worst way. She wanted them to be a family again like they were. Even at the young age of ten, Ava knew there were things that had always been wrong between her parents.

She'd lost count of how many times she'd been awakened in the middle of the night to her parents arguing. Ava never knew exactly what they were arguing about and would put her pillow over her head and hide under the blankets, usually drifting off to sleep and waking up that way. By now, she was used to her mother's hysterical phone calls to her father, but she wasn't used to Brooke being there when they happened. Ava had done such a good job of making everyone think everything was okay. She was the one keeping the house clean, using the step stool in front of the sink to wash the dishes and knew how to run the sweeper, and dust. She knew how to order pizza and microwave frozen dinners. Her mom had to get a job after Dad left because he'd stopped sending money, but she'd gotten fired and was now free to drink all day long. Ava didn't dare look at Brooke as her eyes filled with tears of frustration and embarrassment. What was her best friend thinking? Would she run home and tell her mom and then her mom would never let her stay at Ava's house again?

"It's okay, Ava. We can stay at my house next time." Brooke put her arm around Ava and Ava rested her head on her shoulder and cried silently as the show *Even Stevens* played on the TV.

FIFTEEN

LIA

I was sitting in my rental car in front of Natalie Hammond's house wondering how I was going to ask her about what Mavis Brady had told me, and asking myself who else knew. Mavis Brady could not have been the only one who'd known about Natalie borrowing money from scary people to save her home. Admittedly, it was a very nice home, a two-story brick colonial with a well-maintained lawn on a quiet tree-lined street of similarly well taken care of homes. Was it this house or what it represented that caused Natalie Hammond to make such an extreme choice to hold on to it? I had a contact within the Elmhurst Police Department, but I had no idea where I currently stood with this guy. He seemed eager enough to help me when I first approached him.

Though I suspected he was now dodging my calls, most likely afraid he'll get into trouble for things he'd shared with me about the Peters case, and the evidence that he'd let me see that he shouldn't have. In reality, I'd most likely scared him off because I thought everybody wanted to be on TV. I'd dangled the possibility of him being interviewed about the case for my documentary in his face thinking he'd agree to anything I asked him for. I didn't realize how wrong I was until he'd stopped returning my calls. So now there was only one way to go about this. As much as I was dreading it, I had to go talk to Natalie Hammond, hence being parked in front of her house. I'd already rang her doorbell and gotten no response and had just gotten back behind the wheel when her burgundy Honda Civic pulled onto the driveway. I got out again, but she was not happy to see me.

"I gave my daughter your business card and she said she'd contacted you." Natalie Hammond was struggling to remain polite.

She was a slim attractive woman in her late fifties with brown skin and hair worn in a curly bob. In her gray and black paisley print wrap dress and black pumps, she looked polished and professional. Ava looked a lot like her.

"I'm sorry to bother you again, Ms. Hammond, but I've recently been given some information that I need you to clear up for me."

"Me? What would you have to talk to me about?" Confusion narrowed her eyes and hardened her lips into a tight line.

"I think it would probably be best if we spoke inside."

She let out an exasperated sigh and then turned to head to her front door with me trailing her like a puppy. Once inside the brightly lit foyer, she turned and set her keys down in a bowl on the side table just inside the entrance.

"We're inside. Now, what's this all about?"

There was no reason to hesitate. So, I went for it. "I was recently told that you owed a lot of money to some very scary people and because you didn't pay them, Brooke Peters may have been abducted when it was Ava they were after." I took an involuntary step back as Natalie's face contorted with rage making a mental note of how close the door was in case I had to flee.

But as quickly as the anger popped up on the other woman's face, it dissipated and she sank down onto a bench next to the table and burst into tears. I let her cry for a couple of minutes before pulling a tissue from my purse and handing it to her.

"I am so sorry, Ms. Hammond, but I had to ask. By your reaction, can I assume the rumor is true?"

"Yes," she said before wiping her eyes and blowing her nose

with a tissue. "I was stupid enough and desperate enough to borrow some money at an extremely high interest rate to save this house. I wasn't getting any kind of support from Clay, my ex-husband. So, yes, I was desperate. And, yes, I did borrow that money. When Brooke was first abducted, I did think that maybe they'd been after Ava and got Brooke by mistake. So, you're not telling me anything that hasn't gone through my mind for years." She looked down at the floor as another tear trickled out of the corner of her eye.

"Why are you so sure they wouldn't have taken Ava?"

Her head whipped up and she glared at me. "What would they possibly have to gain by taking my daughter?"

I stared at her like she was stupid. "Do I really have to spell this out for you?"

"No." She shook her head vigorously. "Those people were into a lot of illegal things, but not that. They never would've gotten a single dime out of me if they had. There was no incentive for them to take my daughter if they wanted their money back."

"Maybe taking her would have been their way of making sure they got their money back, like an insurance policy."

"I made a deal with them and before you ask, I'm not telling you what that deal was."

"Why is that?"

"Because it's none of your business and has absolutely nothing to do with Brooke's disappearance."

Her hostile stare didn't intimidate me. Instead, I was angry. "As a mother, how could you not share this information with the police, even privately? Ava would have never needed to know. It could have shed a whole new light on Brooke's abduction."

"How do you know I didn't? How do you know they didn't look into it and found out the people I owed money to didn't have Brooke?"

"And how do I know you're telling the truth and not trying to keep me from telling Ava?"

The hostile look Natalie Hammond gave instantly turned into

a blank stare as her face went slack. She held her left hand out to me, palm side down.

"What am I..." I began before I saw it and gasped. Half her pinky finger, up to the knuckle, was gone.

"They didn't take Brooke, but they took this when they found out I'd led the police to their doorstep."

"Oh my god," I whispered as my hands flew to my mouth.

"This is nothing," she said in a flat voice. "They could have cut off my head."

SIXTEEN

AVA

It's been three days and Dana is still staying with us. Not because she wants to but because she can't find any place else to go with no job and no money, and also because every time she tried to leave, I gave her a reason to stay. Evan still isn't thrilled, but when I pointed out that I was afraid after Adele's murder and I didn't want to be alone in the house when he was away at his job site, he reluctantly relented.

I was scheduled to undergo my first IVF treatment in two weeks and could tell he was willing to agree to anything to keep the process going. Although he was polite to Dana, he wasn't exactly enthusiastic, and she knew deep down he didn't want her there, but I refused to let her sleep in the woods again. She didn't even have a car to live in anymore since she'd sold it. I could tell she'd rather be anywhere but at my house.

Unfortunately, her spot at the shelter had been given to someone else. I was now working every morning at the shelter. One of the other part-timers, a woman named Janine who I only crossed paths with on my way out the door every day, had been chosen by Selma to take Adele's place. She was currently at home recovering from a hip replacement so wouldn't be available to take over Adele's position for two more weeks, which was perfect timing and coincided with my first

IVF treatment. I had no idea how I'd feel during the treatment and didn't want to commit to the shelter once the IVF process got going.

According to Selma, and what I was reading in the newspapers, the police had no leads in Adele's murder. I could tell by how drawn Selma's face looked and the weight she'd lost, that Adele's death was messing with her. I thought about James. How was he holding up? I didn't know the man at all and had barely known Adele, but knowing he was cheating on her and with her boss at that, I hope the guilt was eating his ass alive.

I was cleaning up the kitchen after Dana cooked dinner. Veggie lasagna. It was good, too.

"Are you sure you were okay with no meat?" Dana eyed my empty plate dubiously. While I was a hardcore carnivore, the lasagna was better than I thought it would be. But I was glad Evan was in Columbus until tomorrow because he would not have been feeling lasagna with no meat.

"It was great. Seriously," I assured her truthfully. "I didn't realize you were a vegetarian." I remembered Mrs. Brady's comment about the box lunch and a veggie and cheese sandwich for the people who didn't like meat and realized she must've been talking about Dana.

"I still eat meat when I can afford it, but being vegetarian is just cheaper when you don't have any money. I can get a jar of chunky vegetable spaghetti sauce and a box of spaghetti for two dollars and eat off that for a week. That's the reason I wear my hair buzzed. Don't have to worry about wigs, weaves, or relaxers. Just wash and go."

It never even occurred to me how many of the choices we made every day were dependent on our financial circumstances, and I was more determined than ever to help Dana whether it turned out she was Brooke or not.

"You know, you never told me where you were from. I know you told Evan you came here a few months ago from Dayton, but where were you born? Do you still have family there?"

"No clue. I've been gone so long I have no idea where my family is or if they're still there."

"And by family you mean...?"

"My mom and brother." She stared at her plate intensely, making a show of winding up her last bit of spaghetti with her fork before shoving it into her mouth.

That she didn't want to talk about her family was clear, but the fact she said her family consisted of a mother and a brother was also pointing in the direction of her being Brooke. I knew I was going to have to tease the information out of her bit by bit before I scared her off for good.

"I'm sorry. I know I'm being nosy. I just want to know a little more about you, that's all. I'll answer any questions you want to know about me. Just ask."

She instantly smirked before coming to the other side of the kitchen island and leaning against it with her arms crossed.

"Okay. What's the deal with you and your man? Why is he so damned grumpy when I hear you guys getting busy all the time? I would've thought that would've put a smile on his face."

My face burned with embarrassment because Evan and I had been so careful and quiet, or so we'd thought. The look of mortification on my face caused Dana to throw her head back and laugh loudly.

"I'm sorry. Have we been keeping you awake?"

"No, not at all," she said, holding up her hands. "This is your house, and you can do whatever the hell you want in it. If you guys want to swing from the chandelier naked and oiled up, that ain't nobody's business but yours."

Now, it was my turn to laugh and before I knew it, we were both laughing so hard we were crying. It took us a few minutes to compose ourselves.

"We hit a bad patch a while back and it's taking a minute to work through it, that's all."

"Do you think you'll be able to?" I saw real concern in Dana's eyes and felt touched and a little weepy. I took a big gulp of white wine to mask it.

"I think so."

"Is this about that empty nursery?"

Her question surprised me, but I answered her honestly.

"Yeah, we've been trying for over a year and I even took a leave of absence from my job. We went through a round of a fertility drug called Clomid and we're still not pregnant. I had no idea how this experience would expose the cracks in my marriage."

"I'm sorry, Ava." She came over and sat back across the table from me, then grabbed my hand and squeezed it.

"Are you sure you want to have a baby with this dude?"

"Why would you ask that?"

Dana shrugged. "Just wondering if you want to be a mother with all that entails, and still deal with the cracks if they don't mend themselves. People think babies fix relationship problems. They don't."

"Do you have kids, Dana?" I couldn't help but notice how her eyes slid away from my face the minute that question was out of my mouth.

"No," she said a little too quickly. "Dealing with my current situation is hard enough without worrying about a kid, too."

We were silent for a little while before I picked her empty plate and went to clean up the kitchen. We had fallen into a routine pretty quickly with us taking turns cooking and cleaning up. I sipped on my wine when it suddenly struck me that she still hadn't answered my question about where she was from.

It was after midnight when I heard the scream and nearly fell out of bed, rushing to get to the door. It was Dana, and she was shrieking. I ran to the guest bedroom only to find it empty and then paused to listen when another ear-splitting shriek filled the air. I ran downstairs into the kitchen to see Dana trying to get out the back door unsuccessfully. When she couldn't open the door, she proceeded to start banging her hands against the glass.

I rushed over to her, afraid she would break the glass and cut her hand. I put my hands on her shoulders to pull her away from the door. She turned around, her hand swinging out, missing my face by millimeters. Her eyes were open but focused on nothing. I took a step back, and she went back to trying to get out the door. That's when I realized she was asleep.

"Dana!" When she didn't respond and continued to keep trying to get out of the door, my assumption was confirmed. She was sleepwalking. Combined with the screaming, I recognized she was in the throes of a night terror. I had no idea what to do because I'd always heard you don't wake up sleepwalking people. If it's a night terror, you could be putting yourself in danger as well. Instead, I did something I wasn't sure was the right thing to do, but I was terrified she was going to break the glass.

I stepped to her side and reached past her to unlock the door, expecting her to rush outside, but she just stood there with me silently by her side, watching her as she stared out into the backyard. Soon the peace and quiet of the night was shattered once again when our house alarm went off. I rushed over to the panel by the front door and keyed in the code to stop the alarm. Once the alarm was off, I went back to the kitchen. Dana was curled up on the floor in front of the still open door fast asleep.

I started to walk over to her when I heard my phone ringing upstairs and knew it was the alarm company checking to see if everything was okay. I quickly shut the back door, locked it and ran upstairs to tell the alarm people that everything was fine. Knowing there was no way I could drag Dana back upstairs and put her in her bed, and not wanting to wake her for my own safety and hers, I grabbed a blanket from the hall closet and a cushion from the couch to stick under her head, then put the blanket over her and curled up on the couch and fell asleep myself. I woke to the smell of coffee brewing and sat up abruptly. Dana was in the kitchen with a mug of coffee. When she saw I was awake, she sat her coffee cup down and gave me an apologetic look.

"What did I do last night? How bad was it?"

"Not as bad as it could've been. You were screaming and banging your hands on the glass trying to get out. Then I opened the door, afraid you were going to hurt yourself and it set off the alarm which would have woken the dead, but you still didn't wake up. Instead, you just curled up on the floor in front of the door and fell asleep."

"Damn." She swore softly under her breath and looked away from me.

I got up and went into the kitchen and poured my own mug of hot coffee. I took it to the kitchen table and sat down, gesturing for her to join me, which she did. She still couldn't look at me.

"How long have you been having night terrors?"

"As long as I can remember. Some crazy shit went down when I was younger and now whenever I'm stressed or upset, I get them."

I was momentarily silent as I studied her face, realizing I truly did not know this woman. Even if she was Brooke, ten-year-old Brooke was long gone, and I knew nothing about the woman she was today.

"I hope I'm not the one stressing you out. If I am, I am so sorry."

Her head suddenly jerked up and she gave me a very intense stare. "Are you kidding me? You letting me stay here is the nicest thing anyone has done for me in a very long time. I really appreciate you, Ava, for letting me stay here. I even appreciate your grumpy ass husband. Don't ever doubt that."

The sudden lump that had formed in my throat prevented me from answering her, and I was afraid I would embarrass us both if I started crying. So, I merely nodded, reaching out and squeezing her hand.

"How often do you get these night terrors? And what should I do the next time it happens? I'm in new territory here."

"You did exactly what you were supposed to do. They don't last long. I've never hurt myself and as bad as I wanted to get out of any door, I never go. I'm lucky. I've heard of people who have run off and hurt themselves, or died during night terrors."

"And what do you think caused this one? When was the last time you had one?"

"At Haver House the first night I was there. The stress usually comes when I move to a new location and haven't gotten used to everything yet. I was trying to get out of the shelter, but the front door was locked."

"You went all the way down three flights of steps, then tried to get out the front door, all while you were asleep," I said, more to myself than her. I was in awe of the fact she was able to do all of that while asleep and not fall down the steps and break her neck.

"Yeah. They found me sleeping on the floor in the foyer, just like you did this morning. Can we change the subject?"

"Of course. I'm sorry, I just wanted to know what to do next time. Do you want some breakfast?"

I didn't even wait for her answer and got up and got busy getting eggs, veggies and cheese out of the fridge to make us omelets.

"You're not sorry you invited me here, are you?"

"Not at all. I'm not in the habit of inviting people into my home that I don't want here."

I started cracking eggs into a bowl when the doorbell rang, and I asked Dana if she could get it for me.

A minute later, Dana came back into the kitchen followed by my mother who had a tight smile on her face. I knew from years of experience that she was trying to be polite because she didn't know what was going on.

"Hey, you're just in time for breakfast. Want an omelet?"

"I just stopped by to see how you were doing since I haven't heard from you in a few days and you're not returning my calls. I didn't realize you had a guest."

"Mom, this is Dana Shields. Dana, this is my mom, Natalie Hammond."

"Nice meeting you, ma'am." Dana stuck her hand out to my mom. My mom glanced at her hand briefly before giving it a quick shake.

"Nice to meet you, too, Dana. Did you two have a sleepover?" She looked over at the blankets still on the couch and folded up by the back door.

"Dana is staying with us for a little while."

"Just for a little while until I get back on my feet. And your daughter is so sweet for taking me in. You should be very proud of her."

"I am very proud of her. She is a wonderful person who loves to help people. I just worry sometimes that she's letting the wrong people in."

Dana and I both turned to stare at my mom, who was usually polite to a fault. What was her issue with Dana? But deep down I knew. After what happened to Brooke, she'd been very protective of me. She still felt guilty for how she'd spiraled after Dad left, and had been asleep at the wheel, so to speak, for months, leaving me to fend for myself. Still, she had no right to say that in front of Dana.

"Hey, Dana, why don't you run up and take your shower and get dressed? By the time you get done, your omelet will be waiting for you."

"Sounds good. Nice meeting you, Mrs. Hammond."

We both watched Dana head up the steps to the second floor. We both knew to be silent until we heard the bathroom door open and close.

"What was that about? Why were you so rude to her?" I had set my spatula down and glared at my mom.

"Where is that woman from? Please don't tell me you brought some stranger from that shelter into your home."

"What if I did? It's my home. I can have whoever I want here. I'm an adult, remember?"

"What *you* need to remember is to watch your tone when you

talk to me. Doesn't matter how grown you are, I'm still your mother and I have a right to be concerned about you when you're making stupid decisions. What does Evan think about this?"

"He's fine with it and since when do you care about his opinion? You've never liked him."

"Let's stick to the topic at hand, shall we?" she said, setting her purse down in one of the stools at the kitchen island.

"You're the one who brought up Evan. Not me."

Mom let out a frustrated sigh and continued her rant. "You want to know how I know that you're not sure whether this was a good idea or not?"

"Would it matter if I didn't?"

"The fact that I haven't heard from you in days, and that you didn't tell me about any of this shows me that you already know this wasn't a good idea."

"Who I have in my home and why is not up for debate, but I do have some news that should make you very happy." At least I hoped it would because I was so over having to justify my decisions to my mother.

"And what is that?"

"I called Lia Quinn back and I'm going to participate in the documentary, and she's already paid me enough for one IVF treatment."

A big smile broke out across her face. She came around the island and gave me a hug. "Oh, baby, I am so happy for you. I think participating in this documentary is going to be good for you, but just a word of warning."

I quickly pulled out of her grasp because she was doing what she'd always done my entire life. No matter how happy or excited I was about anything, she always found a way to make me second-guess my decisions.

"Don't look at me like that, Ava. Lia Quinn came to see me the other day, and I just want you to be careful because she's trying to stir up a bunch of mess."

I hadn't spoken to Lia since I had met with her and agreed to participate in the documentary. I remembered what she'd told me about the gossip she heard about Brooke's brother Sam, but I had no idea she was still bothering my mother with old gossip. I had no choice but to participate because I had already received and spent the payment.

"What mess is she trying to stir up?"

"Asking me about old gossip about Brooke's family and other stories she's heard. I know she has to look into these things, but don't let her smear the reputations of innocent people."

She wouldn't quite look at me when she said that, and it instantly put me on my guard, making me wonder what she was talking about.

"You know you really don't have to tell me that. I would never go along with anything that wasn't completely factual when it comes to Brooke or her family. You know that, right?"

Lia had left me a couple of messages that I had been intending to return when Adele had been killed. I was going to make it a point to get back to her today and hopefully talk to her about whatever my mother was talking about. Plus, I knew it was no use trying to get any more details out of my mom when I wasn't sure what her motives were for even telling me this information. Suddenly, I was confused. She was the one who told me I needed to talk to this woman to possibly get some closure about what happened to Brooke. Now, here she was showing up at my house unannounced to tell me not to trust Lia Quinn, and she was trying to make me feel paranoid about giving Dana a safe place to stay. I love my mother to death; we've been through a lot together, but I didn't need this right now.

"Do you want an omelet?"

"Do I want...Girl, stop trying to change the subject. I'm serious. You need to be careful about who you trust."

"So, who shouldn't I trust, Mom? Lia Quinn or Dana?"

"You shouldn't truly trust anyone until you figure out what their motives are. All I'm saying is, be careful. Miss Quinn just wants to do a documentary to capitalize on a tragedy, but I don't know who this Dana woman is. Participating in a documentary for cash is one thing. Inviting a stranger you know next to nothing about into your home is something else entirely."

"We were almost homeless once. You remember that, right?" I blurted it out without thinking and watched all the light go out of my mom's eyes, and was instantly ashamed. I quickly reached out to grab her hand when she pulled it away. "I'm sorry."

She started to walk towards the front door, but stopped and turned to me, looking beyond weary.

"I know better than anybody that we were almost homeless once. I also know that it was my fault. You don't need to remind me of that."

"Mom...I..." But she held up a hand, cutting me off.

"I don't know this Dana person or her story, but I was willing to do anything to keep a roof over our heads."

I couldn't tell if she was angry or hurt or both as she marched out my front door. It wasn't lost on me that this was the first time she had ever alluded to what she had done to keep a roof over our heads. I briefly wondered what she was talking about before realizing I probably didn't want to know.

For the first time in a long time my shift overlapped with Kerri's, and we had a chance to talk, which we hadn't been able to do since I'd started. I'd seen her at Adele's memorial service but hadn't talked to her much because I left after witnessing the clinch between James and Selma. Understandably, she wasn't in the mood for much conversation either, and was distracted to the point that I wondered if something else besides Adele's death was bothering her.

"How are the wedding plans coming along?" If there's anything that could distract her from what happened to her colleague, it was her upcoming nuptials. And I was right. She instantly perked up.

"I had another fitting for my wedding dress. It's going to have to be taken in again because I've lost ten more pounds."

I had noticed that she'd lost more weight. I actually thought she was getting a little too thin, but I wasn't about to say this to her.

"I bet you look beautiful in your dress. I remembered how I felt in my wedding dress. Evan and I had a small wedding, but I still made sure to wear my dream dress."

"I feel like a princess in my dress. It's all I ever wanted. My only requirement was that I feel like a beautiful bride on my special day. And I know I will."

"Men have it so easy. It took Evan all of an hour to pick out his suit. It took me weeks to pick out my dress as well as everything else that went into planning the wedding. All he had to do was show up."

"Really?" she said, looking genuinely surprised. "Josh has been very active in our wedding plans. He picked out the invitations and the venue, and he gave me ideas on what kind of dress he wanted to see me in."

I was momentarily speechless. What kind of dress he wanted to see her in? Why was he involving himself in her right to pick her own wedding dress?

"What kind of dress is that?" I purposely kept my tone light so she wouldn't pick up on the judgment I was feeling towards her fiancé who I'd yet to meet.

"You know? Modest. Nothing too low cut or revealing. He said he wanted a bride walking down the aisle to him, not a lingerie model. I know how that sounds, but I trust Josh and value his opinion. He's a man of faith. That's one of the things I love so much about him, that and how brutally honest he is. He just wants what's best for me and our relationship."

I noticed Kerri's smile was tight and her words of praise for her fiancé weren't reflected in her eyes. Her fingers immediately went to the pendant around her neck, rubbing it between her fingers the same way I'd seen her rubbing it at Adele's memorial. I recognized a stress response when I saw it. I simply nodded and smiled. There was so much I could've said but didn't because it was really none of my business. So, I changed the subject.

"That's a beautiful pendant, Kerri. I meant to tell you that at Adele's memorial."

"Oh this," she said, instantly taking it off and handing it to me. "It was my grandma Kay's, one of the things she left me in her will."

I was surprised it had some weight to it, and I turned it over in my hand. It was a round gold pendant the size of a quarter with the letter K in old English script engraved on the front. I flipped it over and saw there was a tiny round symbol on the back. When I saw it, I did a double take. Was I mistaken or did this symbol look just like the birthmark on Brooke and Dana? Without thinking I held it up to the light to get a better look when Kerri abruptly took it from my hand and slipped the thin chain back over her head and tucked the pendant inside her T-shirt.

"Sorry," she said, her face reddening. "It's really old. I probably shouldn't be wearing it so much. I just feel closer to my grandma when I do."

"No worries." I held up my hands and took a small step back, suddenly embarrassed. "I was just curious about the symbol on the back."

Kerri pulled the pendant out and looked at the back, squinting at the symbol much the way I had. "I have no idea what that is, but if I had to guess, it's some kind of Buddhist symbol. My grandma was big into stuff like that."

"Sounds like she was a woman ahead of her time."

"She was. For years she owned a little shop here in town that sold herbal remedies. She made them herself. Then she suffered a fall and broke her hip and couldn't work anymore, and she had to sell her shop. I think that was the beginning of the end for her. That shop was her life."

Kerri looked like she might start crying again. So, I snapped her back to reality.

"I'd never met Adele's husband James. He seems really nice. My heart just broke for him at the memorial service. He was really torn up."

"Yeah, he's nice." The lack of enthusiasm in her response was evident.

"Uh-oh. I'm sensing a but. What's wrong with James?" Of course, I already knew what was wrong with James, but I wanted to hear what Kerri had to say.

"He's nice. He's just a little too nice sometimes. You know

what I mean? He's a flirty guy. I'm sure he doesn't mean anything by it, but sometimes he makes me a little uncomfortable."

I knew exactly what she was talking about. I'd known plenty of men like James in my life. Men who always seem to be casting a net for whoever they could catch under the guise of simply being a nice friendly guy. From what I had seen right here in this office, James had caught Selma in his nice guy net. Again, I wondered if Adele had known. I realized she probably didn't because why would she be working for a woman who was having an affair with her husband?

Kerri apparently didn't want to talk about James anymore because she gestured to a stack of two cardboard boxes with handles sitting in front of Adele's desk.

"We got our files back from the police, and I could really use some help putting these away before I leave."

"Sure. If we each take a box, we should be able to get through them pretty quickly."

Without waiting for her to respond, I grabbed the box that was marked N through Z. Then I grabbed a cart, loaded the box on top of it along with the corresponding drawers from the filing cabinet and pulled up a chair to get to work while Kerri stood at the actual filing cabinet putting away her part of the alphabet. While her back was turned, I grabbed the file that I really wanted to see but quickly realized Dana Shields' file was not in the box. Where had it gone? Then it hit me. She had given up her spot at the shelter right before Adele was killed. Her file was probably pulled since she was no longer a resident. Was it still here?

"What happens to all the old files for the previous residents? How long do we keep those?"

"I think for tax purposes we have to keep those files for at least three years. So, all previous resident files are pulled and put into storage."

"I didn't realize we had storage. Where is it?"

"Down in the basement, but I've never been down there. Adele and Selma were the only ones with the keys to the storage room. Why are you asking?"

"No reason. Just curious."

We worked for another hour before Kerri had to leave and then I settled myself behind Adele's desk and wondered how long I would see this as Adele's desk. I glanced at my watch and realized I still had three more hours until I had to pick up Dana from the library. She'd been headed out the door at the same time as me for the bus stop. I insisted on giving her a ride to the library so she could use their computers to look for a job. I'd once again asked her about her ID, and she simply shrugged and stared out the window without responding.

I wanted to shake her and tell her she wasn't going to be able to accomplish anything without a picture ID. I knew Evan would have a fit if I offered to volunteer our address for her to receive her new driver's license. I knew the law. Once someone started receiving mail at a residence, it was considered their home, and it was next to impossible to get them out without eviction proceedings. I was thinking about how I could help her when a man suddenly appeared in the doorway, knocking softly to get my attention. It was Detective Avery and the sight of him made my breath quicken.

"Detective Avery? How can I help you?"

"Mrs. West. Actually, you're just the person I came to see."

"Me? Why?" I was suddenly on high alert as he walked into the office, looking around.

"Just a couple questions. Do you have time?"

"Do I have a choice?" I didn't mean to sound rude. I was just surprised and more than a little concerned that the police were wanting to talk to me about anything.

"I didn't realize until I was going over your statement that you are formally Ava Hammond, Brooklyn Peters' best friend."

I was a little taken aback but not completely surprised. This was the kind of reaction I got from everyone when they found out what happened when I was ten.

"I am. What does this have to do with what happened to Adele?"

"Probably nothing. I was just wondering if you knew that Adele's body was found in that same section of the park where Brooke was abducted. Same parking lot."

"Yes, Detective. I did know that, and I still don't understand what it has to do with me."

"Maybe nothing, but I don't believe in coincidences. Did Mrs. Mackie know about your past?"

"If she did, she didn't hear it from me. It's not something that I talk about, especially with people I don't know well."

"I completely understand. That is a disused area of the park since what happened to your friend all those years ago. It's actually been slated to be dug up and a new garden put in next spring."

"Well, maybe that was the point of her being there."

"Meaning?"

"Meaning, maybe she went there because she knew hardly anyone went there and she wanted to be alone and was in the wrong place at the wrong time and someone attacked her."

"For what purpose? Nothing was stolen."

"You of all people should know that people don't need a reason to kill. It could've been purely opportunistic."

Detective Avery stared at me with a neutral expression, not speaking, which made me very uncomfortable. I'm betting that was his intent, but why was he asking me about this? I had no idea where Adele had been found exactly. Did this have anything to do with whatever her issues were with Dana? It was right on the tip of my tongue to tell him about what I'd witness between Adele and Dana. However, something was stopping me. I got the distinct impression that this man needed some kind of an answer from me, or he wouldn't leave me alone. So, I gave him one.

"Detective Avery, did you know that Adele used to be a practicing psychiatrist?"

"Her husband informed me. He also told me she stopped practicing a decade ago because of something that happened with a former patient."

"He told me the same thing. Are you looking into this former patient? Could someone closely connected to this former patient have a grudge against her?"

"We're looking at every avenue, Mrs. West. You have my word on that. That's why I came to see you because I thought it was too much of a coincidence considering you witnessed your friend being abducted in almost the exact spot that Adele Mackie was murdered twenty-five years later."

"If I didn't know any better, Detective, I would think you thought I killed Adele."

"Did you?"

"No." I tried to keep the contempt out of my voice because he had every right to ask me this question. "I did not. I liked Adele and got along very well with her. I would've had absolutely no reason to harm her in any way."

"You know I had to ask, right?"

"I know. That doesn't mean I have to be happy about answering these questions."

"To clarify, you still cannot think of anyone who would want to harm Adele, residents or staff?"

Residents or staff. Did he know about Adele's husband and Selma Ross? Well, he wasn't about to hear it from me. Sure, plenty of people have killed their spouses to be with another person, but the majority are content to keep their secrets and keep having their cake and eating it, too. Most people did not kill their spouses for an affair partner. Besides I could've been completely wrong about what I'd witnessed here in the office the night of her memorial. If James Mackie was as flirty and friendly as Kerri said he was, he could've been the one to take advantage of Selma when she went to embrace him in his grief. I realized Avery was still staring at me.

"And again, no. I have no idea why anyone would want to hurt Adele and I know of no conflicts that she had with residents or staff here."

"Then I'll not take up any more of your time, Mrs. West. Thank you for talking to me and you have my card if you need to contact me in case you happen to remember anything."

I nodded at him and watched him leave. I couldn't shake the feeling that this would not be the last time I would see Detective Michael Avery. Two minutes after he left, my cell phone rang. It was my doctor from the Asher Clinic, and it wasn't good news.

"Man, that sucks. I'm sorry, Ava."

Dana was trying unsuccessfully to console me after I picked her up and proceeded to burst into tears when she asked me how my day had gone after seeing my red-rimmed eyes. The phone call I'd gotten earlier that day had been from Dr. Glen's nurse at the Asher Clinic, informing me that the doctor was currently in the hospital in Switzerland after suffering a major accident while skiing. She would be laid up for the foreseeable future with a head injury and two broken legs. All of her colleagues at the clinic who would have gladly taken over my case were booked out until the end of the year. Evan and I had been lucky to get the appointment that we got. Now, everything was pushed back for six months or more. When I saw the Asher Clinic's number pop up on my phone, I thought they were scheduling our first treatment. How was I going to tell Evan? More importantly, how would he react?

"Thanks," I told her in a flat voice devoid of emotion.

"Well," Dana began tentatively. "At least now you have more time."

More time? What was she talking about? I gave her a quizzical look, and she hesitated just an instant before pressing on.

"You told me that you and your husband were having issues. Doesn't this give you more time to resolve those before you bring a baby into the picture?"

What she said made perfect sense, but I wasn't in the mood to hear it, and I had to practically bite my tongue to tell her to mind her own business. How could I tell her that when I was the one who'd told her my business? I had opened that door and let her in.

"Sorry. That's absolutely none of my business."

"No, it isn't, but you're not wrong," I agreed. "As much as I hate to admit it, maybe this just isn't in the cards for us. Maybe this is some kind of sign that we need to slow our roll and reconnect."

"Isn't that what I just said?" she said with a smile, and we both laughed.

We were three blocks from my house when I drove past a newly opened ice-cream shop that I'd been wanting to try. Nothing like drowning your sorrows in dairy.

"Hey, cheer me up and have some ice cream with me." I didn't wait for her response before pulling into the parking lot of Delphine's ice-cream parlor.

"Not a big ice-cream person. If they've got sorbet, I'll have some of that."

It took me a long time to start eating ice cream again after Brooke was abducted since I blamed myself and that chocolate ice-cream cone for her abduction. It has only been in the last decade that I'd started eating it again. One thing I did remember with crystal clear clarity was that Brooke had loved ice cream. She wasn't a chocolate lover like me. Strawberry was her favorite. My heart instantly sank.

"Really? I don't know too many people who don't like ice cream."

"I didn't say I didn't like it. I can't eat it. Lactose intolerant, but I used to love it as a kid."

"Really? What was your favorite flavor?"

"Chocolate," she replied and headed into the shop ahead of me.

Ten minutes later, we were seated at a table outside. I'd gone all out and gotten a banana split while Dana dug into her pineapple sorbet. We were half finished when I brought up what else had happened to me that day.

"The detective in charge of Adele's case came to see me today."

"Why?" Dana hadn't even bothered looking up and continued to scoop a big spoonful of sorbet into her mouth.

"He keeps asking me if I know of anyone who had any problems with Adele."

That seemed to have gotten her attention, and her spoon froze halfway to her mouth before she set it down and gave me her full attention.

"And you told him about me, right?" She leaned back in her chair and her look was a hair's breadth away from hostile.

"No. I didn't tell him anything. It's not my place to tell him, but you should."

"Nope. I'm good. I don't have a damn thing to tell any cops about Adele."

"I saw you two arguing downtown. If I saw you, then most likely other people saw you guys, too. Wouldn't you rather talk to the detective yourself to clear the air? Before they show up at the shelter with your description wanting to know if we know who you are. Even if I don't say anything, other people at Haver House will." I pulled Detective Avery's card from my purse and slid it across the table to her. She stared at it and then at me.

"Didn't you hear what I said?"

"I'm serious, Dana. You really need to talk to this man." But she would barely look at me, let alone pick up the card. I reached out and snatched it back, sticking it into my purse.

Dana was finished with her sorbet. I was only halfway through my banana split when she stood up.

"Thanks for the sorbet. I don't have time to sit here all afternoon, so you don't get brain freeze, but I'll see you later."

"Dana?" I called out after her, but she tossed up a hand and walked out the door.

She crossed the parking lot and got to the corner just in time for the city bus to arrive. I watched her disappear onto it before it registered what she'd just said to me. Brain freeze? How did she know I got brain freeze when I ate ice cream too fast?

I was finishing up my banana split when a minibus pulled

into the parking lot of the ice-cream shop and a dozen or so kids who looked to be between twelve and sixteen years old got out, laughing and horsing around. They filed past me into the ice-cream shop, but it was the man who was driving the van that surprised me. It was James Mackie. I hadn't seen him since his wife's memorial, and he certainly looked better now. He didn't notice me and started to walk right past when I called out to him.

"Mr. Mackie?"

When he turned and saw me sitting at a table outside, his face broke into a grin and he walked over to me. "Hello. It's Ava, right?"

"That's right." I stood up to face him.

"I was hoping to see you after the memorial to thank you for coming, but you'd already left."

"I had a prior commitment I had to get to. It was a lovely memorial."

"Thank you. I understand about prior commitments. I volunteer with my church's youth group, and we've had a trip to a Reds' game scheduled for months. I know Adele wouldn't have wanted them to miss it. It keeps me from sitting at home missing my wife."

It sure didn't look like he'd been missing her when he'd been in clench with Selma Ross, but I quickly pushed that thought away. With the state of my marriage, who was I to judge?"

"What church do you belong to? Looks like you guys had fun."

"Grace United. We did have fun even though the Reds lost."

We both laughed and I noticed another person get off the bus and approach us. She was a light-skinned black woman who looked to be in her forties with a sleek updo, wearing tight black jeans, red trainers, and an oversized Reds jersey. She was looking from me to James with a tight smile and hard eyes. I instantly knew what her problem was. She thought I was competition. I'd never forgotten my mother telling me about all the church ladies who were after my grandfather when my grandma died. They kept his fridge full of food for weeks afterwards. The man's wife wasn't even in the ground yet and women were already staking claim to him. I wondered if Selma knew. Once she'd reached his side, the woman, whoever she was, just glared at me.

"Mrs. West, this is Suzette Harper, our church's youth services coordinator. Suzette, Mrs. West worked at Haver House with Adele."

"Nice meeting you," she said, looking me up and down.

"Nice meeting you as well. It was also so nice to see you again, Mr. Mackie. Please keep us posted about the funeral."

I walked quickly towards my car, and when I looked back, they'd already disappeared into the ice-cream shop. I wondered if one of James Mackie's lady friends could have been behind his wife's murder.

Evan took Dr. Glenn's accident a whole lot better than I thought he would. He was home cooking dinner when I got home from the ice-cream parlor, unable to finish my banana split. He pulled me into his arms and hugged me tight, and I realized just how much I'd missed my husband.

"We'll get there. I promise. This time next year we'll either have a baby or one on the way. This is just a minor setback. If it doesn't work..." he said, shrugging, and gave me a big smile. "There are always other options."

"Other options as in fostering or adoption?"

He nodded slowly. "Yeah, as in fostering or adoption, but only as a last resort after all other options have failed."

I stared at him in shock. Yes, I could definitely tell he still wanted his own biological children. After his confession about his childhood, I now knew why it was so important to him, but this turnaround gave me hope and I squeezed him back.

"I love you."

"And I love you. If we didn't have a guest, I'd swing you over my shoulder, take you upstairs and show you how much I love you."

"Well, it's not like she hasn't heard us lately."

"Seriously? Coz that's not creepy at all." He pulled back from me and gave me a horrified look. "Speaking of which, where is our guest?"

I wasn't about to tell him that she took off and left me at the ice-cream shop or what she said about the brain freeze. I hadn't told anybody about my suspicions, least of all Evan.

"Not sure. I know she was at the library earlier. Maybe she's still there."

"Well, if she's not back by dinner, I'm eating her share of barbecue chicken. I outdid myself, babe." He headed over to the oven and pulled out a big casserole dish of baked barbecue chicken, setting it on top of the stove.

The spicy aroma quickly filled the entire house. Next, he pulled out a dish of macaroni and cheese and my mouth watered even though I was still full from my banana split. Mainly, though, I was thinking about what Dana had said. The only way she would've known about my brain freeze is if she was indeed Brooke, but there were other things that weren't adding up, either. I was getting a headache trying to wrap my head around it all.

"Why don't I whip us up a salad," I told him as I pulled salad fixings out of the refrigerator. "By the time I get done, if Dana's not here, we can go ahead and eat, and I'll put her plate in the fridge."

"Sounds like a plan to me." He gave me a kiss on the forehead and headed upstairs to shower.

By ten o'clock that night Dana still hadn't shown up and I felt myself getting irritated. She had my number. If she was going to stay out, didn't I deserve a phone call letting me know? I wasn't about to treat her like a child, but some common courtesy would've been nice.

I waited up until midnight for Dana before falling asleep, only to wake up at 2 a.m. and not be able to go back to sleep. I hadn't given her a key, so there was no way for her to get back into the house. Sure enough, I went down to the kitchen and saw her asleep on one of the deck chairs on our back patio. I got irritated all over again, wondering why she didn't just ring the doorbell or call me so I could let her in. As I stood over her, looking down at her sleeping form, I realized this was probably something she was used to. Sleeping rough. I remembered her telling me she'd slept in the woods after she left Haver House. I reached down to touch her shoulder to wake her when I saw her eyes were open and she was staring at me. I snatched my hand back.

"Sorry. I thought you were asleep. Why didn't you call me? I would've let you in?"

She sat up and yawned, stretching her arms and rubbing her eyes like a little kid. Just like Brooke used to do when she had sleepovers at my house. It was so hard to wake her up, but when she was awake, she always looked confused for a few minutes. Just like Dana did now. It didn't seem like she knew where she was, and she looked around with an alarmed look on her face before recognizing me and giving me a sheepish look.

"I didn't mean to be gone so long."

"Where were you? I was getting really worried."

A look of irritation flashed in her eyes momentarily. She stood up and walked past me into the house. It was late and I was tired, but I realized I needed to put some ground rules in place if she was going to continue staying with us.

"Well, are you hungry? Your dinner is in the fridge. I can heat it up for you."

"Thanks. I'm starving."

Once I'd heated up her plate of dinner, I sat with her at the kitchen table while she ate. When she was finished, she finally answered my question.

"I was looking for a new place to crash."

It was on the tip of my tongue to ask her why she felt the need to leave so soon when she had no job and no money, but I decided to leave it alone. "And did you find one?"

"No. The money I got from selling my car won't cover the first and last month's rent anywhere in this town. I can't even afford to rent a room right now. Plus, they all want proof of employment to show you can pay your rent."

"I can't loan you..." I began.

"I'm not borrowing money from you," she snapped. "Not a loan. Not gifts. Nothing. What I need right now is a job. Can you help me find one of those?"

When she saw the look on my face, her tone suddenly changed. She was instantly embarrassed. "I'm sorry, Ava. I appreciate everything you've done for me. I'm just really kind of desperate right now."

The wobble in her voice told me she was close to tears. I briefly looked away so she could pull herself together. I was honestly at a loss as to how to help her, and her not having a picture ID wasn't helping anything. I'm sure she was probably eligible for some kind of assistance but again, she needed identification.

"You have my word that I will help you get back on your feet any way I can. Let me ask around at the shelter tomorrow." I grabbed her plate to rinse it and put it in the dishwasher when another thought hit me. "You said you got your license renewed, right?"

"Yeah, why?"

"What address did you give them to send your new license?"

"I gave them my old address over in Dayton, but I've been calling and calling my landlady and can't get a hold of her."

"I can drive you over there tomorrow to check and see if they sent it."

I was interested in her response because I was pretty sure I'd been lied to and couldn't understand why she was being so evasive about her driver's license. If this was the reason, she and Adele argued I could understand Adele's frustration. Then again, there was an obvious reason for this behavior. Could it be because her name was not Dana Shields?

"That would be cool, but don't you have to work at the shelter tomorrow?"

"Not until tomorrow afternoon. We can get up there in the

morning if you want. Maybe we can stop and have breakfast some-place. How's that sound?"

Dana was silent for a few seconds, and I could clearly see she was wrestling with my suggestion. But why?

"Sounds good, but I need to get to sleep."

It was almost 3:30 in the morning and I needed to get to bed myself.

"We'll leave at about nine. Good night." She merely nodded and I started to leave the kitchen, then stopped and turned to her.

"Hey, how did you know that ice cream gave me brain freeze?" I wasn't sure what I was expecting her to say, but it certainly wasn't what she finally did say.

"I didn't. It was just a guess based on how long it was taking you to eat that ice cream. Why?"

"No reason. Just wondered, that's all. Good night."

I headed to bed still wondering who this woman was and whether I'd made a mistake in letting her stay here.

By 9:45 the next morning, we were sitting at an IHOP in Dayton having breakfast. At least I was. Dana had barely touched her cinnamon pancakes while I was powering through my steak tips and eggs.

"Everything okay? It's a sin to leave cinnamon pancakes sitting untouched on your plate."

She gave me a weak smile and dug into the pancakes, managing to eat half of them before tossing her napkin onto the table and letting out a sigh. "Look, I've got something to tell you."

"Your name isn't Dana Shields, is it?"

I could tell she hadn't expected me to figure it out and instead of getting mad, she looked relieved.

"How did you know?"

"It didn't take a genius to figure out when you were being so weird about your driver's license."

"I'm sorry I lied. I just don't have any form of ID with me currently. I left it all behind when I fled this town a few months ago."

"What is your real name?" I was gripping my fork so tightly in anticipation of her answer, I'm sure I looked like I was about to stab someone. Dana, or whatever her name was, didn't seem to notice.

"Cindy Ford. At least that's the name I was given. I don't know what my birth name is."

"What do you mean you don't know what your birth name is?"

"Ten years ago, I was found wandering down the side of I-70 one night only wearing a nightgown. I had a head injury and was bleeding. I was taken to the hospital and my head injury healed, but I never regained my memory. I have no idea where I'd been before they found me and I have no idea what my name was. No one ever came looking for me, or responded to any of the reports about me in the paper. I was told by social services to pick a new name. I always liked the name Cindy. I picked that name and social services was on Ford Street. I became Cindy Ford. All of my identification is under that name."

I tried not to let my disappointment show. Had I really been expecting her to say her name was Brooke Peters? Then again, if what she was telling me was the truth, she had no idea what her birth name was. She really could be Brooke and just not remember the life she had before whatever accident robbed her of her memory. There was so much more I wanted to ask her. But I could tell by the way she was drumming her fingers on the table and the tight set of her jaw that she was getting irritated. So, I waited a few more minutes until she relaxed and leaned back against the booth before asking my next question.

"Why go by Dana Shields then? Where did that name even come from?"

"That was my landlady's name when I was still living here in Dayton."

"Who are you running from, Cindy?"

"My ex. I stole some money from him, and it was enough that he hasn't stopped looking for me."

"Must've been a lot of money."

"It was and before you ask, that money is long gone, and he knows it. He's still pissed off and wants to hurt me. That's why I left him, to begin with. He was abusive. I hadn't seen him in a couple of years, and he showed up at my old job. I just left every-thing behind and ended up homeless in Elmhurst."

Now, it was my turn to sigh and shake my head. "You know you could've told me all of this."

"I was just trying to survive. I don't really know you and you don't know me. I didn't want to involve you in my mess."

"Have you seen him since you've been in Elmhurst? Do you think he could've followed you here?"

She shook her head. "No. I haven't seen him. Then again, I don't really go to a lot of places, especially now that I don't have a car."

"Did you ever file charges against him for the abuse?"

She wouldn't look at me and I instantly got a bad feeling.

"No."

"Well, if it's been in the last few years, you could still press charges against him. If he shows up in Elmhurst looking for you that is."

"He's a cop." Dana picked up her fork and started picking at the remainder of her stack of pancakes.

"He's a cop? Oh my god, Dana. I mean Cindy. That's not good."

"You don't have to tell me. I know I'm screwed. Unless I can get some money together to get far away from that lunatic. He can use police resources to find me, probably anywhere I go."

"Then you still need to be Dana Shields. At least, until we can get you a new identity."

She stared out of the window and didn't reply, but when she looked back at me, she gave me a bewildered look.

"Why are you helping me? I mean, I get it in your line of work helping people is what you do, but there were a lot of women at Haver House that needed help. Not just me. Why are you trying so hard to help me?"

There was no reason not to tell her, although I wasn't ready to tell her who I thought she could possibly be. I could tell her why I was so drawn to her.

"Because you remind me of my best friend from when I was ten. Her name was Brooke."

"And what happened to her?"

"She was abducted from the playground we were playing in, right in front of me, and I couldn't do a damn thing about it."

Tears sprung up in my eyes and I took a napkin and dabbed them away. Once again, I was disappointed by her response. Had I really been expecting her to suddenly get her memory back at the mention of the name Brooke and abduction, and this would turn into a teary reunion? Dana continued to stare at me blankly. Nothing I just said registered in the least bit to her.

"And you feel guilty about what happened to your friend, right?"

"Yes. My therapist back then called it survivor's guilt."

"What about now?"

That was a very good question. Was I still feeling guilty about what happened to Brooke? Well, one thing was for sure, while I still did feel guilty about what happened to Brooke, it had been twenty-five years and I had done a good job of putting it in the rearview, at least I had until I met Dana, or whoever this woman was.

"Let's just say I'm better than I was." I took a sip of my coffee and stared out the window.

"Then it's not true what they say about time healing all wounds?"

"Have all your wounds been healed?"

"Not even close," she said with a bitter laugh.

Dana polished off the rest of her pancakes, probably not because she wanted to, but to avoid having to talk with her mouth full of food. That was fine by me because her situation had suddenly become so much more complicated. Memory loss, a violent cop ex-boyfriend, no license, no money, and no home. Under normal circumstances I would've been able to help her, and I still wanted to because I still thought she might be Brooke. Where did I even begin?

"If you just give me her address, I could go to your landlady's house to see if your driver's license arrived at her house. Will you at least let me do that for you?"

Dana shook her head vigorously. "Too dangerous. My ex is probably watching her house."

"I'm not suggesting you go. I can go and tell her that I'm there from social services to check on you if anyone asks me why I'm there."

She was silent for a few minutes as she contemplated what I said, and I could tell she was conflicted. She really did need her driver's license, but then what? If her ex-boyfriend really was after her and he was a cop, what would stop him from tracking her to Elmhurst?

"What's your ex's name?"

"Why do you want to know? What difference will it make for you to know his name?"

Up until that point Dana had had my sympathy, but now she was dodging questions and being evasive. A knot of apprehension was forming in my stomach.

"Alright. I'll leave it alone, and you're right, we don't want him tracking you to Elmhurst. At some point, though, you're going to have to try and get your license. Can you keep calling your landlady to see if she'd be willing to mail it to you?"

"Yeah." She nodded in agreement, clearly relieved, but I wasn't going to try to make her go to this woman's house. "I can keep trying."

"I guess we came here for no reason. Probably best to get home."

We left with me wondering if this had been the plan all along, to deter me from going to this woman's house. What was she hiding?

"Thanks, Ava. I know I'm not easy to deal with, but I really appreciate all your help." She got into the passenger side of my car and once I was behind the wheel, I turned to look at her.

"I don't even know what to call you anymore. Do you still want me to call you Dana or would you prefer I call you Cindy?"

"You can call me Dana. I left Cindy behind when I came to Elmhurst."

Back in Elmhurst, I told Dana I needed to go to the shelter and dropped her off at the library. Then I proceeded to look up the address of the real Dana Shields. I needed to know who the hell was living in my house, and maybe this woman could tell me.

NINETEEN

LIA

I couldn't get Natalie Hammond's stump of a missing pinky finger out of my head. I wished I'd never gone to see her. If she were telling the truth, that meant she had owed money to some very dangerous people. How far was I willing to go to uncover the truth of what really happened twenty-five years ago? One thing was for certain, if I got on the wrong side of these people, I might not survive to even make a documentary. I came to this town with a clear vision of how I wanted to make this documentary, but now I found myself on another path. Time to pursue another angle.

TWENTY

AVA

Only one Dana Shields was listed on the internet white pages. She lived in a dicey area near downtown Dayton that made me hesitate over parking my car in front of the two-story house that had once been white. Now, most of the paint was hanging in strips, exposing warped wood underneath. The majority of the houses in the neighborhood were in a similar condition, but I could tell that this had been an affluent neighborhood seventy-five years or so ago. A brown and white pit bull mix in the next-door yard jumped on the fence and wagged its tail. I walked over and patted him on the head, and he licked my hand.

"He likes you," said the elderly woman sitting on the porch of the house in question. I hadn't even seen her there and the sound of her voice made me jump.

"He's very sweet." I gave the dog a final pat on his head before returning my attention to the middle-aged white woman in a wheelchair. She wore a pink tracksuit with fluffy black house slippers. She peered curiously at me from beneath a white baseball cap that hid most of her hair.

"Are you Ms. Shields?"

"Depends on who's asking. And don't say a salesperson because I have no money."

"No, ma'am. I'm here to ask you a question about a former tenant of yours, Cindy Ford?"

"Is she okay?"

"She's fine. Would I be able to come up on the porch and talk to you about her?"

"Come on up."

I walked up the cracked stone path that led to her porch and carefully walked up the steps onto the porch, avoiding the places that were missing wooden slats.

"What did you say your name was?"

"I'm sorry. My name is Ava West."

"And you're a friend of Cindy's?"

Should I tell her the woman that she knew as Cindy was using her name and identity in Elmhurst? I had no idea if I could trust this woman even though Dana seemed to. So, I told her a form of the truth.

"I'm her social worker. She applied for benefits a while back and I'm here to assess her eligibility. Is she home?"

"You're out of luck if you're looking for Cindy cause she's long gone. I haven't seen her in months. She rented my upstairs apartment and skipped out on the rent. Loaned her my car because she said she had a job interview in Indiana and would be back in a few days and I ain't seen her since."

"Did you report her missing or your car stolen?"

"Why? Damned thing was on its last legs, and as you can see," she slapped the arm of her wheelchair, "I have no use for a car. Not when Door Dash and Instacart exist. And I'm not related to her. She's an adult and can do and go anywhere she wants."

"I got the impression from certain things she told me that she had been in an abusive relationship. Could her leaving have had something to do with the man she was involved with?"

"The man she was involved with?" Dana Shields snorted with laughter. "Cindy lived here for five years, and I never knew her to date anybody. She kept to herself. Went to work at her job over at

Phil's Diner and came home. I don't even think she had any friends. I certainly never saw her getting any visitors."

"Do you know where Cindy was before she came to live here? Is she from Dayton?"

"Shouldn't you know that? Didn't you say she applied for some assistance, wasn't there some kind of application that would have told you that?"

"Yes. I'm just checking up on what she filled out on her application."

She took a sip from a glass of what looked like iced tea sitting on a table next to her. "No clue where she came from. She just turned up here a few years ago needing an apartment to rent. My son Donnie's in prison and won't be getting out anytime soon. He lived in the apartment upstairs, and I needed a renter to help pay my bills. I rented to her against my better judgment. And she was a good tenant. Quiet, clean, and kept to herself. Best of all she paid her rent every month on time. I couldn't believe it when she skipped out on me and left me high and dry. Are you sure you don't know where she is?" The welcoming smile that had lured me up to the porch was gone now, replaced with a suspicious glare.

"Ma'am, I assure you I wouldn't be here if I knew where she was."

"Yeah," she said, looking me up and down. "I guess that makes sense."

"And no one has come looking for her since she skipped out on the rent?"

"Not a single soul. I just figured she slipped back into the same crack she crawled out of when she turned up here."

"Did she leave anything behind that could point to where she could be now?"

"Nope, because if she did, I'd be making sure I got my money back."

"How?"

"Small claims court. Just as soon as I find out where she is, I'm gonna be filing those papers. I'm on disability and it barely covers my expenses. I need my $600. So, if you see her, I'd appreciate it if you would tell her that."

"I certainly will, ma'am. Thank you for talking to me."

I headed back to my car feeling like the biggest sucker, but I was still holding out hope that some part of her story could be true. I got in my car and pulled out my phone to pull up Phil's Diner on Google and found out it was four blocks from where I was now. Maybe someone there would know or remember Cindy.

Phil's Diner was a hole in the wall a block from downtown Dayton. When I walked in, an older black woman with box braids wearing a blue uniform told me I could sit anywhere. Two minutes later, she was back with a glass of water and a menu.

"I'll be back to take your order in a sec, sweetie."

I started to tell her that I was there to talk to the owner, but she left so quickly I didn't have a chance. Two minutes later, she was back. I ordered a piece of banana cream pie even though I wasn't really hungry after my big IHOP breakfast.

"I'll be right back with that pie." The server, whose name tag read Brenda, turned to go, but I stopped her.

"Hey, I was wondering if Cindy was working today."

Brenda gave me a startled look before shaking her head. "Cindy left here months ago. A damn shame too because she was a really good server. Could wait on multiple tables and would even fill in the kitchen when our cook was out sick."

"Well, I haven't seen her in a while and had no idea she was no longer here."

"You a friend of hers?"

"More like an acquaintance."

"That sounds about right. As long as I knew Cindy, she never had any friends. No boyfriends. No girlfriends. No friend friends. Nothing. Sometimes, I wonder if that's the best way to be."

There it was again. Cindy not having any friends or family. Could she have been telling the truth when she told me about being an amnesiac found wandering down the side of I-70? I thanked Brenda and watched her head off to greet another customer and then dug into my pie, savoring the creamy goodness when an older white man slid into the booth opposite me. He was of medium build and looked to be in his early fifties with thick brown hair going gray at the temples and a bushy mustache. He wore a blue and gray plaid button-down shirt and jeans.

"Sorry to bother you, ma'am, but I couldn't help but overhear you talking to Brenda about Cindy. Do you know where she is?"

"It's Ava West." I held out my hand across the table for him to shake and his face reddened with embarrassment.

"I'm sorry. I'm Henry Cox, I own the place."

"You mean Phil's Diner isn't owned by a man named Phil?" I said it with a smile because Henry Cox looked so tense.

"Phil was my dad." He instantly relaxed and gave me a small smile. "This is a family-owned diner. My older brother Phil Junior inherited when my dad died and then seven years ago, he passed away without any kids, and that left me."

"And you guys make a mean banana cream pie." I put another forkful of pie in my mouth, purposefully ignoring his question until I could figure out what to tell him.

Dana had lied to me, but that didn't mean I trusted this man enough to tell him where she was. Henry must've sensed my hesitation and looked around briefly before turning back to me.

"Look. I won't contact her if she doesn't want to be bothered. I just need to know that she's okay."

Then it finally hit me. This man had a thing for Dana/Cindy or whoever the hell she was.

"I would tell you where she was if I knew. I'm looking for her myself."

"Do you mind if I ask why?

"I befriended her recently. I've been trying to help her get back on her feet, but then she took off and I haven't seen her since. Someone told me she used to work here and that's why I'm here. If you don't know where she is, either, I'm at a dead end."

Henry Cox looked disappointed. His face fell and I figured he'd had it bad for Dana. He slid out of the booth.

"Would you happen to know if she had a boyfriend who was abusive, who she could've been running from?"

Henry Cox shook his head. "If she did, she never told me. I know I shouldn't have, but I asked her out a few times and she told me she wasn't looking for a relationship. So, I settled for just being her friend."

"Well, if I see her again, I'll tell her to get in contact with you." I wiped my mouth and started to grab my purse to leave.

"I'd appreciate that. The pie is on the house. Also, tell Cindy not to worry about the money and that I understand."

"Money? What money?"

"She stole all the money from the safe before she left."

TWENTY-ONE

LIA

"Does this mean you're going to participate in the documentary?" I asked Detective Michael Avery as he stepped inside my Airbnb in downtown Elmhurst.

Avery had been my secret contact at the Elmhurst Police Department ever since I decided to do this documentary. So far, he had nixed all my offers to appear on camera to talk about the case. That told me he knew the Elmhurst Police Department had dropped the ball when investigating the Brooke Peters' abduction. He looked around the Airbnb I'd been renting and then gave me an unamused look.

"You know I can't do that, Miss Quinn. And I can't stay long. I'm on a case. Why did you want to meet with me?"

"That murdered woman found in the park?"

"That would be it. I'm working on an open homicide investigation, and I don't have a lot of time to spend on a twenty-five-year-old cold case."

"That's what you say, but you're also the one who gave me information about that so-called cold case that you had no business giving me. So, why don't you cut the act and just admit that you want this case solved as much as I do?"

"Oh, so you're trying to solve the case now? I thought you were just doing a documentary, and please don't tell me you're one of those damn podcasters digging into old cases and muddying the waters."

"I am not a podcaster. Although doing a podcast on this case would probably be a really good idea, and cost a whole hell of a lot less than this documentary is costing."

"Be that as it may, Miss Quinn. I'm still a busy man. What do you want that you couldn't talk to me about over the phone?"

"I heard some very interesting gossip about Natalie Hammond and her connection to dangerous people she owed money to and..."

"And people think whoever she owed money to may have grabbed Brooke by mistake when they really wanted Ava, right?"

"Then you knew about this?"

"This is strictly off the record. I'll admit mistakes were made in this case, but we weren't complete screwups back then. The people in question were brought in for questioning and their facilities searched. We came up with no trace or link between Brooke Peters' abduction and these people."

"Why doesn't anyone want to say who these people are? Are we talking about organized crime?"

"Hardly," Avery said with a chuckle. "Try drug dealers. Most of whom are now either dead, in prison, or in the wind."

I let out a low whistle. Natalie Hammond must've been crazy to borrow money from drug dealers. Either crazy or just plain desperate.

"Then you're positive they weren't involved?"

"They were strictly low level, there was no trafficking involved, mostly drugs and guns and money laundering."

"What made you look into them in the first place?"

"Brooke's brother Sam got mixed up with these losers. He was selling weed and got robbed. He also owed these people money and we thought maybe there might've been a connection, but there wasn't. He was lucky he just got off with a beating from them. He had to tell his mother what he was doing, and she paid them back the money he owed them, but we never found a connection to Brooke being abducted."

That completely knocked me for a loop. I hadn't heard anything about Sam Peters dealing drugs. Everything I'd heard about him was that he'd been a straight A student and a protective older brother.

"What about the father, Nate. Did you ever track him down? I heard Julia threatened to kill him over something he did to Brooke."

"Now, that's a new one on me. I hadn't heard that. All I ever heard was that Nate Peters was a junkie and out of the picture for good. No one had seen him in years. Never could track him down. It's like he disappeared into thin air. No activity on his Social Security number. Zero social media presence. Just gone and that was a few years before Brooke was abducted. Are we done?" He was antsy to be gone, and I wondered what would happen to him if his superiors knew he was feeding me information, although not a ton of it, to be honest.

"Just one more question." He was already at the door and turned and gave me a slightly annoyed look.

"Why are you helping me? You act like this case is a lost cause, but yet you're here. Why?"

"This case was my first case as a detective, but I wasn't the lead. I didn't have much authority. A missing ten-year-old black girl wasn't the priority it should've been and it's bothered me ever since. I'm hoping this documentary will jog somebody's memory so we can finally find out what happened to that little girl."

He left, not bothering to close the door behind him. I shut and locked the door, more determined than ever to find out what happened to Brooke Peters.

TWENTY-TWO

AVA

Henry Cox was the third person to tell me that Dana was a thief. Granted, she hadn't stolen directly from her former landlady, but she'd skipped out on a $600 rent which amounted to the same thing, not to mention stealing the woman's name and car. Henry Cox was so lovesick he was willing to overlook the fact she'd stolen money from the diner safe. She most likely used that money to live off of, but why would she be bothered to steal change from Adele's desk? Aside from bus fare, what could she have done with several dollars' worth of change? Haver House had laundry facilities, so she didn't use it at the laundromat. Adele clearly had not wanted to admit to any connection to Dana. Had she lied about the change?

Unfortunately, given Dana's history, I had to believe that Adele was telling the truth. I tried to pull up any articles about a woman with amnesia found wandering along the highway. Dana said it had been ten years ago and most news articles, even online, were archived at that point and I had to pay for a subscription to access the newspapers archives. I guess I could've gone to the public library to look at their newspaper archives, but right now I didn't have time. I was running late for my afternoon shift at the shelter.

When I arrived, the first person I saw was Selma. Our eyes met and mine shifted away from her as I gave her a tight smile and held up a hand in greeting before heading into what we were still calling Adele's office. Selma followed me into the office and closed the door behind her, and my heart fell into my stomach. Whatever was going on between her and James Mackie was none of my business.

"Can I talk to you, Ava?"

"Sure. What's up?" I sat down behind the desk and Selma took the seat in front of the desk.

"I just..."

"I saw you and James during the memorial service here in this office," I blurted out. I hadn't intended to say anything about what I'd seen, but I couldn't get the image of them out of my head. I knew it was going to be a problem while I continued to work here.

"Um...wow...okay." She looked completely mortified, but quickly recovered her composure and sighed. "Look, Ava, you have no reason to believe me, but I never slept with James. We bonded over our love of vintage cars. I own a 1965 Camaro. We both belong to the same vintage car club and became friends. An attraction developed and I know I should've shut it down, but I was newly divorced and lonely, and things just went farther than they should have."

"Did Adele know?"

"If she did, she never said anything. The night of Adele's memorial was the first time I'd seen James in over a month. Seeing him in so much pain, I got a little carried away. I shouldn't have kissed him."

I remembered the way I'd seen her lips pressed against his neck and his hand on her lower back. Either she was lying to me, or to herself, probably both.

"Trust me, Ava, I know how this looks and how bad it makes me look. This is hard to believe, but James really loved Adele. Over the years they had grown apart and I think our friendship filled the void that was missing in his marriage. I am not justifying what happened. I know it was wrong and like I said, I never slept with James. I understand if you no longer trust me, nor want to work here anymore."

Her voice sounded very strong and assured, without the hint of a tremble or a crack, but she looked like a wreck with dark circles under eyes, swollen from crying. This isn't how I wanted things to be. Whatever was going on in James and Adele's marriage as well as Selma Ross's choices in her private life, were none of my business.

"Selma, I love working here and would like to continue. So please don't think whatever may or may not have been going on with you and James Mackie has any bearing on my desire to work here. Before you ask, I have not told Detective Avery what I saw in this office the night of Adele's memorial service, but I hope you have because I'm not the only one who's noticed how close you and James are. I think Detective Avery needs to hear all about that from you and not someone else."

Selma looked shocked, her swollen eyes widening in surprise, but she nodded like she understood. I hope she did because I didn't want to have to be the one to tell Detective Avery about my boss and her murdered employee's husband. She and James both needed to tell the detective about their "friendship".

"It's...a little more complicated than that," she said.

"What do you mean?" Did I really want to know?

Selma let out a breath before answering. "Look, I never told anyone this, but there have been some discrepancies in our accounts."

"As in?"

"Missing money." She gave me a pointed look, and I instantly understood what she was implying.

"You think Adele was stealing money from the shelter? Are you sure? I thought you handled all the shelter's money."

"I handle payroll and all our state and local funding, but Adele offered to take over our smaller accounts for supplies and groceries and she paid the shelter's bills."

"And you think she was stealing from those accounts?"

"I don't know," Selma said, throwing up her hands in exasperation. "It's just that we received a small local grant recently and

Adele used that money to buy the new window air-conditioning units. She never provided any receipts. I kept asking and she kept putting me off. I finally called the store, and they only had record of one air-conditioning unit being sold to her. She was supposed to have purchased eight. So, what happened to the rest of that money?"

My heart instantly dropped into my stomach. I ran my hand over my face before telling her how I discovered all the air-conditioning units except for the one in her office were used. "Is it possible she was trying to save the shelter money?"

"If that was the case, then the rest of that grant money should be in the shelter's bank account, and it isn't. She had to have pocketed it. I'm afraid of how this will look if I tell Detective Avery. I don't want him thinking I'm smearing Adele's reputation because I had the hots for her husband. He'll think..." her voice trailed off and she didn't need to finish her sentence. She knew what she'd just told me made her a suspect in Adele's murder.

"He still needs to know, Selma. If Adele was stealing from the shelter, who knows what else she was into that could have contributed to her murder."

Selma looked torn but finally nodded. "You're right. I promise I'll tell him. Maybe he can figure out what happened to that grant money. I'll let you get back to work." She got up to leave.

I suddenly remembered she said there was something she wanted to talk to me about before I brought up what I had seen that night. "Was there something else you wanted to tell me?"

"Yes," she said, sitting back down. "I wanted to let you know that Kerri will no longer be volunteering here, effective immediately."

"What? Why?" Kerri had seemed just fine the last time we'd been in the office together.

"I don't know. I got an email from her this morning telling me she'll no longer be working here, and I don't have to tell you how much we're going to miss her around here. I do have a couple more volunteers starting next week, so please don't think that things will be this short-staffed permanently. I'll be taking over the shifts that you can't work here in the office while I train the new volunteers."

"Of course. Please let me know if there's anything I can do to help. I know I haven't been here long, but I could definitely help train any volunteers that are starting."

Selma looked very relieved, and I realized she must've thought that I might quit too after what I'd witnessed between her and James.

"Thank you, Ava. I really appreciate that, it'll be a big help." She got up to go and then paused at the door and turned back. "Would you be interested in a full-time position here? I'm in desperate need of an assistant director. I know you're on leave from Child and Family Services and we may not be able to match your salary right away, but it would be a much more flexible schedule than you're used to working for the county, and I think you could make a real difference here."

I didn't know what to say. Being offered a full-time position with Haver House wasn't anything I was expecting, but now that the possibility was there, I realized I liked the idea.

"Well, at least think about it and let me know."

Selma had mistaken my silence for indecision when in reality it was a no-brainer. "Yes," I blurted out, stopping Selma who turned and smiled at me. I got up from the desk and walked towards her.

"I'll be perfectly honest with you, my husband and I are trying to have a baby. I'll need time off for appointments as well as paid maternity leave once we conceive. Will that be a problem?"

"I don't see why it would be. This would be a job like any other with a benefits package including healthcare, sick days, and vacation days."

"Then I'm in. I would be honored to be Haver House's assistant director."

"I am so glad to hear that, Ava. Now, it's time I got back to my office because I'm sure I've got a ton of emails to go through, and I need to get the paperwork started."

She left me standing there smiling and excited about the

opportunity. Then what she told me interrupted my thoughts. Kerri wasn't coming back. Why? I headed to the kitchen and the one person who would definitely know what was going on.

"Yes, Lord, I heard about Kerri. Wish I could say I wasn't surprised."

I had caught Mrs. Brady in the middle of fixing lunch which consisted of a baked potato bar, salad, and a large pan of apple crisp. She was pulling a tray of steaming baked potatoes from the kitchen's large oven when I walked in.

"What happened? Did something happen between her and one of the residents?"

Mrs. Brady shook her head as she pulled her oven mitts off and leaned against the counter, giving me a disgusted look that I almost thought had been meant for me. "It's that man of hers."

"Josh?"

"Yep. He doesn't want her working here anymore because of what happened to Adele. At least that's the official excuse. I think Kerri is afraid he's gonna call that wedding off if she doesn't do what he says. I knew that man was a control freak when she spent an hour crying on my shoulder the other day about her wedding dress."

"Her wedding dress? What about it?"

Then I remembered what Kerri had told me about Josh being involved in the wedding planning and giving her criteria for what her dress should look like. I thought it was odd that she wasn't allowed to pick out the dress of her dreams, but I had no idea it was even worse than I thought.

"She took him to the bridal shop with her for one of her fittings and he had a fit. He said the dress wasn't bridal and insisted she get her money back. That child is gonna be wearing a lace potato sack down the aisle if that man has his way. And you should see that mess she's been bringing in for her lunch. Some kind of vegetable stew that looks like mush. Told me it was Josh's weight loss specialty. He ate it to lose fifty pounds and has kept it off for years."

"She doesn't need to lose any more weight, and that dress is gorgeous. She looks beautiful in it. What's his problem with the dress exactly?" Kerri had shown me a selfie of her in her dress from the fitting she had a week ago, and I wondered why she'd even shown him the dress.

"This has absolutely nothing to do with the dress. He's controlling and she can't see it. All I see is a lifetime of misery for her if she marries that man. If she thinks he'll just be happy with her no longer volunteering here, she's got another thing coming, because I guarantee you once he puts that wedding band on her finger, he's gonna be pressuring her to quit working altogether."

I thought about taking leave from my job to start a family and for the first time wondered what would happen after I got pregnant. Evan and I never really discussed how long I would stay home. Was he secretly hoping I would never go back to work? I pushed the thought out of my head because this was hitting a little too close to home.

"Have you met Josh?"

"Don't need to meet him. I already know his type. My daddy was just like this man. Never would allow my mother to work outside the home, but those were different times back then and women didn't have a whole lot of opportunities. Times are different now."

"I wonder if I talked to her, would it make a difference?"

"Talk to her and say what? Because I'm telling you all that girl can see is being that man's wife. She won't hear anything against him. She thinks she's lucky to have him."

"I'm not going to say anything about him. I just want to check to make sure she's okay and she knows she can always come back here whenever she wants."

"Good, because as much as I hate to say it, she's got a hard lesson ahead of her. It might take ten years and two kids before she realizes he's no Prince Charming."

I didn't disagree with her because I was hardly one to talk given the tenuous state of my own marriage. Would Evan really agree to adopt if I couldn't conceive, or did he just say that to appease me? I was also aware of how much worse things could be between me and Evan.

"When you talk to her," Mrs. Brady said, turning to a nearby cabinet and opening it, pulling out a plastic container, "give her these."

She handed me the container which turned out to be full of lemon bars.

By the time I tracked Kerri coming out of her last class of the day at Elmhurst Community College, I had eaten almost half the lemon bars.

"Ava? What are you doing here?" The color drained from her face. She looked around quickly before pulling me into the now-empty classroom.

"I came bearing gifts from Mrs. Brady. Selma told me you weren't coming back. Are you really not coming back to volunteer?" I sat the now-half-empty container of lemon bars on one of the desks, but Kerri barely glanced at them.

"Sorry I didn't say goodbye, but I talked it over with Josh and he feels like the shelter might not be the safest place for me to be spending time until they catch whoever killed Adele. So, I'm focusing on my wedding and my course load. I'm sorry you came all the way down here. I hope you weren't trying to convince me to come back because my mind is made up."

In all the time I had known Kerri, I had never known her to be anything but friendly, kind, and caring, but the woman standing before me looked like she lost even more weight since the last time I've seen her. She was on edge and clearly not happy that I was there. Given what Mrs. Brady had told me about her fiancé, she had to be under a lot of stress trying to please this man as well as keep her obligations to her job. I wanted to grab her and give her a big hug, but I knew she wouldn't appreciate it.

"You know you're always welcome to come back at any time, right? Selma offered me the position of assistant director and I'm going to take it."

Kerri's face instantly lit up, reminding me of the Kerri that I knew, but then the sound of a voice behind us from the doorway instantly wiped the smile off her face and she looked even more tense than when I arrived.

"Are you ready to go, hon?" The man in the doorway was a medium-height, medium-build white guy with thinning brown hair and a sharp featured face, the thin lips of which were now pressed into a hard line at the sight of me. I had assumed Josh was Kerri's age of late twenties, but this man looked a good decade or so older than her.

"Honey, this is my former coworker from Child and Family Services, Ava West. Ava, this is my fiancé, Josh Turner."

"So nice to meet you, Josh." I stuck out my hand for him to shake, which he did, reluctantly.

I also noticed that his grim expression quickly turned into a charming smile that didn't quite reach his eyes. I could almost see the thoughts running through his mind. He was wondering exactly who I was and what I was doing there.

"Nice to meet you, Ava. You wouldn't happen to be related to Evan West, would you?"

"Yes, I'm his wife. How do you know Evan?"

"We went to high school together. We were both on the wrestling team."

"Really? I didn't realize Evan played sports in high school."

In fact, Evan didn't talk much about his past at all and now I knew why. I'd been right. If Josh had gone to school with Evan, he'd be forty-one, more than a decade older than Kerri.

"Well, it was only freshman and sophomore year. Then he got injured and had to drop off the team. Please tell him I said hi, and it was nice meeting you."

He said it in such a dismissive way my face burned with embarrassment. He gave Kerri a look that could've frozen water and made me flinch, and he wasn't even looking at me. What was this asshole's problem? Then it occurred to me that Kerri did not tell him that we volunteered together at Haver House. She simply told him that we used to work together at Child and Family Services. Why the lie? I figured if Kerri was lying to him, it was for a good reason, and I didn't want to get her into any more trouble with him than she probably already was. He was eyeing the container of lemon bars with a frown on his face.

"It was so nice to see you, Ava. It's been too long." Kerri pasted a phony smile on her face and started edging towards the door, but Josh wouldn't be rushed.

"How long has it been?" Josh looked from Kerri to me.

"Not since her going-away party when she left to come to work here last year. I just happened to be in the building. I passed by and saw her. I couldn't believe my luck."

"Really?" he said, clearly not buying my story. "What brings you to campus today?"

"I graduated from here and one of my old professors, Dr. Martin, asked if I could come in to talk to her class. I even brought lemon bars." I just gestured towards the plastic container sitting on the desk. "Would you guys like one?" I nervously snatched the container from the desk and opened the lid. Josh looked into the container with a grimace, like I was offering him crack.

"No, thanks," said Kerri. "I've got a wedding dress to fit into."

She let out a nervous laugh that set my teeth on edge. Why was she so afraid of this man? Was he physically abusive? I gave her arms and legs a quick once-over to see if I could see any visible bruises and was happy to see nothing but toned, tan skin, but in the few minutes I'd known him, I deduced this man's abuse was most likely emotional.

"Sugar is a vice I quit a long time ago and my life is much better for it. Kerri, are you ready to go?"

He held out his hand which she quickly took, and I watched

the two of them leave the classroom without so much as a backwards glance. I knew I probably wouldn't be invited to the wedding. After leaving the classroom, I gave the remaining lemon bars to a group of students studying in the common area down the hall. What had Kerri gotten herself into? Since I didn't want to make any problems for her, and had a feeling her asshole fiancé would check, I swung by my old professor's office, happy to see that she was there, and appreciated the big smile that lit up her face when she saw me in her doorway.

Paulette Martin had been my favorite professor during my time at Elmhurst Community College. It had been a long time since we'd spoken, and I hated that this was the reason I was coming to see her now.

"Ava Hammond? Get in here and give me a hug."

I quickly stepped into the room and into Dr. Martin's warm embrace. "Hi, Dr. Martin. You have no idea how wonderful it is to see you. And it's Ava West now."

"That's the kind of thing someone says after they didn't get such a warm welcome from somebody else. Let me guess, Josh Turner?"

"How did you know?"

"Because I saw him and Kerri walk past a few minutes ago and he was chastising her like a child for not telling him she knew you."

"Are you kidding me? What is up with that guy? Why would he care if she knew me?"

"Aside from being a colossal controlling jerk with an ego as big as Texas and as fragile as peanut brittle, I'm not sure. You know there was another woman that he was dating here before he met Kerri. She had to leave the state to get away from him. A few people tried to warn Kerri about him, but she wouldn't listen. Not much we can do if she doesn't want to hear it." Dr. Martin shook her head, settled herself back behind her desk and waved me into the chair in front of it.

"I just came to check if she was okay because she quit the

women's shelter we both volunteer at, but he was acting so weird, and she never mentioned that she knew me from Haver House, so I figured I better keep my mouth shut about that. By the way, if he happens to come by here and ask if I spoke to one of your classes, can you please just tell him yes? I don't want to make any more trouble for Kerri."

"It's nice to see you, Ava, but you didn't have to ask me that. I would've backed you up no matter what. Isn't Haver House where that woman who got killed in the park worked?"

"Yes. I worked with her. She was a sweetheart. No one knows why she was even in the park. Last I heard, the police have no suspects or a motive."

"You know her husband works here, right?"

"James Mackie works here?"

"He's one of our part-time adjuncts. He teaches Life Skills. I figured he was out on leave because of what happened to his wife, but I saw him heading into class this morning."

"I didn't know that. Is the adjuncts' office still on the fifth floor? I might pop up and see how he's holding up."

"No. They moved it because of construction. It's down in the basement. I'm headed that way to class, so I'll walk you out."

We were about to leave when another question popped into my head. "Hey, do you know what kind of church Josh Turner belongs to? Kerri told me that he was a man of faith and that was one of the things she loved about him."

Dr. Martin snorted with laughter. "I wouldn't exactly call the place he goes every Sunday a church, but if that's what she wants to call it, whatever."

"What do you mean?"

She pulled open a drawer in the filing cabinet next to her door and riffled through one of the folders, pulled out a pamphlet and handed it to me.

"He was leaving these all over campus until he was told to stop."

It was a brochure for someplace called the Infinite Horizons. I flipped through it and quickly realized it had very little to do with traditional religion of any kind. It was more like a series of self-help classes for everything from weight loss to drug addiction, touting hard physical labor, saunas, and dietary changes to free oneself from destructive behavior, but it was the logo on the front of the brochure that made me do a double take. It was a star-shaped symbol. It looked exactly like the birthmark on the back of Dana's right shoulder.

"You okay?" Dr. Martin put a hand on my shoulder when I continued to stare at the brochure.

"Yep. Let's go." I tucked the brochure into my purse and followed Dr. Martin out the door.

After Dr. Martin and I parted ways, I took the elevator to the basement. I'd never had a reason to come down here when I was a student and was glad because it was dimly lit with water-stained carpeting and concrete walls painted industrial gray. Having to work down here must feel like punishment. I followed the sound of voices, passing by some group study rooms, a classroom, and the speech lab before finding the adjunct instructor's office. The office was two classrooms where the wall had been knocked out to make one big space filled with cubicles for about thirty people. A young woman with glasses was coming out as I was walking in, and gave me a smile.

"Can I help you?"

"Yes, I'm looking for James Mackie. Is he here?"

The young woman's smile instantly turned into a smirk as she looked me up and down. I knew exactly what she was thinking. She thought I was one of James's admirers. How many women like Selma did he have special "friendships" with?

"He's got class until this afternoon. If you want to leave him a note, his cubby is in the back right corner."

She left before I could thank her, and I stared after her wondering how many other women were showing up here looking for James to offer comfort and condolences. Even if I hadn't been told where James's cubby was, I would have been able to find it by the sheer abundance of condolence cards, flowers, and stuffed animals covering the top of the desk. There was even a large fruit basket sitting on his chair.

Not sure why I'd even come, I was about to leave when I spotted something familiar in his trash basket next to his desk, and plucked it from the trash. It was a framed degree just like the one I'd found in Adele's office, showing that James Mackie had received his medical degree in psychiatry from Prime University in Las Vegas, Nevada. James never mentioned being a psychiatrist, too. Why hadn't he mentioned it when I'd asked about Adele's psychiatry career? And why was this in the trash?

I turned to go and almost jumped out of my skin to see an older white woman with gray hair in a sleek chignon carrying a platter of cookies. She didn't look happy to see me and sized me up like I was competition.

"He's in class until this afternoon," I told her, for lack of anything better to say.

"I know James's schedule. And you are?"

"I worked with his wife Adele and stopped by to see how he's doing."

"Oh, that was horrible, wasn't it? We still can't believe it."

"Did you know Adele?"

"Not at all. This is only James's second semester teaching here. I think I met her when he first started. She seemed nice enough."

"I was surprised to hear he was back at work so soon."

"Knowing James, he's behind on something and needs to get caught up."

"What do you mean?"

"Don't get me wrong. I like James, but he's the worst Life Skills instructor we've ever had. Doesn't teach from the textbook. Spends all his class time talking about himself. Can't get grades in on time. His classes have a rep amongst the students as an easy A if you can endure his endless stories about his glory days in New York."

"Why hasn't he been fired?"

"Are you kidding? It takes an act of Congress to get fired from this place."

"Well, he seems to be popular." I looked over at his loaded desktop.

"Only to a certain demographic if you know what I mean."

I looked pointedly at the platter of cookies in her hands.

"Oh, these are for a meeting I'm headed to. My desk is over there. Take care."

I watched her head to a desk in the opposite corner and grab a sweater from the back of the chair. She was halfway to the door when I stopped her.

"Hey. How'd he get hired if he's such a crappy instructor?"

She let out a snort of laughter. "He came highly recommended by another staff member."

"Can I ask who?"

She looked torn and then shrugged. "A math instructor named Josh Turner."

My surprise must have registered on my face because she laughed again.

"Do you know Josh?"

"Just had the pleasure of meeting him today."

"Then you have my sincerest apology."

I left the building and was headed back to my car when I spied a dumpster full of office chairs that looked to be in perfect condition. I realized they must be from the part of the building they were doing construction on and would be replaced with new ones. I resisted the urge to grab one and toss it into my car. Then I saw what was written on the underside of each chair: Property of ECC. The same thing had been written on each of the air-conditioning units at Haver House. ECC were the initials of Elmhurst Community College, meaning the units must have been the old units the college had gotten rid of. If that was the case, James Mackie had to have been in on Adele stealing that grant money. What else had those two been up to?

TWENTY-THREE

LIA

I was sitting in the same diner where I'd met Mavis Brady, going over my notes when one of the waitresses, a woman whose name tag read Becky slid into the booth opposite me, startling me. She was an older white woman who looked to be in her sixties and her jet-black hair hung in a ponytail down her back. Her uniform strained over her large chest, and I could see her lacy white bra through the gaps between the buttons. Her face was slightly flushed, and she gave me an apologetic look.

"I am so sorry, ma'am, but could I talk to you for a minute?" She looked around quickly making sure there were no customers waiting at the hostess station, but it was 2:30 in the afternoon and I was the only one in the diner. The lunch rush was over, and it was way too early for dinner.

"Sure." I sat my pen down and closed my notebook to give her my full attention. "What can I do for you?"

"Well," she said, looking around once again before giving me her full attention, "I couldn't help but overhear when you were in here talking to Mavis Brady. Are you really doing a documentary about that poor Peters girl that got abducted?"

"I am. Did you know Brooke Peters or her family?" I was trying to remain calm because I had a feeling this woman was about to tell me some very valuable information.

"Not me, but I know someone you need to talk to."

"And who is that?" I found myself leaning forward in my seat, causing Becky to lean back in hers.

"My cousin Vivian Barnes."

"Why would I need to talk to your cousin?"

"Because for twenty-five years she swore that she saw Brooke Peters a good two months after she was abducted, but no one, including the police, would believe her."

Now that knocked me for a loop. I thought she was going to tell me that the Peters family ate regularly in this diner and had some kind of heartwarming story to share about them, but nothing prepared me for this. I just stared at her without speaking. Too shocked to say anything.

"I already told her about you being in here with Mavis the other day and that you were doing a documentary. She's really anxious to talk to you." She slid a piece of paper across the table to me with a phone number scrawled on it with the name Vivi underneath. "Just give her a call anytime. She's hoping to hear from you."

Becky quickly slid out of the booth to go seat a couple that had just walked in. I stared at the scrap of paper before snatching it off the table, hoping it wasn't too good to be true.

It wasn't. An hour later, I was at Vivi Barnes's home. We sat out on her back patio with lemonade and sugar cookies and watched her two granddaughters, Callie and Caylee, play in the backyard. I'd already been there for twenty minutes and Vivi had yet to tell her story. I could tell she was hesitant, probably because of what Becky had told me, that no one had believed her.

"Your cousin Becky said you've been telling the same story for twenty-five years?" I prompted, hoping she would finally tell me what I had traveled all the way across town to hear.

"I'm sorry. This is just still so hard for me, even after all of these years." She picked up her lemonade glass to take a sip and I noticed her hands trembled slightly. So I settled myself in for as long as it took, not wanting to push her away in my excitement to get her story.

"You just take your time, Mrs. Barnes. I've got all evening."

"Well, I've just got a couple of hours. My youngest daughter Hannah lives over at that homeless women's shelter Haver House. I take care of her daughters during the day while she works and then we all go have dinner with her when she gets off."

Vivian Barnes lived in a very spacious ranch home, which I'm sure probably had at least three bedrooms. I wondered why her daughter and granddaughters were living in a homeless shelter. She must've read my mind.

"I'd have them here in a heartbeat if it weren't for Hannah's addiction issues. I already went through it with her sister Crystal. I can't have that in my home again. She's doing well right now, but that could turn on a dime just like it did for her sister."

"Where's her sister Crystal, now?" I asked not really caring about the answer, just trying to be patient until she told me what she had to tell me about Brooke Peters.

"Dead. They said it was an overdose. I didn't believe it then and I don't believe it now. Crystal is the reason why I saw Brooke Peters two months after she was abducted."

"What do you mean?" My heart started hammering in my chest and I willed myself to calm down.

"Like I said Crystal was an addict. She was my oldest and got caught up with a man who got her hooked on drugs. She was only twenty at the time, and I blame me and my husband Earl for sheltering her too much. As soon as she was old enough, she went wild. She went from being her class valedictorian to her first stint in rehab in just two years. We tried everything. Court ordered rehab, interventions with the entire family and her friends, letting her go to jail for drug possession. None of it worked. Finally, Earl had enough when she stole one of his shotguns and tried to sell it for drug money. He put her out of the house and told her she couldn't come back, and we couldn't have anything to do with her until she got herself together."

"But she didn't?"

"Not then. I'm not sure where she went or what happened to her, but two years later, she showed back up on our doorstep looking healthy, saying that she had gotten a job that she loved that kept her so busy, that it was such hard work she didn't have time to think about drugs. Earl let her stay for dinner and we had the best time with her since before she graduated from high school. I honestly thought it was the start of a new beginning for us as a family. My daughter Hannah was in her final year of high school, and I was so happy that Crystal had gotten herself together so she could be there for Hannah who had been missing her like crazy over the two years she'd been gone."

"What happened?"

"A few months later, she was found dead on the side of the road out in the county. I couldn't bear to go identify her body with Earl, and when he came home from the morgue, he was never the same again. He said she looked like she'd weighed all of eighty pounds and was covered in bruises and calluses."

"I am so sorry," I said softly, resisting the urge to squeeze her hand. "What was her cause of death, an overdose?"

"No. Starvation and dehydration. She'd starved to death. They tried to tell us that she was so high she must've forgotten to eat and starved to death, but I read that autopsy report and there were no drugs or alcohol in her system." A sob escaped her throat, and she buried her face in her hands.

I let her cry for a few minutes, but a shriek from the girls caught her attention, and she immediately pulled herself together. "Calm down, girls, I told you about all that screaming." But the girls were having too much fun to pay attention to their grandmother and their peals of laughter continued to fill the air.

"I am so sorry for your loss, Mrs. Barnes, but what does this have to do with Brooke Peters?"

Vivian Barnes sighed, took off her glasses, wiped her eyes, and cleared her throat before continuing. "The last time we saw Crystal, she said she had been working on a farm. She didn't say where the farm was or who owned it. Every weekend after her funeral, Earl and I would drive around out in the county, approaching farms with her picture to see if any of them had employed her. We didn't get lucky until we found one about ten miles away called Infinity Farm. We went up to the gate and saw that it was heavily padlocked, and we couldn't get access to the road up to the farm, but there was a bell you could ring. I stood there and rang it. We waited and rang the bell for a good fifteen minutes when all of the sudden, a little black girl showed up at the gate. She had pigtails, but she was filthy and thin."

"Brooke." My voice was barely a whisper, but Vivian didn't notice and kept talking.

"I remember asking her if she knew someone who could let us in, and she started crying. That's when she told us her name was Brooke Peters, and she wanted to go home, and asked if we could take her to her mommy. Before we could even say yes or no, she tried to squeeze through the gate. She almost made it when a young guy with a shotgun showed up and snatched her, dragging her off screaming. We showed him Crystal's picture, and he told us he had no idea who she was and that we needed to get off the property before he set his dogs on us."

I listened to the story and didn't realize that I was barely breathing until I got a little light-headed and sat back in the seat, letting out my breath. "What did you do?"

"Nothing we could do. We were trespassing and we had to leave. You better believe we reported what we saw to the police because as soon as she told me what her name was, I remembered that there was a little girl that had been abducted from a park in Elmhurst named Brooke. We actually showed back up on the property two hours later with the police. The same man showed up with a little black girl with him who said she was just kidding and that she was sorry. She never made eye contact with us. I knew immediately it was not the same little girl. I'm no racist," she said defensively, draining the rest of her lemonade. "I'm not one of those white people that thinks all black people look alike. That was a completely different little girl than the one we saw just a few hours before."

"Let me guess. The police told you to stop wasting their time and accept the fact that your daughter died because of her addiction, right?"

"Not only that," she continued, indignantly slamming her glass onto the table. "They said if I bothered those people again, they would charge me with trespassing and wasting police time."

"Did you leave them alone?"

"I went back a week later, parked on the road and walked up to the property. This time, the gate was unlocked because there was nobody there. They were all gone and they never came back. They took Brooke Peters and any answers they had about my daughter's death with them."

"Unbelievable," I said for a lack of anything better to say.

"Earl died five years ago, and I made him a promise on his deathbed I would find out what happened to our girl. Hannah was just as lost as her sister and never got over her death. She started using drugs as a coping mechanism, and I'll be damned if I see her end up like her sister."

We were silent for a few minutes as we watched the girls play. I was still trying to wrap my head around everything that Vivi had just told me, but I realized this woman wanted something from me that I wasn't sure I could give her.

"What is it you're hoping to accomplish by telling me all of this?"

Vivian Barnes's head whipped around so fast it surprised me. She was staring at me so intently it was like she was staring a hole into my soul.

"Put me in your documentary. Let me tell my story. Maybe we can kill two birds with one stone because there's nothing you or anyone can say to me that will convince me what happened to my daughter and what happened to Brooke Peters aren't connected and the answer is out somewhere on that abandoned farm."

I should've been excited to have Vivian's story, but did I want to open this can of worms? This wasn't a bigger plot twist than the possibility of the people Natalie Hammond owed money to could've kidnapped Brooke by mistake. If I put Vivian Barnes in my documentary, she would essentially be accusing the Elmhurst police of incompetence for not getting a warrant to search Infinity Farm. On the flipside, how could I not put her in the documentary after what I had just been told? It was certainly a compelling enough story. But was it true?

I thought about the case file that Detective Avery had let me take a peek at. He wouldn't let me have it, but I did take some photographs of the report and had read it front to back multiple times. Numerous people claimed they'd seen Brooke as far away as California, but there had been no mention of what Vivian Barnes claimed she saw that night when she and her husband went to Infinity Farm. Which is why, after I left Vivian's house, I drove out to the address she gave me for Infinity Farm. It was indeed abandoned, but there were cameras everywhere at the entrance and signs warning that trespassers would be prosecuted.

I parked across the road from the padlocked gate where Vivian said she and her husband encountered the little black girl who said her name was Brooke. In the field next to where I was parked was a large billboard announcing a new housing development coming soon called Bristol Estates with homes starting a $275,000. Tears filled my eyes as I thought about how scared and desperate that little girl must've been to beg strangers to take her home to her mommy. What had happened to her once they'd dragged her away from that gate?

As I sat in my car, I pulled out my phone, pulled up a browser and searched for Infinity Farm. Only finding one mention of it in publicly accessible records of registered businesses, but it didn't give me any information on the owner of the business. I drove back to my Airbnb and pulled up Elmhurst counties probate website on my laptop to access property records which were available online and searched the address 2850 Hilltop Road. The owner came up as Infinity Corporation. No name was attached to the property record. These people did not want to be found. If they were responsible for the abduction of Brooke Peters and the death of Crystal Barnes, what else had they done and where did they go?

I decided to check the public library to see if they had any information since Infinity Farm was a local business. I watched as the older male reference librarian checked their database for any archived news articles about Infinity Farm, and came up empty.

"Well, thanks for checking." I started to walk away when he called after me.

"Ma'am, you might try our pamphlet file. It's over here in our local history room." He got up from behind the counter and gestured for me to follow him into a small room across from the reference desk. He stopped in front of a long, low, black metal filing cabinet. Each drawer was labeled with a range of the alphabet.

"Are things filed by alphabetical order?"

"No. They're assigned call numbers and subject headings. They don't show up in our card catalog, but you can consult the index." He pointed to a small wooden card catalog with four drawers that sat on top of the filing cabinet.

"Thanks." I watched him go and pulled open the first drawer quickly scanning the subject headings.

I had expected to find mention of Infinity Farm in the agriculture section. But no luck. I didn't get lucky until I got to the third drawer under local businesses and found a single entry that mentioned Infinity Farm. Unfortunately, what I thought was going to be a brochure about the farm turned out to be a faded, yellow, single-page flyer for a business called Helen Kay's Herbals, a store that sold herbal remedies for all kinds of conditions from colds to hair loss owned by a woman named Helen Kay Sikes. There was a tiny notation at the bottom of the flyer letting customers know that the herbs Helen Kay used were sourced from Infinity Farm. Apparently, Infinity Farm had been a working farm that grew medicinal herbs. I saw there was an address for Helen Kay's Herbals. I drove past it on my way back to my Airbnb, only to find that small storefront located between a laundromat and a tattoo parlor was now a barber shop. I gave up and went home.

TWENTY-FOUR

AVA

When I got home that night, I was happy to see Evan and Dana working together to make dinner. Evan was grilling some steaks on the back patio while Dana was in the kitchen putting a salad together and checking on the baked potatoes. I wanted to hold on to this peace for as long as I could and decided telling Evan about the job I'd been offered at Haver House could wait until tomorrow. I didn't want to ruin what was looking to be a very pleasant evening. At least that's what I told myself. In reality I was still reeling over the Infinite Horizons' logo. Was I imagining that it looked like the birthmark on both Brooke and Dana's shoulders?

"Hey, can you grab that sour cream and an avocado out of the fridge? I'm going to make myself some homemade avocado ranch because I'm not feeling that vinaigrette you and your husband are into on my salad."

"Only if you make some for me, too; I buy that vinaigrette because Evan likes it and it's just easier to use it on my salad, too."

I handed her the container of sour cream from the fridge and pretended I didn't notice how she rolled her eyes when I told her I only used vinaigrette because of Evan.

"Everything good with you?" she asked as she got busy whipping together the dressing.

"Why do you ask?"

"You forgot to pick me up from the library. It's no biggie. I caught the bus, but I was just worried something had happened."

"Oh my god, Dana! I completely forgot. I am so sorry!" I slapped my hand against my forehead. "I got caught up in a situation at work and it completely slipped my mind."

"Nothing too serious, right? Nobody else got hurt or anything, right?"

"No. Nothing like that. Just something unexpected came up and I had to go check on the person in question."

"I guess you can't tell me what it was about, huh?"

I was really surprised she wanted to know since she hadn't asked me a single thing about Haver House since she'd come to stay with us. It was almost like she'd forgotten that she'd lived there for a short amount of time. I figured it wouldn't be a big deal if I told her since both she and Kerri were now no longer associated with Haver House. I quickly explained what had happened but stopped short of telling her about Kerri's fiancé Josh, let alone the brochure Dr. Martin had let me keep.

In addition to the extreme diet, they also didn't believe in western medicine and relied heavily on plant-based concoctions for illnesses. The fact I saw nothing in this brochure about modesty or a woman's subservience to men told me it was Josh and not his so-called religion that was causing him to behave the way he was towards Kerri. Mrs. Brady was absolutely right. He was just controlling and obnoxious. She was also right about the fact that this was going to have to be a lesson Kerri learned on her own because she wasn't going to let anybody keep her from marrying this man. And that made my heart hurt for her. All I could do was be a friend to her, and be there if ever she needed me. Speaking of so-called friends, why in the world would Adele have introduced Kerri to the likes of Josh Turner? How could she not have known what kind of a man he was?

"Kerri's the redhead with man problems, right?"

"Yes, that's her. Why would you say she has man problems?" How did Dana know about Kerri's relationship issues?

"Kinda hard not to notice when she's sitting in her car crying on the phone. I was in my car a few times and overheard her arguing with someone about a prenup."

"A prenup?"

"Yep. From what I could hear, it sounded to me like she wanted her fiancé to sign one and he told her he would cancel the wedding if she didn't trust him."

"Well, they must have worked it out because as far as I know, the wedding is still on."

"If the wedding is still on, that means she gave up trying to get him to sign it because from what I overheard, her lawyer was really pushing for her to get a prenup. Sounds like a lot of money's at stake."

I suddenly remembered Kerri telling me she was struggling with her grandmother's death and everything that came with it, and how Adele had been there for her. I'd wondered what she'd meant by everything that came with it. Had she meant an inheritance? Is that why Adele wanted to be there for Kerri? Because she knew Kerri had money? If Selma was right and she'd been stealing from the shelter's accounts, it wouldn't be a stretch to think she'd have befriended a grieving young woman who'd just inherited a large sum of money.

"Earth to Ava. Come in, Ava," deadpanned Dana, giving me an odd look. "You okay?"

"Sorry. I didn't mean to zone out."

"No worries."

Dana turned to put the sour cream back in the fridge and her birthmark was in full view. I took a step closer to get a better look.

"You know I've been meaning to ask you about that birthmark on your shoulder. I don't think I've ever seen one like that before."

"Birthmark?" She turned to stare at me. "That's not a birthmark. It's a brand."

"A brand? As in somebody branded you?" Had I just heard her right?

"And before you ask, I have no idea how I got it or who did it and when. I didn't even realize it was there until after I was found and taken to the hospital. One of the nurses asked me about it and I had no idea what to tell her because I just don't remember. I'm not sure I want to remember."

I could tell she didn't want to talk about it anymore. I left it alone, but I couldn't get it out of my head for the rest of the night.

Evan and I were lying in bed watching TV and I'd almost fallen asleep when I remembered meeting Josh Turner earlier that day.

"Oh, I can't believe I almost forgot to tell you. I ran into someone who says he knew you in high school."

"Who?"

"Josh Turner. He's the fiancé of that girl I used to work with named Kerri, remember her?"

"I remember enough about her to know she's too nice to be involved with Josh Turner. Where the hell did she meet him?"

"They both teach at ECC. I didn't know you went to high school with him. Was he any nicer back then?"

"That dude has always been an asshole. We also went to elementary school together and he was an entitled little jerk even then."

"He said you guys were on the wrestling team together. You never told me you wrestled in high school."

"That's because my wrestling career didn't last very long, and Josh Turner is the reason why."

"Alright." I sat up, giving him my full attention. "Out with it. What happened between you two back in high school?"

"The whole wrestling team was at a party at our coach's house after we qualified for the state championship. Josh's parents let him do whatever he wanted, but the rest of us had curfews and had to be home by midnight. Josh had his mom's minivan. We knew he'd been drinking, but he swore he was okay to drive. He wasn't. Ended up crashing into a telephone pole. They had to use the jaws of life to get me out of the passenger side."

"Oh my god, Evan. How are you still alive?"

"By the grace of God along with the seatbelt and airbag. I broke my leg in three places and fractured a couple of vertebrae and had to wear a cast and a back brace for months. That was the end of my wrestling career. Thanks to Josh Turner's drunk driving, and me being stupid enough to get in a car with him."

"Was he charged with DUI or underage drinking?"

"No. The Turner family has some pull in this town. He got off with having to attend a youth outreach program for substance abusers in lieu of jail time. I was the one who paid the biggest price. Not that my wrestling career was going to lead to anything life-altering, but still. That was four months of my life that I'll never get back." Evan yawned, which was his signal that he wanted to go to sleep and not talk about this anymore. "Do me a favor."

"I know. Stay away from Josh Turner."

"I'm not kidding." His voice suddenly turned serious, and I looked over at him to see the hard set of his jaw. "He's bad news, Ava. An arrogant, narcissistic, racist jerk. Promise you'll stay away from him."

"I promise." I put a reassuring hand on his arm. He picked up my hand and kissed my fingers.

That Josh was a jerk was pretty obvious. If he was racist, why had he recommended James Mackie so highly for the Life Skills instructor position at ECC?

We kissed good night. I turned out the light on my bedside table, plunging the room into darkness, and settled myself against my pillow, feeling even more sorry for Kerri than I already did.

TWENTY-FIVE

DANA

Dana stood on the sidewalk staring at the two-story brick colonial wondering if she had the nerve to ring the doorbell. It was after midnight, and a conversation was in order with the owner of this house. She marched up the driveway and rang the doorbell. Seconds later, a disembodied female voice came over the doorbell camera.

"Yes? Can I help you?"

"I know you can see who it is. Open the door, or would you like me to tell your daughter why you really don't want me in her house?"

A minute later, the door opened a crack and Natalie Hammond appeared wearing a green silk robe and looking even less friendly than when Dana saw her at Ava's house.

"What are you doing here? And what kind of game are you playing with my daughter?"

"Trust me it's nothing like the game you participated in twenty-five years ago."

Natalie opened the door wider, looking quickly up and down the street like somebody gave a damn who was visiting her in the middle of the night.

"Come in and make it quick."

Dana stepped inside a nice, tidy foyer with bright white walls and a chandelier hanging from the ceiling that looked like a work of art.

"I've actually got all the time in the world because I know you don't want to end up like Adele."

Natalie's eyes instantly narrowed as she sank down onto the bottom step of her staircase.

"Did you...?"

"Kill her? I wouldn't risk my place in the upper room for that spineless bitch. We both know she got what she deserved."

"Then I'm assuming you know who did it?"

"No. I actually thought you did."

Natalie jumped to her feet, eyes blazing, and pointed at the door. "Get out of my house!"

"All these threats, but you haven't threatened to tell your daughter who I really am and how we know each other. Now that would be a very interesting conversation."

"I was a victim, too!"

"Don't act like you're the same as me. I was just a kid. What was your excuse when you were a grown ass woman?"

"I said get out!"

"I'm going, but watch your back because karma comes for us all. Just ask Adele. Oh, that's right, you can't because she's dead."

Dana didn't wait to be told to leave a third time and marched out the front door and down the driveway towards the corner to catch the last bus back to Ava's house before they realized she'd snuck out.

TWENTY-SIX

NATALIE

Natalie paced back and forth in her foyer, glad to see the back of her uninvited guest, who she hoped she would never see again. What she'd said had disturbed her. Was Adele Mackie's murder connected to what happened all those years ago? How was she going to keep this from Ava? She had only done what she had to do to keep a roof over their heads. How could she be blamed for that? Any mother would've done the same. It wasn't like she had a choice when she'd had to borrow so much money and then couldn't pay it back.

All of those thoughts and more were swirling around her head when her doorbell rang again. Thinking her visitor had come back to harass her some more, she flung her front door open only to be met by a figure dressed in a dark hoodie with the hood pulled low over their face. She couldn't even get a word out before the knife sliced into her side and hot breath hissed in her ear.

"You knew and you did *nothing*. All those innocent people being fooled, abused, and taken advantage of and you did *nothing*. You said...*nothing*."

Natalie screamed as her assailant pulled the knife out of her, poised to stab her again when a voice rang out from across the street and the figure in the hoodie took off running.

"Natalie! What's going on over there? Are you okay?" It was Mr. Hernandez, her neighbor from across the street.

But Natalie couldn't speak. The searing pain snatched all the breath from her lungs as she pressed her hands to her side to staunch the flow of blood. Mr. Hernandez and his wife were at her side in an instant. He ripped a strip off his T-shirt to press it to her side.

"Call 911!" he told his wife as he lowered Natalie to the floor of her foyer, commanding her not to move or speak.

"Ava..."

"Don't speak. We'll make sure to call Ava after we get you to the hospital."

"Tell her...I'm...sorry," was the last thing Natalie said before it all went black.

TWENTY-SEVEN

AVA

My mom was lucky. Whoever stabbed her had missed major organs but nicked her liver. Another few millimeters and the knife would've penetrated her gall bladder. I've been practically living in her hospital room for the past two days trying to wrap my head around who in the world would've wanted to kill my mom. She didn't seem to have any idea, either. Mom said she had no memory of the attack beyond opening her front door. They had her on pain meds so trying to get any kind of conversation out of her was difficult. The newspapers were having a field day connecting what had happened to my mom to Adele Mackie's murder, theorizing that some kind of serial slasher was stalking Elmhurst.

My mom's doorbell camera hadn't been charged in months. So, while she was able to use it to see who was at her door, the camera was not recording and didn't pick up her attacker. When I checked the doorbell camera app on her phone, I saw the camera had registered two people at her door within nine minutes of each other. One of these people was definitely her attacker as Mr. Hernandez, her mom's neighbor, had seen the person at Mom's door when he'd been rolling his trash dumpster down to the curb. He thought the person was a man in a black hoodie and jeans who ran off on foot as soon as he yelled across the street. Police had already been to take my mom's statement but realized they would have to come back later as she was still groggy from surgery and couldn't remember much of anything.

Thankfully, the police had an officer stationed outside her door in case the freak who stabbed her tried to come back and finish the job. I was thankful she was still alive and felt horrible for getting so irritated with her the last time she'd been to the house. Dana has been a godsend. Cooking up food and bringing it to the hospital for Evan and I, and keeping an eye on the house. She wouldn't come into my mom's hospital room, and I figured it was probably because my mom had been so rude to her when they met.

"Ava?"

My mom was attempting to sit up, wincing at the effort it took. I was out of my seat instantly, crossing the room in two strides to get to her side.

"Mom. Don't try to sit up. Let me just adjust the bed for you."

I grabbed the remote that controlled the bed, pressing the button and gauged by my mom's facial expression how far to raise the bed before her wound started bothering her.

"Do you want some water?"

"No, but can you scratch my back for me? I don't want to rip my stitches trying to reach it and it's driving me crazy."

"Can you lean forward just a little?"

My mom grimaced as she leaned forward just enough for me to get my hand behind her back. In the process her hospital gown came loose, exposing her back and right shoulder and I did a double take. On the back of her right shoulder was the same star-shaped brand that Dana had on her shoulder. The one that looked just like Brooke's birthmark. I knew it was a birthmark because that's what Brooke had told me. Where did this come from? I couldn't remember seeing it before. Granted, I hadn't seen my mom in any kind of state of undress in years. Not since I was a little kid.

"Mom, what's this on your back?" I ran my index finger over it and my mom flinched like I'd shocked her.

She didn't answer and instead doubled over and cried out in pain. I immediately jumped up and ran into the hall to find a nurse. I had the strangest feeling that my mom wasn't in that much pain, she just didn't want to answer my question.

Three people with the same marks on their backs. Dana said hers was a brand but either didn't remember or just didn't want to tell me who put it there and why. Now, my mom had the same brand on her shoulder. This wasn't a coincidence anymore. I also knew my mom was in no shape to answer my questions right now. But there was one person I could ask even though I had promised my husband I'd stay away from him.

The nurse gave my mom more pain meds which put her to sleep, and I stretched out on the couch in her room and shut my eyes. I was asleep and dreaming in minutes.

TWENTY-EIGHT

AVA AND BROOKE

July 2000

"What's that on your back?" Ava asked, reaching out to touch the raised star-shaped mark on the back of Brooke's right shoulder. It was darker than the rest of her light brown skin.

"That's my birthmark. My mom told me I got it from my dad. He had one just like it on his arm."

"Does it hurt?"

"No. I've had it since I was a baby. Lots of people have them. Don't you have one?"

"No. I guess I'm just boring."

Both girls laughed. Ava was spending the night at Brooke's house. Something she'd rarely been allowed to do, but lately Ava had the feeling her mother might have a boyfriend. She pushed the thought out of her head because if her mom had a boyfriend, it meant she and her father were definitely getting a divorce. Her father wouldn't be coming home, and they wouldn't be a family again.

She'd overheard her mom talking and laughing on the phone to somebody and then when she let Ava spend the night at Brooke's, she cooked up a big dinner that wasn't meant for her. Ava knew something was up and she was glad she wasn't in the house that night because she didn't want to be a part of whatever it was. She didn't want to meet any man trying to take her dad's place. Even though her dad had stopped calling her like he used to, he was still her dad, and she missed him.

"Here. Now, you've got one, too."

Brooke reached out and pressed something onto the back of Ava's right shoulder. Ava reached behind her and pulled it off to see what it was. It was a small circle of brown construction paper. Brooke had put a tiny piece of tape on the back and drawn a star shape with a black ballpoint pen on the front. When Ava gave Brooke a weird look, her friend burst out laughing.

"What's the matter? Now, you've got a birthmark just like me. Don't you like it?"

Brooke started tickling her and soon both girls were shrieking with laughter until Brooke's mother Julia called up the steps commanding them to settle down.

Detective Michael Avery just stared at me, not speaking, when I confronted him about Vivian Barnes's story. He looked away, embarrassed as well he should be. We were sitting in my car around the corner from the Elmhurst Police Department. I'd brought him a coffee to lure him out, which was now sitting untouched in my cupholder.

"I'm not sure what else we could've done, Miss Quinn. We had no legal recourse to search that farm after another little girl swore she was the one who'd talked to Vivian Barnes and that she never told Mrs. Barnes her name was Brooke Peters. Did Mrs. Barnes also tell you the little girl was with her mother when she talked to the police?"

"It's been twenty-five years, Detective. She can't be expected to remember every detail." I was reaching and I knew it, but Vivian Barnes absolutely believed she'd seen Brooke at that farm, and I believed her.

"You also have to remember that Vivian Barnes was a grieving mother looking for answers about her daughter's death."

"And you didn't find it at all odd when she swore it was a different little girl to the one she saw?"

"Even Mrs. Barnes agreed that it was late, and it was dark. She admitted she could have made a mistake. I know you had to have noticed the thick glasses she wears. She has a pretty serious vision impairment which, if I'm remembering correctly, prohibits her from driving at night. Take all of that into consideration and pour a heaped helping of emotional distress on top of it, and it's a recipe for an honest mistake."

"You didn't find it suspicious at all when the people living on that farm just up and left without a trace? That looks pretty damn guilty if you ask me. Why would they just leave like that? Was the farm searched after they left?"

"Again, we would have to have a warrant which we had no reason to get."

"Was this what you meant when you said mistakes were made in this case? And if it was up to you, things would've been done differently?"

He sat stone-faced and refused to answer, then finally looked over at my big tote bag which was lying on the console between us slightly open and I realized what he was thinking.

"Don't worry. I'm not recording this. So, your answer will be strictly off the record."

"Then hell yes. I wanted to take a team in and search that farm top to bottom for that little girl, but like I said, my hands were tied because I wasn't the lead. I was a rookie detective and had to do what I was told. I was told to back off and not go back out to that farm. And I backed off."

"Why do you think that was? Did someone on the force have a connection to that place that they didn't want exposed?"

"Infinity Farm was a very big contributor to Senator Kirk Conrad's campaign at the time. So, yes, I'm sure that had more to do with it than the lack of evidence. That's not to say I didn't do my due diligence. At least to the best of my limited abilities." He picked up the cup of coffee which had to be cold now, took a swig, grimaced and set it back in the cupholder.

"You mean you went out and searched on your own behind the backs of your superiors?"

"I did."

"And?"

"And nothing. I found no trace that Brooklyn Peters had ever been on that farm. Now, that's not to say she couldn't have been there because I was only one guy sneaking around in the dark with a flashlight and there were only so many places I could get to in one night. Lots of locked doors and no idea what was behind them. I left that farm fairly certain that that little girl was not there."

"Any idea where they could've gone?"

"No. And, to be honest, they may not have actually gone anywhere. They may have just disbanded their operation, and everyone associated with that farm moved on to other places."

"Is there any way I can find out who owns Infinity Corporation? I can't find any information about them."

"Just because a business has the word Corp at the end of it doesn't mean it was actually registered and licensed as a real corporation. I'm guessing that's what happened here. They probably weren't a real corporation. Just because someone has a business card doesn't make them a business owner."

"Well, that's just great. The biggest lead I have in the documentary, and I can't find anything about them."

"Do you think it's a good idea to track these people down? If they did abduct a ten-year-old twenty-five years ago, then they're capable of anything and you might not want these people to know you're looking for them."

"Detective, I have survived more than you will ever know. I think I can handle myself, but thanks for your concern."

He gave me a neutral look and then shook his head. "Just be careful and don't say I didn't try and warn you."

"Hey," I said, before he could get out of the car. "Is it true what they're saying about a serial slasher in Elmhurst?"

"No comment."

"So, what happened to Adele Mackie and Natalie Hammond aren't connected?"

"I wouldn't tell you if they were. Have a nice day, Ms. Quinn, and watch your back."

He got out of the car and took off down the alley to get back to the police station. A chill ran down my spine because I knew a warning when I heard one.

When I got back to my Airbnb, I realized Avery's claim that Infinity Corporation might not be a real business simply didn't feel right. Since I'd found out next to nothing about who was behind Infinity Corp, I took another route. I hopped on my laptop and did an internet search for the address of Infinity Farm. With the exception of the address showing up in multiple online realty sites, I came up with a single mention in the *Elmhurst Daily Citizen* from five months ago under the probate courts property transfers section stating that the address in question, 2570 County Creek Road, had transferred from a Helen Kay Sikes to a Kerri Sikes. Helen Kay?

Why did that name sound so familiar? Then I remembered and grabbed my phone. I'd taken a picture of the flyer I'd found at the library for Helen Kay's Herbals. Though the flyer didn't mention her last name, I was pretty sure this was the same Helen Kay. Apparently, she hadn't just sourced her herbs from Infinity Farm, she owned it. Excited at having finally caught a break, I did a search for Helen Kay Sikes only to find her obit. She died at the ripe old age of eighty-five six months ago and Kerri Sikes was listed in the obit as her grandchild and only survivor. My heart deflated like a punctured tire. Helen Kay was dead and whatever she may have known about Brooke being on that farm died with her. Would her granddaughter know anything?

I found Kerri Sikes's LinkedIn page showing an attractive redhead in her late twenties. Her bio said she was born in Elmhurst and raised in Cleveland. She currently taught at Elmhurst Community College. She wasn't even living here when Brooke was abducted, but it couldn't hurt to talk to her. I found her office phone number and campus email address on the college's website and called. There was no answer, so I left a message and then called the department of Arts and Sciences and asked about her.

"Are you one of her students?" asked a woman with a nasal voice who answered the phone.

I started to say no, but realized I'd probably get more info if I pretended I was one of her students. "Yes, ma'am. I forgot what her office hours were and wondered if you knew."

"You should have gotten a message on your class portal letting you know Ms. Sikes is out sick for the rest of the week."

"I must have missed that. Thanks." I hung up, disappointed I wouldn't be able to talk to this woman anytime soon.

THIRTY

AVA

The sound of shattered glass and our alarm going off woke Evan and me after midnight. Evan was instantly on his feet while I rubbed my eyes in confusion having had so little sleep after my mom's attack.

"What...the?"

"You stay here. I'm going to check it out." Evan grabbed a gun from the nightstand on his side of the bed. I hated that gun, but he insisted we needed it.

Normally, it was locked in a gun safe. When and why did he move it to the bedside table? I heard him calling me from downstairs. I immediately got up, threw on my robe and slippers, and quickly headed down the steps. I stopped at the sight in front of me.

Dana was standing at the back door like she had been the night I'd found her sleepwalking. Only this time she had put her arm through the glass and was bleeding profusely. Evan was trying to staunch the flow of blood with a kitchen towel while Dana stood there staring straight ahead, clearly still asleep, as blood trickled down the inside of her forearm onto the floor.

"Dana!" Evan shouted right in her face. That seemed to do the trick because she finally woke up, looked down at her arm and all the blood, then started screaming.

I rushed over and pulled her into my arms as Evan continued to apply pressure to the gash. We both carefully maneuvered her over to a kitchen chair, trying to avoid the broken glass on the floor.

It was close to four in the morning when we got back from the ER. It took twenty stitches to close the cut in Dana's arm. We were all exhausted and I helped her into clean clothes and into bed. Evan had barely said a word the entire time, and I waited to ask him what I really wanted to know until after we were behind the closed door of our bedroom.

"Why is your gun out of the safe? When did you put it in your bedside table? I thought we agreed if you were going to have one, it would always be locked in the safe."

"That was before you brought a stranger I don't know from Adam into this house. Now, I find out this woman has mental health issues. What the hell were you thinking, Ava?"

I hesitated for a moment, but it just made no sense anymore to hide how I was feeling and what I was thinking regarding Dana. I sat down next to him on the bed. I couldn't face him.

"Evan, I think Dana might be Brooke."

"Brooke? Are you serious right now? How the hell can she be Brooke?"

When I continued to stare at my hands and refused to answer him, he got up and knelt in front of me, taking my hands in his. "Babe, look at me," he commanded until I finally raised my tear-filled eyes to his.

"I'm sorry. I should've told you about this when I first suspected, but I really do feel like she's Brooke. She's about the same age. She has the same birthmark on the back of her right shoulder, and she even has an old stuffed turtle named Willa just like Brooke had when we were kids."

Evan let out a sigh and then stood to sit next to me again, wrapping his arm around me. I laid my head against his shoulder.

"All of those things could just be coincidences. If they aren't, then where has she been for twenty-five years?"

"She told me she doesn't remember much of her life before ten years ago when she was found wandering down the side of a highway, and she still has no idea who she is or where she came from."

"That sounds awfully damned convenient if you ask me."

I stood up abruptly and glared down at him. "You think she's dead, don't you?"

"So did you before you started volunteering at Haver House and met this woman who could be anybody. Didn't you tell me she doesn't even have any kind of picture ID?"

"Don't you think I know how this all sounds, but something in my spirit is telling me that this woman is Brooke. And if she is, I have to help her because..." I couldn't continue as a sob tore out of my throat, and I buried my face in my hands and wept. Evan pulled me into his arms and stroked my hair.

"Because you couldn't help her the day she was abducted. I know, babe. I know how guilty you've felt all of these years because you couldn't help Brooke that day, but you've got to stop this. I don't know who the woman in our guest bedroom is, but I guarantee you she is not Brooke and you're going to tear yourself apart trying to fix something that can't be fixed."

I couldn't deny his logic and was too tired to try.

"And we've got another problem." He reached out and tucked a strand of hair behind my ear.

"What now?" I groaned, not wanting to hear about any more problems.

"Your mom is getting out of the hospital at the end of the week. I don't think she's going to want to go back to her house right now. She can't be by herself, and our guest bedroom is occupied. Don't you think it's time Dana found another place to stay? I know you want to help her because you think she's Brooke, but family comes first."

I fell asleep that night with Evan curled around me, realizing he was absolutely right. At the same time, I knew my need for answers wasn't something that was going away any time soon.

THIRTY-ONE

AVA

I managed to track Josh Turner down twenty minutes before his office hours ended. He shared a small office on the third floor of Roslyn Hall with another math instructor who was working at her computer with headphones on and had her back to us. Having another person in the room was probably the only reason why Josh Turner was as civil as he was when he looked up and saw me standing in the doorway. He smiled like it caused him physical pain. I took that as my cue to walk on in.

"Mrs. West? What a surprise. What brings you to my part of campus? Dr. Martin's office is in Collins Hall."

"I know that, but it's you I came to see."

"Me?" He was genuinely surprised. "Are you thinking about taking a math class?"

"No," I said with a laugh and parked myself in a chair by his desk uninvited.

I quickly glanced at his desk which was actually two desks pushed together. There was a computer with a double monitor on one side, and on the other side piles of books, papers, file folders, and framed photographs of him with groups of people, some looked like students and others with what looked to be other faculty members. None of them were photos of Kerri, the woman who was about to become his wife.

"If you came looking for Kerri, she's feeling much better. She'll be back on campus soon."

"Kerri? She's sick?" There was no way I could have known what was going on with Kerri, especially given what I've been through the past several days.

"Nothing a few days off won't take care of. She's been working herself to death with her course load and with the wedding planning."

"Really? She told me you were being such a big help to her with the wedding planning. Why would she be so stressed out if you're helping her?" I struggled to keep the accusatory tone out of my voice because it would accomplish nothing but make more problems for Kerri. Her attraction to this man was something I was probably not meant to understand.

"Ours is a partnership. More men need to be taking an active role in wedding planning because, after all, it's our day too, right? And you women do tend to get carried away. Someone needs to rein you all in, but I know you didn't come here to talk about my wedding plans. So please tell me how I can help you."

I pulled the brochure that Dr. Martin had given me for Infinite Horizons from my purse and held it out to him, noticing he looked truly shocked.

"I had no idea any of these were still floating around campus. How'd you get this?"

I didn't bother answering his question and asked what I'd come to ask. "I wanted to know about this star symbol on the front. What kind of symbol is this?"

Josh Turner let out a harsh bark of laughter that irritated me like nails on a blackboard. When he finished laughing, he gave me a smug smile. "For starters, this isn't a star. This is a Dharma wheel."

"Dharma wheel? What's that?"

"It's a Buddhist symbol that represents transformation and rebirth."

"And you're using it as a symbol for Infinite Horizons? Why?"

"Because our members come to Infinite Horizons deeply troubled and in need of a restart. A renewal if you will. And that's what they get from our programs. As a matter of fact, are you interested in signing up for any of our programs?"

I could tell by the way he was eyeing me up and down with a smirk that he was about to suggest the weight loss program, which would have been the quickest way to earn himself a punch in the throat.

"No, thank you." How I managed to keep a smile on my face I'll never know and now that I had my answer there was no reason to hang around this idiot any longer.

"May I ask why you're asking if you're not interested in any of our programs?"

"It's just I've seen a handful of people lately with this symbol on the back of their shoulder and wondered what it was all about, and then I remembered seeing this brochure with the same symbol on the front. I figured if anyone would know, it would be you." There was no reason to lie to him about having seen the symbol, but I wasn't about to tell him my mother had been one of these people.

"And the people who have the symbols weren't able to enlighten you?"

"No. Everyone seems to develop amnesia whenever I ask them about it."

"Well, what does that tell you?"

"Not a damn thing which is why I am asking you."

"Mrs. West, there are answers to every question that you want to know. Just know that the people you're asking are not obligated to share those answers with you."

"Did you just tell me to mind my own business?"

"How very astute of you. Now, if you'll excuse me," he said, grabbing his big ass leather briefcase and walking past me towards the door. "I've got class. You know the way out."

"My husband said hi."

He paused briefly, giving me a tight smile. I watched him leave and as soon as he was out the door, his office mate, a young white woman with a bright pink bob, pulled off her headphones, turned to me, rolled her eyes and shook her head. She must have been listening. We didn't have to say anything to each other to know what the other was thinking about her office mate.

"Girl, I am so sorry," I told her as I walked out the door.

As I headed to my car in the parking lot, I heard someone calling out my name. I turned to see Dr. Martin rushing towards me with concern on her face.

"Ava, how is your mom doing? I heard about it on the news."

"She's on the mend. She gets to come home on Friday. I'm just so thankful that her neighbors were able to intervene before that lunatic killed her."

"And they have no idea who did this to her or why? People are saying it's connected to what happened to James Mackie's wife."

"They're not sharing any information and they have no idea who did this. I think someone is picking random victims, and my mom was the unfortunate winner this time around."

"If there's anything I can do, just let me know. I'm there for you, you know that, right?"

I hugged Dr. Martin. "Thank you. I really appreciate that." She started to head back towards the building when something Josh Turner said popped into my head.

"Dr. Martin?" She turned and I walked over to her. "I heard Kerri was sick. Do you know what's going on with her?"

"We haven't seen her all week. I tried calling her, but it just goes straight to voicemail. Josh always stops into the department every day to give us an update on her. I trust him about as much as I trust straw rain boots. I would feel so much better if I could actually talk to her."

"If you hear from her, please let me know. I'm worried about her, too."

Dr. Martin nodded and headed back into the building.

I decided I'd been dodging Lia Quinn's calls for long enough and it was time I got busy doing what I had agreed to do when she paid me. I was now sitting in the dining room area of the Airbnb in downtown Elmhurst, where she was renting while she was working on her documentary about Brooke. It was just the two of us. I didn't know why I thought there would be a camera crew there. It was just Lia and I sitting across from each other at the dining room table. I had a mic clipped to the lapel of my blouse, as did Lia. There were three cameras, one behind me facing Lia and one behind Lia facing me, as well as one sitting on top of the dining room table to capture a side view of both of us as we talked.

"I'd like to thank you for agreeing to sit down for an interview, Ava. I know this has to be such a hard time for you with what's going on with your mom. Is she going to be alright?"

"Physically, yes, but we're all afraid whoever did this might come back. I'm just relieved Elmhurst police officers are guarding her room around the clock, but I'd like to request that you don't include anything about my mom's attack in the documentary."

"Of course not. This is strictly about Brooke's abduction," Lia assured me, making me feel a bit more relaxed.

"Great, and I'd like to thank you for giving me the opportunity to finally tell my story." I actually meant it, especially now that I thought there was every possibility that Brooke was alive and had found her way home to Elmhurst.

It was not my intention to reveal this revelation on camera. It wanted to cooperate fully with the documentary and then, when it came out, sit Dana down, have her watch it and then share my theory with her afterwards. I was hoping the documentary would jog something that would unlock her memories as Brooke.

"Well then, are you ready to get started?" Lia had a remote in her hand that I assumed turned on the cameras. I nodded. I was suddenly nervous and took a quick sip of my bottled water sitting on the floor next to my chair.

"Tell me about your first memory of Brooke."

"We met when we were both eight years old and in the third grade at Pleasant Street Elementary school. Brooke was very popular, outgoing, and fun-loving. She was a really sweet little girl. She was in a bigger circle of friends that I had at the time, but over the next couple of years that circle dwindled until it was just me and Brooke. By the time we were ten years old, we were best friends."

"And everyone loved Brooke?"

"Absolutely. Everyone loved that little girl. She was so special."

I could already feel the lump in my throat and the tears forming in my eyes. This was going to be hard to get through, so I took a deep breath and straightened my spine; otherwise, I would be having to take breaks every few minutes and I wanted to get this over with.

Lia seemed to sense my emotional state and paused before the next question to give me time to pull myself together.

"What were some of Brooke's favorite things to do?"

"She loved being outdoors. She loved exploring the woods near our neighborhood, and she loved animals. She couldn't wait until she was twelve because that's when her mom told her she could have a dog. She loved watching the Nickelodeon channel. *Even Stevens* and *Rugrats* were her favorite shows, and she loved to swing. She was always challenging me to swing set races. I only ever beat her one time."

Lia would probably love hearing about me beating Brooke in that swing set race, which led to our being in the park that day. I'd certainly punished myself enough over the years about winning that race. If I'd let her win, would she still be here? But I wasn't about to bear my soul in that way on camera for anybody.

"Would you say that Brooke was a happy, well-adjusted little girl?"

"Yes, I would. She always had a smile on her face and a laugh that made everyone around her laugh, too."

So far nothing I had told Lia Quinn had been a lie, but there was another side to Brooke, one that I didn't like much and thankfully didn't see often. With the six-year age gap between her and her brother Sam, and with her being the youngest, Brooke was spoiled and could be difficult to deal with when she didn't get her way.

There was a time the year before her abduction when her mom took us to the movies, and we couldn't agree on what to see. She'd wanted to see *Stuart Little*, and I wanted to see *The Iron Giant*. We'd gotten into a huge argument and neither one of us got to see what we wanted. Brooke's mom took us to see *Inspector Gadget* instead, and Brooke refused to speak to me the entire time we were there, and I didn't see her for three days afterwards.

Then one morning she popped up at my front door all smiles, acting like she hadn't thrown the biggest tantrum over not getting to see the movie she wanted, and blamed me. But that was Brooke, and I accepted the fact that sometimes she wasn't very nice. I wasn't going to bring up that side of her because even though she was ten years old, some idiots out there in the viewing public would say she deserved what she got for not always being nice.

"How well did you know Brooke's family?"

"Not as well as I knew Brooke. Her brother Sam was a teenager. I rarely saw him because he was always with his friends. Her mom was really nice, but she worked two jobs to support the family. I never knew her dad because Brooke told me he'd died in a motorcycle accident when she was six."

"Are you sure about that? In my research into the Peters family, I never found an obit for Nathaniel Peters."

Was she kidding? Why would Brooke lie to me about something like that?

"Uh, I don't know how to explain that. Brooke had a picture of her father on his motorcycle in her bedroom, and I distinctly remember asking her about the picture. That's when she told me her father had died, and she barely remembered him."

Lia Quinn didn't look up from her notes to acknowledge what I'd just said, and I was inexplicably angry.

"Are you putting that in a documentary?"

Lia picked the remote up from the table and switched off the cameras. "Whatever you say here today on camera will be edited and your contribution will be shared for you to review. Anything you don't want to appear in the documentary, you'll have a chance to let me know and I will edit it out if you don't feel comfortable sharing it. Is that okay with you?"

"That's fine, but I was telling the truth when I said I thought Brooke's father was dead. If he's not, then I don't understand why her mother would've told her that."

"My research into the Peters family uncovered rumors of abuse."

"Abuse? You mean Brooke's father abused her?"

"According to the rumor, Brooke's father did something to hurt her, so her mother banned him from ever seeing her again, and told Brooke that he died. That information seems to be backed up by the fact I've not been able to find an obituary for Nathaniel Peters. I found an obit for his mother Abby Peters, but there was no mention of him predeceasing her in her obit. He had an older brother who predeceased the mother. So, there's no one that I can ask about his whereabouts currently."

I felt sick. Why would a father hurt their child? Brooke must have blocked out the trauma because why else would she have had a picture of her father in her room if he had hurt her so badly that her mother told her he was dead? Of course, after all these years, whatever story Lia Quinn had heard was the equivalent of a twenty-five-year-old game of telephone. Who knew how much of what she had been told was true, but if Nathaniel Peters was dead, there should've been a death notice even if there was no obituary. Could he have died in another state or country, and his family had never been informed? I didn't know anything about Brooke's father aside from his name. I had no idea if he even had family here in Elmhurst.

"I don't know what to say. I had no idea about any of this."

"Would you like to take a break?"

"No. I'm good. Let's keep going."

"Take me through the day of Brooke's abduction. Everything that happened up to the time you guys walked into the park."

I closed my eyes and thought back to that day. Then proceeded to tell Lia Quinn about how we hung out at Brooke's house that morning, but we couldn't hear the TV over the vacuum cleaner that Brooke's mom was running. Her threatening to put us both to work helping her clean the house is what sent us out that day looking for something to do. I had change jiggling in my pocket for an ice-cream cone, but Brooke didn't want ice cream, she wanted payback. I had beat her in our last swing set race and she wanted a rematch. I barely ever got my way with Brooke, but that day I was adamant I wanted an ice-cream cone. Ice cream first and then a swing race rematch. As I thought back on that day, my eyes flew open. I remembered something. Something so small at the time, it had been buried in my memory because no one had asked me about anything that had happened before we got to the park until now. The recollection came flooding back like a tsunami.

THIRTY-TWO

AVA AND BROOKE

July 2000

"Hurry up. I can't believe you don't want any ice cream. It's so hot out and it'll cool you off," Ava said to Brooke as she quickly walked down the street in the direction of the park.

There was an ice cream truck permanently parked at the entrance to the park, and Ava could already feel the chocolatey goodness of the ice cream melting in her mouth. Chocolate was her favorite. Brooke just looked bored and impatient because Ava was insisting on getting ice cream first when she wanted to wait until after the swing race. Ava ignored Brooke's bad mood. She was in such a hurry to get to the ice cream truck, she wasn't watching where she was going when she stepped off the curb in front of the entrance to the park. Suddenly, the sound of screeching tires filled the air, and Ava felt herself being jerked backwards by her tank top.

"Watch out! You almost got hit." Brooke let go of the back of her shirt.

If Brooke hadn't been there, the car that was now heading around the corner would've hit Ava. It was a brown car with a rusted-out hood.

THIRTY-THREE

AVA

It was the same car Brooke had been dragged into; her abductor's car had almost hit me that day. They had been following us. Probably looking for an opportunity to snatch Brooke. I suddenly remembered something else. The face of another little black girl looking out the back window at me as they drove away. Her big brown eyes were wide with fear. I abruptly stood up as those new memories assaulted me and I knocked over the bottle of water in the process.

"I'm...Sorry...I got to go." I grabbed my bag from the kitchen counter on my way to the front door with Lia Quinn hot on my heels.

"You remembered something else, didn't you?"

"I can't do this right now. I'll call you."

I hurried out of the house like I was being chased by the devil. I couldn't get the key into my ignition because my hands were trembling so badly. Brooke's abduction hadn't been a random crime of opportunity. Her abductors had been stalking us. How long had they been following us that day? Who was that other little girl? And how could I have forgotten all this?

I leaned against the headrest and thought back on when I'd been in therapy after Brooke's abduction. I'd been struggling in school at the time and overheard my therapist telling my mom that the trauma I'd experienced could be affecting my memory and ability to retain information. Had trauma blocked out those other memories as well? Would remembering this at the time have led to them finding Brooke? Was it my fault, after all? I burst into tears and buried my face in my hands and sobbed.

When I got home, I poured myself a glass of Moscato and almost drained it in one gulp. I had to tell somebody. But who? And would it even make a difference when Brooke's case had gone so cold. What about that other girl I saw? Had she been abducted as well? I certainly don't remember hearing about another little girl going missing around the same time as Brooke, but that didn't mean anything. She could've been from another city, state or even country. Since missing black people didn't usually make mainstream media, it wouldn't be hard for anyone not to have known about this other child. I thought about Brooke being dragged into that car and thought about how loud her screams were, how they seemed to be coming from everywhere. But was it just Brooke's screaming that I heard? Did I also hear that other girl's screams as well?

I could feel a tension headache coming on. I turned and almost jumped out of my skin to see Dana standing there. She was dressed in a nightshirt of mine with her right forearm bandaged. When I left that morning, Dana was still in bed. She looked tired with dark circles under her eyes. She also looked uncertain, like she was unsure about whether she had worn out her welcome or not.

"Morning, sleepyhead. Do you want something to eat?"

"I am so sorry about last night. You must be regretting letting me crash here."

"Why would I blame you for something you can't help? I can't imagine you want to have night terrors, do you?"

She shook her head wearily and then took a seat at the kitchen island while I heated up the sausage, gravy and biscuits I had made that morning when I couldn't sleep. I fixed myself a sandwich and sat across from her. We ate in silence for several long minutes.

"I heard you leave the house this morning. Did you have to go to work?"

"I was being interviewed for a documentary about my friend that disappeared when we were kids. Do you remember I told you about that?"

"Yeah," she said nonchalantly. "I remember you telling me about that. How did she disappear?"

"She was abducted right in front of me from a playground when we were ten years old."

Her head jerked up and the stunned look on her face made me think for a split second that she may have remembered something. Again, I was disappointed.

"And you have no idea who did it or where she is now?"

I wanted to scream at her, but didn't. "Her case remains unsolved. No trace of her has ever been found in twenty-five years."

"Seriously? That is messed up."

I couldn't hold it in any longer and finally asked the question I'd wanted to ask her at IHOP. "You know your stuffed turtle, Willa."

"What about her?"

"You said you'd had her since you were a kid, right? But you also told me you didn't remember anything beyond ten years ago when you were found wandering down the highway. So, how do you remember always having Willa?"

I wasn't asking because I was trying to catch her in a lie. I was asking because I thought she might remember being Brooke and just didn't feel safe admitting it. It sounded like an accusation and Dana took it as such as she let out a sigh, wiped her mouth and tossed her napkin on her plate.

"I had her when I was found. Since she looks so old, and the nurses at the hospital told me I refused to let her go, I just assumed I'd had her for a long time. I can tell you think I'm lying. I knew this wasn't a good idea." She hopped off the stool and headed for the stairs.

"Where are you going?"

"I can't stay here. I'm sure helping me is filling some kind of void in you, but I can't stay here if you have to question every single thing that comes out of my mouth. What do I have to do to get you to trust me?"

"I do trust you, Dana. It was just a question. You're allowed to ask me questions, and I'm happy to let you stay here. I'm just trying to make sense of your situation. Though, if this is how you're going to be every time I'm confused about something you told me, then maybe it would be best if you left."

I was bluffing of course. I didn't want her to leave, but there was something about her that triggered the same kind of annoyance in me as Brooke did when she and I were kids, when she wasn't getting her way. Back then she had gotten used to me doing everything she wanted. The only problem was when I pushed back, but she never stayed mad at me for long, and once I was willing to stand up to her, the tantrums reduced. It was working with Dana as well.

She stood poised at the bottom of the steps, then turned to me. Her eyes were filled with tears. She sank down onto the bottom step.

"I don't want to leave, but I don't want to fight with you, either. You have no idea how thankful I am that you're letting me stay here. So, you can ask me anything you need to, but I can't answer how I came to have Willa, because I honestly don't remember."

"It's okay. Come back and finish eating. I don't have to go into the shelter today, so we can do whatever you want to do."

After we'd eaten and cleaned up the kitchen, I gave Dana some plastic wrap so she wouldn't get her bandage wet, and she went to take a shower. While she was in the shower, I took the opportunity to look around her room. She didn't have much and hadn't even bothered to hang up the few items of clothing I'd lent her. Willa the turtle was lying against the pillows of her made-up bed. I picked her up. It was the first time I'd had a chance to closely examine her since I'd seen her.

I examined every inch of her threadbare exterior and froze. There was a small spot on Willa's front foot. It was from when Brooke had Willa on the table at school during lunch and tipped over her juice box. We took Willa into the bathroom and tried to scrub the spot as best we could, but it had left a pink stain behind. Dana's Willa had this exact stain. I was suddenly light-headed and sank down on the edge of the bed as I realized Dana truly was Brooke. If she had been abducted without Willa, how did she come into possession of her beloved stuffed animal after her abduction? That meant that either someone Brooke knew had abducted her, or one of her abductors had gone to her house to get Willa.

THIRTY-FOUR
DETECTIVE AVERY

Detective Michael Avery sat in his unmarked police-issued Crown Victoria in front of the padlocked gate of Infinity Farm. He looked up at the cameras mounted on weathered wooden posts flanking either side of the gate. They were pointed at the winding drive leading up to the farm and he knew none of them were working. It was just a decoy to keep people away. Reluctantly, he got out of the car wondering for the millionth time what the hell he was doing there and why he had let Lia Quinn get under his skin so badly. He didn't know what he was hoping to accomplish by coming here, other than making himself feel better.

He had some bolt cutters in his trunk. It wouldn't take much to cut through the rusty lock, but he wanted to leave no trace of his visit. Instead, he climbed the gate and almost had it cleared before falling flat on his face, realizing he was way too old for this shit. The place hadn't changed much over the years since he'd last been here, except for the decay, the overgrown grass, the thick spiderwebs on the outsides of the windows, and the rusted-out farm equipment.

He walked into a large barn with single beds lined up on either side and shone his flashlight up into the loft of the barn and saw even more beds up there. Pulling the barn door open all the way flooded the space with light. He looked around the room, but the beds were stripped and the mattresses and pillows left behind were covered in mold.

Nothing had been left behind save for a few stray bobby pins, a man's plastic shaver crusted with rust, and a child's tennis shoe. He picked it up and a large spider came scuttling out. Dropping the shoe, he kicked it against the wall; more spiders exited the shoe. Clearly children had been here but had one of those children been Brooke Peters? He walked through the barn to the doors on the opposite end, noticing the two horse stalls on either side at the back of the barn. What he found next shocked him. A late model blue Hyundai had been parked in the stall on the left. It wasn't nearly as dusty and grimy as everything else in the barn. Someone had recently left this here.

The car was locked, and whoever had left it here had driven straight through the barn door and parked it in the stall. The barn had tire tracks in the dust, which he had walked right through without noticing. It shouldn't have surprised him that people were hiding things here. He was sure plenty of the locals knew that this place was sitting empty, and wouldn't hesitate to hide stolen items. He was in the process of looking through the car's windows when he noticed it. The foul stench of decomp. It was coming from somewhere inside the car. He pulled his phone from his back pocket to call it in, while he tried to decide what excuse he could give for him being there.

An hour later, the barn was officially a crime scene. The first officers on the scene managed to open the trunk to find the decomposing body of a man. At least everyone thought it was a man. The body had been in the trunk in a barn in the hot August heat. Avery was surprised the body was still intact as he held a napkin to his nose to block out the stench that now filled the barn.

So far, a search of the car yielded no identification that might tell who this guy was. Even the license plates had been removed, but Avery could tell by the lack of dust and grime on the car, and by the tracks in the dust on the barn floor, the car had not been there for very long. Was the dead guy in the trunk the owner of the car or just the unfortunate victim of whoever owned it?

A search of the other buildings on the property showed that someone had been living in one of the sheds behind the main farmhouse. They found a sleeping bag, a plastic gallon jug of water, some canned goods, beef jerky, and some protein bars. Avery bent to pick up a protein bar wrapper and remembered seeing one that looked just like it inside the trunk. He had a feeling the guy in the trunk had been squatting in the shed, but how did he end up in the trunk? And who the hell was he?

"Detective Avery," said a young, uniformed officer. "We got a hit on the VIN number for the car."

"That fast?" His eyebrow lifted in surprise. "Was it reported stolen?"

"No, sir. The car is registered to Dana Shields, aged sixty-one, of Dayton, Ohio."

He thanked the officer and asked him to text him the address because he knew at some point that day, he was going to make the trip to Dayton to talk to Dana Shields about how her car ended up in Elmhurst, Ohio, hidden in a barn with a dead guy in the trunk.

THIRTY-FIVE

AVA

I insisted on taking Dana shopping for some new clothes because she'd lost the key to the bus station locker where the rest of her things were. The only place she would agree to go was the Goodwill near my house, where she picked out a couple of pairs of jeans, a sweatshirt, two T-shirts, some new underwear and a bra, a pair of sneakers and some sandals.

Once we were back home, she told me she was tired and went upstairs to take a nap. I went to do a load of laundry and found something shiny glinting up at me from inside the washer as I loaded it. It was a locker key. After I started the washer, I headed back upstairs to tell Dana I'd found her locker key. She didn't answer when I knocked so I peeked inside to find she was fast asleep. While she rested, I figured I'd do her a favor and head down to the Elmhurst Greyhound station to get the rest of her things from locker 706, which was stamped onto the key.

I found the locker easily enough but was surprised to see that the only thing it held was her rolling suitcase. I wondered what she'd done with the laundry basket she had. I grabbed the rolling suitcase and put it in my trunk, then realized it would be the only time I could look through her things without her knowing. Not sure what I was looking for, I cautiously unzipped the red suitcase and lifted the lid and was met by the smell of unwashed clothes. Everything in the suitcase looked to have been tossed in in a hurry. Nothing was folded. Nothing was clean. Dried mud caked on the soles of a pair of high-top tennis shoes had flaked off, making everything inside the suitcase even dirtier. I wrinkled my nose and was about to close the lid when something else caught my eye.

I saw the outline of a book or something in the lid pocket of the suitcase. I reached in and pulled out a thick manila envelope, then pulled out the contents. I flipped through and my heart started to pound. They were printouts of newspaper articles. A big stack of just about every article that had ever been written about Brooke's abduction. Something fell out from between the pages of the articles and fell onto the floor of my trunk. I stared at it, already knowing what it was before I reached out to pick it up.

It was a driver's license showing a much younger Dana, only her name was Simone Riley, and the license had expired ten years ago. Hadn't she said she was found wandering down the side of a road with no memory ten years ago? How could that be when I was holding proof of who she was then. Then I noticed something else that broke my heart, and angry tears filled my eyes. It was the date of birth listed on the license: February 5, not April 23, which was Brooke's birthday. What shocked me even more was the year. Brooke had been born in 1990, like me. The woman I'd opened my home to, Simone Riley, was born in 1982. She was forty-three, not thirty-five.

I knew the chances of her being Brooke were slim, even though I'd convinced myself otherwise, but I still felt like the biggest fool. Dana, or rather Simone, had been lying to me all along about everything, from having amnesia to not knowing who she was. Everything about her was a lie. Was it because she was a con woman who had targeted me, knowing I would be vulnerable enough to take her in if I thought she was my missing best friend? I stuffed the envelope back into the pocket, but it wouldn't go in all the way. I reached inside and pulled out a wadded up red tank top.

Then I realized the tank top wasn't red. It was tan and the front of it was stiff with dried blood. But whose blood?

Dana had gotten blood all over herself the night before when she'd cut her arm, but her suitcase had been in the bus station locker for days and I hadn't noticed any cuts on her that would have created a bloodstain this large. So, whose blood was this? All I knew is, I needed answers, and I planned on getting them. I closed my trunk and tossed the envelope onto the passenger seat and tore out of the bus station parking lot so fast I almost clipped a car turning into the lot.

When I got home, I marched straight up the steps and flung the door to the guest bedroom open only to find it empty. Whoever had been staying in my house, eating my food and taking advantage of my hospitality, was gone with only an envelope left on the bed. It read:

I'm so sorry, Ava. It's safer for both of us if I go. Thank you for everything. But here's something you need to know.

Inside the envelope was an old, faded Polaroid picture. It showed a group of men and women with an older man standing in the middle of them. His arms were around the shoulders of the boys on either side of him. The photo was so grainy I could barely make out the faces of any of the other people, but I recognized the man in the middle of the picture.

It was James Mackie.

THIRTY-SIX

LIA

I was in the middle of my fifth cup of coffee of the day, editing the video footage that I had gotten so far from the handful of people who'd agreed to be interviewed for the documentary. Every so often I would look at my phone or at the door, hoping maybe Ava West would come back to finish her interview. So far, she hadn't, and she also hadn't answered any of my texts to see if she was alright. What the hell happened? Everything was going so smoothly and then all of a sudden all the color drained from her face, and she bolted. I went over the footage and what I'd asked her again and again, but could not figure out what I had said or done to cause this reaction. Clearly, she'd remembered something when I'd asked her to go over the day Brooke had been abducted. Her odd reaction was triggered when she was telling me about her and Brooke walking to the park.

As I was getting up to put my coffee cup in the sink, my phone beeped with a text. I snatched it up thinking it was Ava rescheduling her interview, but it wasn't. It was a text from Detective Avery and all it said was:

Turn on the news.

Most people I know got their news from social media these days, but I knew that's not what Avery was talking about and switched on the flatscreen on the wall directly in front of the couch, flipping through the channels until I found a local news station.

As soon as I saw the picture of police cars in front of Infinity Farm, I sank down onto the couch in disbelief. According to a female reporter standing across the road from Infinity Farm, a body had been found on the property that had yet to be identified. Not surprisingly the reporter brought up the connection between the report of the sighting of Brooke Peters at the farm twenty-five years ago. Was she implying that the body found at Infinity Farm was Brooke Peters? Because I of all people knew that couldn't be true.

THIRTY-SEVEN

BROOKE

July 2000

Brooke screamed and screamed until her lungs felt like they would burst before one of the two men in the front seat turned around and swung at her, missing her face by millimeters. She attempted to get as far away from the passenger seat as she could, but she could only go so far. To her left was another black girl who looked about her age. She had wedged herself so tightly into the corner of the backseat and was so rigid with fear, she looked like she might break apart if Brooke touched her.

"Shut the hell up!" shouted the man who had grabbed her at the park. The one she had foolishly thought had puppies to show her. The man driving was black and had a blue baseball cap on.

"I wanna go home! Take me home!"

Fingers dug into her arm, jerking her out of the way as the man swung at her again. She looked at the girl whose eyes were big and frozen with fear as she vigorously shook her head, her eyes imploring Brooke to be quiet.

Spent, gasping and hiccupping on her sobs, Brooke laid her head down on the other girl's lap, shoving her fist into her mouth to block out the sound of her sobs as the car drove on, taking her further and further away from home.

THIRTY-EIGHT

I was relieved Dana was gone. I hadn't been looking forward to confronting her over the license and all the other lies she'd fed me that I'd eagerly lapped up. I had wanted her to be Brooke so bad it had clouded my judgment. I also knew that meant I wouldn't be getting any answers from her about why she'd lied, let alone why she'd left me the photo. Did it have something to do with Adele's murder? Was she trying to tell me James Mackie had killed his wife? I was so confused and did something I probably shouldn't have. With no one else to talk to, I found myself unloading everything on Evan as soon as he walked through the door.

"She had a driver's license all along?"

"An expired one. There's a name on there, different to the two names that I knew she went by at some point in the past. Dana Shields was her landlady's name. Dana said Cindy Ford was the name she took after they found her, and she couldn't remember who she was. How could she not know who she was and still have a driver's license with the name Simone Riley on it? And she can't be Brooke." I couldn't even look at him when I said it.

"Why?"

"She's too old."

"Look, Ava, I know you were trying to help this woman

because you thought she might be Brooke, but from everything you've told me, she just sounds like a straight up con woman who targeted you because she knew she could get your sympathy. Have you looked around the house to see if she's stolen anything?"

I was so shocked to come home and find our guest gone that it hadn't even occurred to me to check to see if she had taken anything. Evan and I made a quick search of the house. He took the upstairs, I took the downstairs. I couldn't spot anything missing, but when Evan came down the stairs, the look on his face said it all.

"What is it?" My voice was barely a whisper.

"My gun. I never put it back in the safe. It was still on the bedside table. And now it's gone."

I grabbed my cell phone from my purse.

"Who are you calling?"

"The police. This needs to be reported. Dana is running around with a gun, and we have no idea why she took it or what she's capable of."

Evan snatched my phone out of my hand and put it in his pocket so it was out of my reach. "You can't do that, Ava."

"What do you mean I can't call the police? You got your gun rights back, didn't you? You said you petitioned the court, right?"

"Not exactly."

"What do you mean not exactly?"

"I petitioned the court. They denied me. I don't have my gun rights back yet, but I'm working on it. I swear."

I just stared at him with disbelief. I had believed him. Why wouldn't I? He was my husband. I trusted him. Now, a woman with questionable motives had stolen a gun he wasn't legally allowed to own because he was a convicted felon, and we couldn't call the police to report it. What else had Evan lied about? How could I trust anything he'd told me?

"I can't believe this. Are you serious right now? How long did you think you were going to be able to hide this from me?"

"Look, I knew you were going to react this way. I swear to God,

Ava. I'm working with an attorney to get my gun rights back, but it takes time."

"Just like you swore to me the court approved your petition, and you were allowed to own a firearm again? How am I supposed to believe anything that comes out of your mouth when you tell me lies?"

"Because you always overreact and make me feel sorry for telling you the truth."

"You mean the way *you* overreacted when I just wanted to take a small break before we explored IVF? Then all I did was mention adoption and you acted like I'd shot you, Evan. You barely spoke to me for weeks. Now, you have the nerve to stand here and tell me that I'm overreacting when I find out you lied about having your gun rights back? Please explain that to me so I'll understand."

"I told you what that was about. You said you understood."

"Fine." I let out a breath and tried to calm down. "I understand about your past and why you didn't want to adopt, but why did you lie about your gun rights? Why do we even need a gun in the first place?"

He stared at me, quickly realizing I wasn't going to let him off the hook, and sighed. "I got it for protection because I was being threatened."

"Threatened? Threatened by whom?"

"Josh Turner." His voice was flat, and he couldn't look me in the eyes.

"Josh...Turner? What in the hell, Evan? Why would...?"

"He's my half-brother, Ava."

I stared at him, too shocked to speak, and waited for him to continue.

"I've known he was my brother since middle school, but he only found out he had a half-black half-brother a year younger than him six months ago when his," he paused and cleared his throat, "when *our* mother died. She cut him out of her will but left me $250,000. He's pissed and has been trying to get me to sign that money over to him ever since. That's the real reason I've had to take construction jobs out of town. He knows I'm a felon. Hell, everyone I went to school with knows, but Josh has been telling my clients about my criminal past, and I've lost jobs because of it."

"But why did she leave you that money? Guilt?"

"That and the fact that Josh blew through a lot of his parents' money when they were alive. He wasn't exactly a son they could be proud of. They were constantly having to bail him out of financial and legal messes. They even shipped him off to some treatment program on some farm when he was a teenager. Nothing worked. He's just a narcissistic jerk."

I let out a harsh laugh I didn't recognize. "Oh, really? And what does that make you? Huh, Evan? You've known about this for months, which means you've been lying to me for months. Were you ever going to tell me any of this? I specifically asked you about where you were going to get the money for the IVF treatments and you copped an attitude and flat out refused to tell me, and then made me feel horrible for asking. So, if your big brother Josh is a narcissistic jerk, then you're a lying jerk. It must run in the family!"

"Babe, please." He tried to touch me, but I batted his hand away.

"Please don't call the police about the gun, Ava. I'll fix it. I promise."

He followed me to the front door, but before I left, I turned to stare at him. "I don't think this can be fixed. I just need to get out of this house right now and it would probably be in your best interest not to be here when I get back."

"Ava! Come back. Babe, I'm sorry. I..."

I slammed the door on whatever he was about to say, tears blurring my eyes. I had to sit behind the wheel of my car for several minutes to calm down, not trusting myself to drive in the state I was in. Where could I go? My mom's was out of the question, and I didn't feel like going to the shelter. That only left one person.

THIRTY-NINE

LIA

It was after eight o'clock when a soft knock came at my door. Had I not been headed back to the living room where I had parked myself in front of the news all day, I may not have heard it. I opened the door to find Ava West on my doorstep.

"I'm so sorry. I know it's late, but I was hoping I could continue my interview for the documentary."

"Of course, please come in." I stepped aside for her to enter and noticed her eyes were red. Had she been crying? Had she heard the news about what was happening at Infinity Farm, too?

"Would you like a glass of wine?"

"A big one if you've got it."

By the time I came back to the living room with a large glass of white wine for her, she was staring open-mouthed at the TV. By the shocked look on her face, I could tell this was the first time she was hearing about the body found at Infinity Farm.

"This has been on the news all day."

She barely looked at me when she took the glass of wine and took three big gulps, almost draining it. "Do they know whose body they found?"

"It's not Brooke, Ava."

"How do you know?"

"Well, I don't know for sure, but it was described as a body and not remains."

I had to rush forward to catch the wine glass that slipped from her fingers, splashing the remnants of wine down my sweatshirt. I gently led her to the couch before getting a dish towel to mop up the wine.

"There was a sighting of Brooke at a farm on the outskirts of town a few months after she was abducted. I remember hearing my mom and Brooke's mom talking about it in our kitchen, and remember how disappointed her mom was when they found out it wasn't Brooke."

"I know all about that. I interviewed Vivian Barnes, the woman who reported that sighting, for the documentary. She still swears to this day that it was Brooke she saw."

"This is just...too much." Tears streamed down Ava's face, and she wiped them away with the back of her hand.

There was no way I could interview her for the documentary tonight and it would be cruel to try as she was clearly emotionally distressed and had been when she arrived at my doorstep.

"Oh my god." Ava suddenly jumped up from the couch and stared at the screen.

I looked too and saw a car being towed down the driveway and out of the entrance to the farm. From the quick glance that I got, it was a blue Hyundai Sonata. "What's wrong?"

"I know whose car that is."

"Please tell me you'll be able to establish a time of death." Avery was looking at Dr. Tate Lang, the interim medical examiner, noting the downward turn of his mouth and the slight lift of his left eyebrow.

He first met Lang at the Adele Mackie crime scene as he'd recently come on board temporarily as their long-term medical examiner had retired recently. Lang was a good thirty years younger, with a slender build, close cropped hair, and dark brown skin. In his denim button-down shirt, khaki dockers, and black Nikes, he looked more like one of their IT guys.

"Might be able to pin it down once we get some of the flies and larva to an entomologist which can take forever. In this heat, it's going be damned hard to pinpoint the precise time of death, but I did find this."

He handed Avery a plastic evidence bag with some type of plastic card coated with bodily fluids that made Avery's stomach lurch slightly. He took a closer look. It was a driver's license and when he saw the name on it, his head jerked back in surprise.

"What's wrong? You know this person?" Dr. Lang asked, stripping off his plastic gloves and shoe covers.

Avery didn't respond because too many thoughts and questions were racing through his head, namely how the hell did Nathaniel Peters' body end up dead in the trunk of a car, which was owned by a woman who lived in Dayton, in the barn of a farm in the outskirts of Elmhurst, Ohio? Where had he been for the past twenty-five years? And why had he been living in a shed on this property, which happened to be one of the places his daughter Brooke Peters had been sighted after her abduction?

FORTY-ONE

AVA

The police were now looking for Dana, or rather Simone Riley. Lia had called Detective Michael Avery, but he was too tied up at the crime scene at Infinity Farm to come and take my statement, and sent two uniformed officers instead. I told them everything that I knew, even gave them her driver's license but stopped short of telling them about the gun. I didn't want my husband to lose everything despite the fact I was extremely angry and disappointed in him. In my heart of hearts, I really didn't think Dana was a threat. She was out in the streets alone again now, and probably needed the protection.

I told the officers that came and took my statement that I didn't think she was involved in whatever happened at Infinity Farm, but I wasn't sure I really believed it. She'd told me she sold the car, but how could she have sold it when it didn't belong to her? She couldn't have had the title. She'd borrowed the car from the real Dana Shields and never brought it back. In her note she's said it was safer for both of us if she left. What had she meant? The news had since reported the body found in the car had been a man. Was that who Dana had been running from, or was whoever she was running from responsible for the man in the trunk?

Ten minutes after the officers left, the doorbell rang and Lia answered it, coming back into the kitchen with a pizza box.

"I ordered this while you were giving your statement. Please stay and help me eat it. I only got a large because I had a coupon and I'm a sucker for a deal."

"You don't have to ask me twice. I'm starving."

Between the two of us we devoured the herb and butter pizza like we hadn't eaten in days.

"This is really good. I'm usually a loaded toppings pizza kind of girl."

"I'm not much of a meat eater except on holidays. I'll eat turkey and ham if it's offered to me."

I was instantly reminded of Dana who also didn't eat much meat. Once we finished the pizza, I helped her clean up the kitchen which took all of five minutes as there were no dishes to wash, and we settled ourselves back on the couch. I wondered how long I could stay here and not have to go back home. If I knew my husband, he had not heeded my request for him to leave and was probably waiting for me at home to plead his case and prove he wasn't a lying asshole.

"What was that you gave the officers?" Lia was sitting on the couch at the opposite end, facing me with her legs crossed. I saw no reason not to tell her.

"The driver's license of the identity thief who's been living in my house for the better part of a week. I met her while I was volunteering at Haver House women's shelter. And..." I took another sip of my iced tea, nervous and feeling like the biggest fool.

"And what?" prompted Lia. "Go ahead. You can tell me. This is just between me and you and not for the documentary," she assured me when I just stared at her.

"I was helping her because I thought she might be Brooke." After everything that happened and finding out about all her lies, it made me feel slightly sick to admit this to Lia.

I'm not sure what I expected her to say, but I didn't expect Lia to stare at me with something very close to horror on her face. "What? Why would you think she was Brooke?"

I went on to explain all the reasons why I'd thought the woman I'd met at Haver House, and had known as Dana Shields, was my missing best friend Brooklyn Peters. Lia sipped her water and stared at me wide-eyed like she was a girl scout sitting around the campfire and I was the scoutmaster telling horror stories. I ended the story with finding the folder in Dana's suitcase with the copies of articles about Brooke's abduction, and theorizing she'd targeted me intentionally.

"I would've loved to have seen her license. Do you remember the address on it?"

"I've got something even better. I reached over and grabbed my purse on the table and pulled out my photos on my phone. I tapped the photo in question and handed her my phone. "I took a picture of the license after I found it."

The instant Lia laid eyes on Simone Riley's license I swore all the color leached from her skin and she looked ashen. With trembling hands, she reached out and grabbed her water glass from the table to take a sip, only to find it empty.

"What is it? Do you know her?"

"No!" her voice came out a harsh bark and I gave her a startled look. "Sorry. And no," she said, sounding more like herself. "She just kinda looks like someone I knew back in the day, and it just surprised me that's all, but I know it can't be her."

"Why?"

She paused for a few seconds before answering. "Because she's dead."

"And why did you want to know what Simone's address was?" Why had things gotten awkward when I'd shown her the license?

"Because she might still have family at that address who might know where she is. Are you up for a road trip?"

"It's almost eleven. I don't think now is the time to go knocking on strangers' doors."

"All they can do is either not open the door or slam it in our faces. We won't know until we try. So, are you up for it or not?"

I got up and grabbed my purse. "Let's go before I change my mind."

FORTY-TWO

BROOKE

September 2000

Brooke lay on the dingy twin bed that she shared with Mika, trying hard to cry quietly before she got into trouble. Tamika sat at the end of the bed crying, too.

"I can't believe you tried to leave me. What were you thinking?"

Brooke instantly sat up and looked at her friend. Both girls were thin and dressed in their work clothes. Dirt crusted their fingernails and calluses had formed on their fingers and palms from working on the farm from sunup to sundown. A tray with two bowls of vegetable stew and hunks of sourdough bread sat on the floor next to the bed.

"I was trying to get us help, Mika. If I can get home to my mommy, she'll come back for you, too. I know she will."

Brooke had been unsuccessful in her attempt to get the white lady and her husband who had showed up at the gate to help her. She'd only been able to talk to them for a few minutes before the boy they called Joshy, the one who'd brought her to the farm, dragged her kicking and screaming away from the gate and threatened the white couple with a shotgun. Hours later, they'd come back with the police.

They'd made Mika's mom Nikki take her to the gate to tell them that she was the girl the couple had seen and that her name was not Brooke Peters. Now, days later, Brooke was being shunned for bringing the police to the farm and they even told Mika not to speak to her, even though they shared a bed and had become instant best friends due to their circumstances. Brooke didn't have anyone but Mika. Her dad had been there when she first got to the farm, but he left less than a week later, and she'd been told he wasn't coming back.

Brooke remembered her old life when she'd had another best friend, sweet, funny Ava, who was always excited to see her and always up for an adventure. She wondered what Ava was doing now. Wondered if her parents ever got back together or if she had a new best friend now. She was desperate to see Ava, her mom, and brother Sam again so much, it was like a constant ache in her chest, but she couldn't leave Mika. Not now when just that morning she'd been told her mother Nikki, who she'd arrived at the farm with the year before, had left and didn't want her anymore. Mika had been crying all day, and Brooke could tell her friend was terrified she was going to be left there all alone.

So Brooke decided right then and there she would not try and leave again unless she could take Mika with her. Once they'd both calmed down, they ate the same dinner they'd been eating for months along with the stale bread, washing it down with a cup of water. The barn door flew open, startling them. It was nighttime, but Brooke could see a large, white passenger van parked outside and saw some of the other residents of the farm climbing into it.

"Time to go, ladies. Put these on and hurry up about it." One of the men who worked as a guard on the farm tossed them a plastic bag of clean clothes.

Brooke looked down at the bag of clothes and then up at the man. "Where are we going?"

"Well, because of your little stunt down by the gate, we need to leave tonight. You've got five minutes to change your clothes and get your asses in that van. And don't make me have to come get you unless you want to end up like Crystal."

"Yes, sir," they both said in unison, remembering how sweet and kind Crystal had been before she got sick and disappeared.

Late one night, Mika had nudged Brooke awake and dragged her over to the barn door where they'd peaked out and witnessed one of the guards carrying Crystal to the van. She looked like a skeleton, and the girls almost didn't recognize her. The guard callously tossed her into the back of the van like a sack of potatoes before driving away. That had been the last time they'd seen Crystal. And, no, they didn't want to end up wherever they'd taken her.

The girls changed quickly and headed to the van. Once the van was filled with all the rest of the farm's workers, they pulled onto the main road with another van following and Brooke realized her hope of escape was dwindling fast.

FORTY-THREE

LIA

The address on Simone Riley's license was for a modest tri-level in Beavercreek, Ohio, a suburb of Dayton. Ava had driven and now we were parked a few houses down. We didn't dare get out of the car yet because there was a police car parked in the driveway of the address.

"Maybe we should just leave," said Ava. We'd been waiting for twenty minutes, but it didn't seem as if the officers were about to leave, and we had no idea how long we would be waiting.

"Wait," I told her as she was just about to turn the key in the ignition. "Looks like they're coming out."

Sure enough two uniform officers were getting into the police car and a minute later were backing out of the driveway. Ava and I looked at each other. Were we really about to do this? Bother some stranger about someone connected to this address?

"Let's get this over with." Ava got out of the driver's side, slamming the door shut behind her as I scrambled out of the passenger seat to follow her.

"Who are we going to tell these people we are?" I was so used to having to bend the truth to get people to talk to me I couldn't help but feel like we were flying blind.

"I don't know about you, but I'm going to tell them the truth.

That Simone Riley has been living with me and lying to me, and I want to know who the hell she is."

She marched right up to the gray front door with two large black terracotta pots of orange marigolds sitting on either side of it and rang the doorbell. An elderly woman who looked to be in her seventies answered the door. She was tall and imposing with bright white hair that was in sharp contrast to her dark brown skin. She didn't look so much angry as she did weary.

"It's going on midnight. What in the world do you want?"

Instead of answering, Ava pulled up the picture of Simone Riley's driver's license up on her phone and held it up to the woman's screen door and watched as her eyes widened in shock.

"You know my daughter?"

"Your daughter lived with me and told me nothing but lies in the process. I'm just trying to figure out who she is and where she went because she stole something from my house, and I need it back."

Simone Riley's mother looked beyond tired. I could tell that as far as her daughter was concerned, this was far from her first rodeo.

"Come on in then."

She stepped away from the door and I tailed Ava into the house. We followed the older woman up the steps into a living room area with white carpet and oversized brown leather furniture that looked old but well taken care of. The house smelled like apple cinnamon candles and a perfume I hadn't smelled in years. Shalimar. My mom used to wear it, and I had to blink back tears as the unexpected memory hit me hard. In between the living room and the kitchen was a dining room where she gestured for us to sit.

"I'm Ava West and this is Lia Quinn," Ava said as she sat down at the oak dining table, with me sitting right next to her.

"I am Amelia Riley. Simone is my oldest."

"When was the last time you saw Simone?" I asked.

"I haven't seen my daughter in twenty-five years. I know she must've done something, or you wouldn't be here, right? First the police and now you two. What has she done?"

I sat there and listened to Ava explain to Amelia everything that she had experienced with her daughter and why the police were looking for her. If I expected Amelia Riley to be upset, I was disappointed.

"You know those cops never told me exactly why they were here looking for her. Just wanted to know if she was here. Thank you for explaining why they came looking for my child."

"Ma'am, can I ask why you haven't seen Simone in twenty-five years?" I asked.

Amelia Riley got up and went into the living room to a bookcase housing knickknacks and photos and grabbed a framed photo. She set it on the table before sitting back down herself. It was a photo of a young black boy with close cropped hair and a big smile who looked about twelve.

"This is my son Amari. This was the last school photo taken of him before he died."

"I am so sorry, Mrs. Riley." Ava had picked up the picture and stared at it before handing it to me.

"What happened to him?" I handed the photo back to Amelia who laid it face down on the table.

"He and Simone were over at the school playing basketball when the little boy she was dating showed up to tell her he'd changed his mind about taking her to the prom. She was seventeen and Amari was twelve. While she was busy arguing with her boyfriend, Amari was shooting hoops and the basketball rolled out into the street. He ran out between two parked cars to get it and was hit and killed instantly. It was an accident, but Simone blamed herself for his death and her life has been in freefall ever since."

"Meaning?" prodded Ava.

"Meaning drugs, alcohol, petty theft. Anything and everything that would dull her pain. Even though she caused problems between me and her father that led to our divorce, she was always welcome here no matter what trouble she got herself into. I'd already lost one child. I didn't want to lose another one, but that's exactly what happened."

"And you haven't heard from her lately?" I asked.

"No, I haven't. The last time I saw Simone she seemed to be in a much better place. She had a job she enjoyed and had been getting treatment to straighten herself out and had stopped all that drinking and drugging. She was excited for her future for the first time in years. But..." Her voice trailed off and she shook her head.

"What happened?" Ava leaned forward and touched the other woman's arm.

"That's just it. I don't know. She never came back. Until those cops showed up here tonight, I didn't know if Simone was dead or alive."

This sounded exactly like what Vivian Barnes had told me about her daughter Crystal. "Did Simone say anything about working for a place called Infinity Farm?"

Amelia Riley thought hard before replying, "Infinity Farm. No. I don't remember her saying anything about any Infinity Farm. What's that?"

"I'm still looking into it, but that's where the car your daughter stole from her landlady ended up."

"Lord have mercy," Amelia mumbled under her breath.

There wasn't a whole lot left to say, and I couldn't tell if Ava was satisfied with this woman's answers or not, but it was late. It was time we both left.

"Thank you so much for your time, Mrs. Riley." I stood up and Ava looked at me in surprise, which told me she had more questions, but I doubted anything else Amelia could tell us would be helpful.

"You said she took something from you?" She directed her question to Ava who nodded.

"A gun."

"Oh my god." Her hands flew to her mouth. "Why would she steal a gun? What is she planning to do?" Amelia Riley looked close to tears, and I mouthed *"let's go"* to Ava who reluctantly stood up.

"Is there anybody we can call for you? I hate to leave you like this. I don't think you should be alone." Ava shot me a look that made me flinch.

"I'll be fine, young lady. Are you two women of faith?" She looked from me to Ava and Ava quickly nodded. I was relieved not to have to answer that question as I wasn't sure what I believed in.

"Yes, ma'am," Ava confirmed, subtly nudging me in the arm and I grudgingly nodded as well.

"Then the best thing you can do is pray for me and Simone. Pray that God has mercy on us."

"Why did you do that? I had more questions for her." Ava shot me a disgusted look once we were back in the car.

"What more could she have told you that would change what has already happened? What answers are you still looking for?"

"For starters, I'd ask her about this." She thrust her phone at me, and I saw a picture of a dingy old stuffed animal. It could've been a turtle, but it was hard to tell. Something about it sparked a memory that I instantly snuffed out.

"You wanted to ask her about an old stuffed animal?"

"I realize now that the woman I knew as Dana is not Brooke, but how the hell did she come to have Brooke's favorite stuffed animal, Willa the turtle?"

"You think there was only one of these turtles ever made? There are millions of those things mass-produced and lots of kids have them."

I could tell Ava wanted to argue with me, but I was tired, and it was late and even though it had been my idea to go on this little expedition, I was mentally worn out.

The drive back to Elmhurst was silent and I could tell Ava was not happy with me. By the time we got back to my Airbnb, she seemed back to her old self.

"It's late. Why don't you crash here on the couch until the morning?"

"Thanks, Lia. And sorry about earlier."

"You have nothing to apologize for. I get it. I do." She had no idea just how much I got it.

It was almost three o'clock before I settled into a troubled sleep, waking at 7:45 the next morning to find the pillow and blanket I'd given Ava folded neatly on the couch. She was gone. It was a little while before I noticed that my folders full of notes on Brooke's case which had been on the dining room table had been disturbed, including the one detailing Mavis Brady's story about Ava's mom Natalie. Shit.

In all the years that Detective Michael Avery had been a cop, he'd never got used to autopsies. It was bad enough when the bodies were fresh, but a body that had been in a hot trunk and was bloated and decomposing was its own special kind of hell.

"You found something?" Avery had his back purposefully turned away from the table with the body of the victim on it.

"I can show you better than I can tell you." Dr. Tate Lang tried but failed to hide his amusement at Avery's discomfort as the older man followed him over to the autopsy table.

Avery was relieved when Dr. Lang pulled back the sheet covering Nate Peters to reveal the corpse was face down on the table, the man's back exposed. It was covered in raised, round scars.

"What the hell is all that?" He took a step closer to the table and leaned in with his hand over his nose and mouth.

"Brands?"

Avery looked up at the young doctor, not sure he'd heard him right. "You mean someone branded this man?"

"Exactly. And before you ask, each brand represents a different spiritual meaning."

"Such as?"

"This one," said Lang, pointing to a brand on the back of the victim's right shoulder, "is a Dharma wheel. And we've also got the tree of life, a lotus flower, the moon..."

"But what do they all mean?" Avery was too impatient to listen to the laundry list of symbols branded onto Nate Peters' back.

"They all mean the same things, transformation, rebirth, and growth."

"He couldn't have done this to himself, right?"

"No, Detective. Someone would have had to have done this to him."

"And how old are these brands? Any of them recent?"

"No. They're all well healed. I'd say at least a decade or more old."

"So, why are you showing me decades' old brands on a dead man's back?"

Lang sighed and headed over to his desk at the back of the morgue and pressed a key on the keyboard. "Because, when my lab assistant was logging the victim's distinguishing marks into our system, the brands got flagged and pulled up another body with one of these brands on the back of their right shoulder. A twenty-four-year-old woman found deceased on the side of a road out in the county back in 2000 by the name of Crystal Barnes. I called you down here because I thought there might be a connection between the two deaths."

"Shit," Avery swore softly under his breath wondering how many botched cases were going to come back to bite him in the ass.

"You okay, Detective?"

"Just fine. And what about the cause of death of Mr. Peters? He wasn't stabbed, was he?"

"Stabbed? No. Try a heart attack."

"So not a homicide?"

"I didn't say that."

Avery followed Dr. Lang back over to the autopsy table and watched him lift up one of the dead man's bloated hands, the fingernails of which were torn and bloody.

"Someone locked this man in the trunk of that car, and he died of a heart attack trying to claw his way out."

FORTY-FIVE

AVA

A quick pitstop at home to shower and change revealed that Evan was not there. But I had more than a dozen missed calls and texts from him. I checked his closet. All of his clothes were still there, including his overnight bag, meaning he would definitely be coming back after work. He was the last person I wanted to see, but all of that paled in comparison to what I'd seen in Lia Quinn's files when I couldn't sleep last night and got up to get some water. I saw the files lying in a pile on the dining room table and couldn't help myself. I read all the statements from people she'd interviewed about Brooke's case, most of which I had already heard before. It wasn't until I got to her notes from talking to Mrs. Brady that it caught my attention and I was nauseous by the time I'd finished reading the account of how my mom owed people money and she couldn't pay it back. These people may have taken Brooke by mistake when I was the original target.

If that was the truth, it would explain so much. I distinctly remembered my mom looking so sad and agitated whenever Brooke's name came up. Brooke's mom Julia leaned heavily on my mom during that horrible time, and I caught my mom crying more than once. At the time I just thought she was sad because she'd loved Brooke, too, but after reading Mrs. Brady's account, I wondered if she had been crying because she felt guilty. She'd always alluded to the fact that she had to do things she didn't want to do in order to save our house, but she never once told me where the money came from and what she'd had to do to get it. Before now I never wanted to know.

Though, I'd always wondered why that house had been so important to her. The only thing I could come up with was that it was a symbol of her love for a man who'd discarded her. I never saw my father again after he left for Seattle, and while ten-year-old Ava was hurt by his abandonment, adult Ava had learned long ago to live without him.

When I arrived at the hospital that morning to see my mom, full of anger and questions, all I saw was how fragile she was. She looked like she'd aged ten years. When she saw me, a smile lit up her face and compassion took the place of my anger. My mom knew me. She'd seen the look on my face and instantly knew that something was wrong. I sat on the edge of her hospital bed and burst into tears.

"Ava? Baby, what's wrong?" She wrapped her arms around me gingerly holding me despite the fact that she was still in pain. It was like she was trying to absorb all of my pain which made me cry even harder.

"I just want to know one thing." I gently pulled away from her. "And then I'll never ask you again."

I could feel her body tense, but she looked me in the eye, like she'd known this day would come and was ready for it. She nodded.

"Did they take Brooke by mistake? Was it supposed to be me?"

She cupped my chin so I couldn't look away. "Ava, I've done things. Things I'm not proud of. Things that were against the law. Things that might make you hate me. You have my word on my life that nothing I did led to Brooke being abducted. And I will swear to that on a stack of Bibles."

. . .

I stayed with my mom all morning, then left for my afternoon shift at Haver House. When I walked through the door, it felt like I've been gone forever and was so happy when some of the residents came up to give me hugs and ask if my mom was okay and how I was holding up.

When I walked into the office, I was surprised to see Selma with Janine, Adele's replacement, who'd decided to come back early from sick leave.

"Ava. How are you holding up? You know you didn't have to come back until you were ready, right?"

"If I don't get back to work, I'll go stir-crazy. I need to keep busy and be active. And I missed you guys."

"Well, it's plenty active today," said Janine. I realized then I'd never really spoken to her before because we were always passing each other like ships in the night.

"Intake?"

"You know it. And it sounds like the first round are here now."

I ducked my head out into the hallway to see a handful of women walking in the front door, looking tentatively around like they weren't sure where to go. It was time to get back to work.

"Good afternoon, ladies, if you're here for your intake appointment, please sign the logbook and then have a seat in the living room area across the hall until we call your name."

Four hours later, I clocked out. I checked my phone as I was leaving to see several missed calls and a dozen texts from Evan. I wasn't ready to talk to him yet and didn't know what I would say when we did finally come face to face. Surprisingly, I had a missed call from Kerri, too, but when I called her back, it went straight to voicemail.

"Ava!" Janine was coming down the steps of the shelter holding a box.

"What's that?"

"We found more of Adele's things. Selma's at a doctor's

appointment and suggested I ask if you could drop them by Adele's house since we can't seem to get a hold of James."

"Sure. No problem."

"Great. Here's the address."

She handed me a slip of paper, and I took the box from her. It was a box of photos, accounting books, and another framed degree that I hadn't seen before. This degree declared that Dr. Adele Mackie had received her medical degree in psychiatry from a different college than the first framed degree I had seen. I was instantly confused. The first framed degree I'd seen, the one she said had been someone's idea of a joke, stated the college she had received her medical degree from was Crestwell College in Niagara Falls, Canada. I'd never heard of this college but didn't think anything of it because it was in Canada and why would I have heard of it? But this framed degree claimed that Adele had gotten her medical degree from a college called Prime University in Nevada. This was the same college on the framed degree in James Mackie's trash basket in his cubby at ECC.

I got into my car and set the box on my passenger seat and instantly pulled up a browser on my phone and looked up Prime University, only to find numerous articles and horrible reviews from the Better Business Bureau claiming Prime University was an unaccredited online for-profit college that basically sold their degrees to students who never attended classes. Next, I looked up Crestwell College, but their website was no longer working, and I could find no other information about them.

This could've only meant one thing. Adele had not been a licensed medical professional and neither had James. Had she gotten caught and that's why she was no longer practicing? Detective Avery needed to see this along with the picture Dana had left me. I got on my phone and called Selma.

"Hey, Ava. What's up?"

"I found something in this box of Adele's things Janine just gave me. I think the police would be interested in it and I'm wondering if I should drop it off at the police station instead."

"What is it?"

"Sorry, but I'm not sure I should tell you in case it might be connected to her death."

"Okay, but I already left a message letting James know you're on your way with that box of Adele's things."

"Why don't I take out the object in question and give James the box with the rest of the stuff?"

Selma hesitated for several long seconds before replying, "I'm on my way back from my doctor's office and I'm only a few blocks away from his house. Would you like me to meet you there?"

Now, why was she offering to meet me there? I'd already been warned by Kerri about how flirty this man was, which had been confirmed by one of his colleagues at the adjunct instructor's office. Was she worried he would try and hit on me?

"Only if you want to. I was just going to hand him the box and then leave."

"Please don't take this the wrong way. I told you the truth when I said nothing happened between me and James, but he's become a dear friend to me, and I'm worried about him. I haven't heard from him all week even though I've been calling. He's never not answered one of my calls before."

I rolled my eyes as I realized that no matter what Selma told me, she was still very invested in this man, especially now that there was no wife to stand between them and she was looking for any excuse to see him.

"Then I'll meet you there in ten minutes. How's that?"

"See you there," she replied before hanging up.

James and Adele Mackie lived in one of the more affluent parts of Elmhurst. One of the older neighborhoods that came along with much higher property taxes. Evan and I had looked at a house in this area when we'd first gotten married, but the unfriendly neighbors and the price tag on the home deterred us. It's not that we wouldn't have been able to afford the house, but that's all we would've been able to afford. And neither one of us was trying to be house poor. Our town house was perfect for our needs, and we only talked about moving once our family expanded. We had no family, so the town house would be where I would be for the foreseeable future at least. Evan's time there was growing short.

The Mackie home was a beautiful mid-century masterpiece at the end of a long asphalt paved driveway. There was no way this house cost less than half a million. With Adele working as an admin assistant and James a part-time adjunct instructor, how could they afford this? I instantly put the question out of my head because it was none of my business and elitist as hell. What they had in their bank account was their business. I noticed Selma pull in right behind me in her blue Camaro. We both exited our cars, and I reached across and grabbed the box having already taken the framed degree out of it.

"Thanks for meeting me. Would you be up for a coffee when we leave to discuss my offer for assistant director?"

"Absolutely." In all the chaos I had completely forgotten that I had been offered an amazing new opportunity.

We both walked up to the front door and Selma rang the doorbell. We heard barking from within the house and a cocker spaniel ran to the door and frantically scratched and whined, but no one came to the door. Selma and I looked at each other before she rang the doorbell again and then proceeded pounding on the door.

"James! Are you in there? James! I'm going to go back to his garage. He's probably out there working on his car with the radio turned up and can't hear us."

"I'll just wait here."

I set the box down on the front porch beside me and waited. No one came to the door. Instead, I heard an ear-piercing shriek from Selma and quickly raced around the house towards the garage at the end of the drive slightly behind the house. I found Selma still shrieking as she stood in the side door of the garage. The sickly-sweet stench of death was wafting out of the door. I shoved her aside and followed her line of sight to see James Mackie dead on the garage floor next to the Camaro he must've been working on. His throat had been slit from ear to ear.

Selma had to be sedated, which left me to answer Detective Michael Avery's questions. Avery looked beyond exhausted himself. With dark smudges under his eyes.

"We meet again, Mrs. West. I hear your mother is going to be released Friday. Is that right?"

"Yes, and I know you're busy, but now there's a second person who's been killed with a knife. There would've been a third if my mom's neighbor hadn't interrupted her attacker. This has to be the work of a serial killer, right?"

"Maybe. I can't confirm that definitively. Everyone wants to throw around the term serial killer, but we don't want to cause unnecessary panic and that's why we are very careful before we start flinging that term around."

I just stared at him and sighed. Although, I didn't know why I felt so frustrated as the police had protocols to follow even in the face of overwhelming evidence pointing to what should have been an obvious conclusion. He knew this was a serial killer but hadn't been given clearance by his boss to admit it. I dealt with it on more than one occasion in my job as a social worker and it frustrated me to no end.

"I might have some information you can use at least in Adele's murder. Might also have something to do with what happened to James," I told him instead of berating him for not seeing the obvious.

"I'm all ears, Mrs. West, because I need all the help I can get."

I retrieved the phony degree from my car and handed it to him. "This is the second framed degree that I found showing Dr. Adele Mackie having received a medical degree in psychiatry. I saw a similar one in James Mackie's trash basket at ECC. Did you know he taught there?"

"I did, but what does it have to do with the Mackies' deaths?"

"One of the colleges was shut down for being a degree mill basically. And the other one doesn't seem to have existed. Could be some of her former clients may have found out and been very angry because I'm sure if they had a psychiatry practice, they weren't treating people for free."

"That makes sense because we haven't been able to find a shred of evidence that Adele Mackie was licensed to practice psychiatry in the state of Ohio or any other state."

"Now, you know why." I was still holding out the degree to him until he finally took it and tucked it under his arm.

"Thank you, Mrs. West. If you've already given your statement to one of my officers, you're free to go until we have further questions."

"What about Simone Riley?" I called out after him as he started to walk away.

"What about her?"

"Well, have there been any sightings of her?" I trailed behind him as he continued walking away from me.

"Not to my knowledge. Now, if you'll excuse me." I watched him lift the crime scene tape that had been erected across the driveway and head back to the garage, then realized I'd completely forgotten to show him the photo Dana had left me.

Selma was in no state to drive herself home. She stared mutely out the window the entire drive to her house. She'd insisted on taking the Mackies' dog Juniper home with her and the dog lay across my backseat looking sad and confused by her changed circumstances. If she hadn't been drinking from the toilet and managed to tear open a bag of dog food in the pantry, she'd have been close to death herself.

"I can stay with you for a while, Selma."

"Thanks, Ava. I'm fine. It's just...such a shock. I've been calling him for days and he was dead the whole time. Who could have done this?"

"Probably the same person who killed Adele. How long have you known Adele?"

"She was my first hire as director for Haver House, and we've been open for about four months. So not long. You know, I almost didn't hire her."

"Really?" My ears instantly perked up. "Why?"

"She interviewed well. Blew all the other candidates out of the water, but I was never able to verify any of her professional references. The phone numbers she listed were disconnected, and none of the messages I'd left on the numbers that were working were ever returned. We were about to open, and I didn't have time to do another round of interviews and just trusted she would work out, and she did. She was amazing at her job until I found out she was stealing from the accounts."

"I think James was helping her."

"What?" Selma's head whipped around, and her eyes widened in shock.

I told her about the used air-conditioning units having come from Elmhurst Community College where James worked and could tell she didn't want to believe it.

"Was anything about them real?" she asked with a sigh.

"I don't think so. And I think they paid for their secrets and lies with their lives."

After I dropped Selma off, I went straight to my mom's so I could grab her some clean clothes to come home in. I purposefully went through the garage ignoring the crime scene tape blocking off the front door as well as the blood stains on her front stoop, but I couldn't ignore the blood stains that were still left behind in her foyer and felt my stomach roil. I grabbed a bucket, a mop and cleaning supplies from under her kitchen sink and got busy scrubbing up the dried blood.

When I was done, I took a bucket of soapy water and poured it over the blood stains on her front stoop and then took the hose to spray away the remaining blood. I wasn't sure if it was the sight of all the blood, the smell of the bleach from the cleaning supplies, the stress, or the fact that I hadn't eaten anything but a banana since early that morning, but once I straightened up after putting the cleaning supplies back under the sink, a wave of nausea hit me hard, and I had to run to the powder room in the foyer, barely making it before heaving my guts up. Afterward, I gargled and splashed cold water on my face before heading up the stairs to pack my mom some clothes.

Within ten minutes, I'd gather toiletries, underwear, shoes, and an outfit for my mom to wear home. I searched her closet for something to put it all in and found her work travel suitcase. It was way too big, so I went in search of an overnight bag. I ended up having to pull a stepladder from the hall closet to search the upper shelves of her closet which were filled with purses and shoe boxes. Not finding what I was looking for, I got off the stepladder and then searched the back of the closet only to find a lone cardboard box with what looked like canvas tote bags folded up and sitting on top. I soon discovered half the box was filled with old files and brochures. Annoyed and overheated from being in the hot closet, I pulled the box out to search it more thoroughly.

Underneath the folded tote bags, the box was filled with glossy brochures with a smiling couple on the front. It was James and Adele Mackie. Only their names in these brochures were Jonathan and Annette Moseby. They were standing outside a house that wasn't the one they lived in; a small brick ranch near a wooded area I didn't recognize. I flipped through it and found out it was a drug treatment program called Infinity's Children. The glossy brochure, which was the equivalent of a magazine, showed pictures of the people in the program, with most of them teenagers and young adults. There were a few older adults but not many.

Annette was listed as a lead psychiatrist, who supposedly had spent more than a decade counseling individuals suffering from all kinds of addictions, from gambling to shopping to drug and alcohol addiction. Meanwhile, her husband Jonathan was listed as the program's director and also a licensed psychiatrist. It wasn't until I was almost at the end that I finally understood what Dana had been trying to tell me when she left me that photo.

The same photo was in this brochure, and I could clearly see all of the people in the picture. The man I knew as James Mackie was in the center with his arms around what I thought at the time were two teenage boys. The one on his right was a young white man who I now recognized as Josh Turner, but the other person on the left-hand side I'd been mistaken about. It wasn't a young black man like I had originally thought. It was a young black woman with short natural hair. It was Simone Riley a.k.a. Dana Shields. Josh was smiling his smug, shit-eating grin that hadn't changed much in the twenty-five years since this picture had been taken, but Simone stared straight ahead at the camera, unsmiling and rigid, her torso angled away from James Mackie.

I didn't recognize anyone else in the picture as they were identified as a mix of staff and members of the program. One of the people identified was a young blonde woman named Crystal Barnes who must've been Vivian Barnes's daughter. Crystal was standing next to a smiling black woman named Nikki Clark. Was this what I was meant to see? Dana had known James and Adele Mackie back when they were Jonathan and Annette Moseby, as well as Josh Turner. Was this some kind of confession? Had she been the one to kill Adele and now James? And why did my mother have this? I put the brochure down and flipped through the rest of the box, finding a framed degree declaring that Natalie Hammond was a licensed therapist who received her degree from Prime University in Nevada. I sat the degree down and groaned.

"Mom, what did you do?" I whispered to myself before I suddenly realized something.

The framed degrees I'd found for Adele had her current name on them, Adele Mackie not Annette Moseby. I remembered Adele telling me the framed degree was someone's idea of a joke. And the caller looking for Mrs. Moseby. Someone had known who Adele used to be. That person was Simone Riley, aka Dana. Had she killed the Mackies and then tried to kill my mom?

As for my mom, she hadn't finished college. She'd done two years at ECC and then became a flight attendant. She wasn't a college graduate, let alone a licensed counselor. What kind of scam had she gotten herself into with the Mackies, Mosebys or whoever the hell they'd been? And all for a house that could've been replaced. A further search of the box uncovered something even more shocking. Pictures of my mom looking very cozy with James Mackie.

I could hear my phone ringing downstairs and figured it was Evan again. I let it go to voicemail. I never did find an overnight bag, so I put my mom's things in a large tote bag along with the box I found in her closet and went back downstairs. Clearly, a conversation was in order with my mom about what all this meant and what her involvement was with two people who had been murdered. Is that why Dana had come to the shelter? Had she been looking for Adele all along over whatever had happened with this Infinity's Children program? My phone rang again and this time it was Lia.

"Did you hear the news about James Mackie?" she asked instead of greeting me when I answered the phone.

"My boss and I were the ones who found him."

"Are you for real? What happened? Was he stabbed, too?"

"Look, I need your advice. I found something at my mom's that I think you need to see, and I have no idea what I should do with this information. I'm on my way."

I pulled up in front of Lia's Airbnb, but before I got out, I finally checked the voicemail I'd gotten while I was still at my mom's. It hadn't been Evan; it was Kerri, but she didn't leave a message. All I heard was muffled background noise and what sounded like labored breathing. Every time I tried to call Kerri back, all I got was her voicemail. I had no idea where she lived as we'd only been work colleagues and never socialized outside of work. Then I remembered. As employees of Elmhurst County Child and Family Services we were required to download an app to our phone that would track our locations when we were out in the field doing home visits alone.

Some of the places we needed to go to could be volatile situations, therefore our locations needed to be tracked at all times. Since Kerri was no longer working for the county, did she still have the app on her phone? I pulled up my phone and tapped on the app which we jokingly called Gypsy. If Kerri was still having her location tracked by Gypsy, she would come up in my contact list within the app. I pressed the app and prayed. I was surprised when Kerri's location came up and even more surprised when I saw the dot tracking her location moving. Was she driving? I called her again and Josh answered the phone.

"This is Josh, Kerri's fiancé…"

"Josh, this is Ava, can I please speak to Kerri?"

"I'm sorry, Ava, but Kerri is unavailable right now. She's not feeling well, but I'll be sure to let her know you called." He hung up before I could say anything else.

Asshole! I continued to stare at the tracking location moving. Clearly, Josh was lying. There was only one way to find out what was going on. And that was to follow that dot. Without even thinking, I started my car and took off just as Lia came out of her Airbnb waving her arms and yelling something I couldn't hear.

FORTY-SIX

LIA

I felt like an idiot standing on the car curb yelling and waving my arms. What the hell? Why did Ava take off without coming in when she'd told me there was something I needed to see? Was she in trouble? She was still at the light up the street when I hopped into my car to follow her, but a sharp rap on my window scared me so bad I almost shot through the roof of my car. It was a brown-skinned black woman with short natural hair making a rolling motion with her right hand, wanting me to roll down my window. Of course, I knew who she was. I recognized her immediately as soon as Ava had shown me her driver's license and told me about her theory that this woman was Brooke. I reluctantly opened the window.

"I know you know who I am because I certainly know who you are and I'm not here to reminisce about the bad old days. I know where Ava's going and it's important you let me in this car if you want to see her alive again," said Simone Riley.

There was no time to discuss our shared past because we needed to get to Ava before her impulsiveness got her killed.

I unlocked the passenger side door, and she hopped in.

"Where am I going?"

"Head to the traffic light and then take a left."

I did as I was told and tried hard to forget about the last time I'd seen Simone Riley.

FORTY-SEVEN

BROOKE

September 2000

Tamika was hungry despite the fact hard boiled eggs had recently been added to their diet as a source of protein. Now, they got two hard boiled eggs along with their daily apple and bread for breakfast, but it hardly mattered when Mika hated eggs. So, she gave her eggs to Brooke in exchange for Brooke's apple. Having an extra apple did nothing to ward off the hunger that was coming later in the day. Her meager portions of vegetable stew and bread were quickly burned off by the day's work and by bedtime she was usually starving.

"We're gonna get caught, Mika," pleaded Brooke as they crept into the kitchen after ten o'clock that night in search of something to eat.

"How? Everybody else is in bed. And I'm so hungry my stomach hurts."

They crept into the dark pantry only to find all of the cabinets had padlocks on them.

"See," said Brooke in a harsh whisper. "All the food is locked up. I already told you that."

"That's not locked up." Mika pointed to a loaf of bread sitting out on the counter.

"Well, hurry up and grab a slice so we can get back to bed."

No sooner had Mika reached out towards the loaf of bread than a light came on, flooding the room with brightness.

"What are you two doing in here?" An older black girl with short hair stood in the doorway to the pantry.

Brooke had overheard someone calling the girl Simone. She always looked angry and barely spoke to anyone at the farm. She was one of the people who had brought Brooke to the farm and her new family. Brooke avoided her, and that mean white boy who lured her to the car, like the plague.

"I was hungry and wanted something to eat." Brooke stepped in front of Mika, instantly angering her friend who shoved her aside and took a step forward.

"I'm the one who's hungry and I want a piece of bread." Mika crossed her arms, glaring at the older girl defiantly.

Neither of the younger girls were sure of what this girl would do, but they didn't expect her to grab the loaf of bread, open it and pull out two thick slices. She handed a slice to Brooke and a slice to Mika who instantly snatched it out of her hand and shoved half the slice into her mouth.

"What's going on in here?"

All three girls whirled around to see the woman they'd been instructed to call Mother standing there at which point Mika almost choked on the remainder of her bread and Brooke tossed the slice she'd just been handed back up onto the counter.

"The girls were just hungry, so I gave them a couple of slices of bread, that's all. No big deal."

The woman stepped forward, staring from the bread to Simone, a tight smile creasing her lips.

"Oh, but it is a big deal. What was your name again?"

"Simone."

"And how long have you been here, Simone?" Mother took a step forward.

"Four months."

"Four months what?"

The older woman and the teenager stared at each other before the other girl realized what was required of her.

"Four months, Mother."

"Then you already know that there are rules around here and one of those rules is that food is only to be consumed during mealtimes. Part of your treatment here is that your meals be strictly regulated. If you're sneaking food that means you're stealing from us, and we do not allow stealing here."

"It's just a couple of pieces of bread for two hungry little kids. What's the big flipping deal?"

"The big deal is you are quite undisciplined and ungrateful, and this is the kind of attitude that landed you here in the first place. It's fueling all of your poor decisions and addictions. This is the kind of behavior that you were sent here for us to stamp out of you. And stamp it out of you we will."

"What are you talking about?"

"Do I need to remind you of the waiver that you signed in order to be allowed into this treatment program? You had no money to pay and agreed to come here to work off the expense of your treatment."

"What if I change my mind and want out of this wack ass program? I've been here four months and have never gotten any treatment. All any of us do is work. You don't even know my name! And I'm not calling you Mother anymore. I have a mother and it's not my fault you can't have kids."

Brooke and Mika thought Mother might explode. Her face got very red. Then she smiled and walked up to Simone who took an involuntary step backwards. "You'll be let out just as soon as you fulfill your financial responsibility and not a minute before. Until then you need to learn some manners."

Mother stepped over to the phone on the wall and picked it up whispering something into it while Brooke and Tamika clung to each other in fear.

When Mother turned her attention towards them, Brooke felt the warm sensation of urine trickling down her bare legs and she looked down at the puddle on the floor in horror before bursting into tears. Even though Simone didn't know what Mother was capable of, Brooke did.

"You two get the cleaning supplies and scrub the entire kitchen floor and then go to bed. And you won't have to worry about having any breakfast tomorrow since you're so ungrateful for the food that you got today."

The girls rushed off to do as they were told when two security guards showed up, each grabbing one of Simone's arms.

"Get off me! What the hell are you doing? It was just a couple of slices of bread. Are you insane?"

Brooke looked back in time to see Simone being dragged from the room kicking and screaming. As soon as they were out of the room, both girls dropped their sponges and ran to the window as Simone was dragged to the discipline shed followed by Mother who had something long and thin that ended in a wheel shape in her hand. All four of them entered the discipline shed. Half an hour later, Brooke and Tamika huddle together in the pantry, covering their ears to block out the sound of Simone's screams.

"Don't worry, girls," came a voice from behind them that made them jump. It was that creepy white boy they called Joshy, the one who brought Brooke to the farm. "When she comes out of that shed, she'll be a new person."

His smile scared them more than Simone's screams.

FORTY-EIGHT

AVA

Ten minutes into my drive out into the county, Kerri's dot stopped moving. As I turned down the narrow dirt road in the direction of the dot, I recognized the name on the signs I passed that pointed further down the road. It was Infinity Farm. I realized the narrow dirt road I was now on was the back of Infinity Farm's property, judging by the abundance of No Trespassing signs. I had no idea how big this farm was. I couldn't even see the main farmhouse from the road I was on. What were they doing out here? The road was covered in deep potholes and ruts and getting more difficult. My car didn't have four-wheel-drive. So, I parked along the side of the road and got out to walk the last half mile to where Kerri's location was marked on the map on my app.

Before long I arrived at a clearing and saw Kerri's red Honda CRV parked near the road. Fifty feet away I could make out a man digging a hole, but it was what lay next to the hole he was digging that made me rush forward as a scream tore from my throat. A pale, thin woman lay unmoving on a dark colored tarp on the ground, dressed only in a dirty white T-shirt and panties. Her limp red hair obscured her face.

"Kerri!"

I was just about to reach the tarp when something whizzed

past my face followed by searing pain that sent me sprawling on my ass and clutching my forehead. Josh Turner, sweating and panting from his exertions from digging the hole, had swung the shovel at me when he'd seen me rushing towards Kerri, and cut my forehead.

"Sorry, but I hope you're not here for a family reunion. That bastard you're married to is not my brother and you're not my sister-in-law."

"Like I'd want to be connected to spineless nutjob like you!" I screamed as warm blood flowed through my fingers and panic gripped my chest.

He started to swing the shovel at me again. I held out my hands to shield myself, but the blow never came. The woman I'd known as Dana was holding my husband's gun to Josh's temple. About ten feet behind her was Lia Quinn.

"Easy there, Joshy. You don't want to do that. Drop the shovel or I'll blow your head off. And since we go way back, you already know what I'm capable of."

"You wouldn't dare." Josh Turner's jaw was so rigid with anger it sounded like he was hissing.

Dana's swift blow to the back of his head with the gun caused him to cry out in pain and drove him to his knees.

"You never learned your lesson, did you, Joshy? That's why you were always in the discipline shed. I only needed one trip, but you were a repeat visitor. Go ahead and admit it. You liked it when Mother used the brand on you, didn't you? You believed all her bullshit about symbols giving us the ability to transform."

Mother? Was she talking about Adele? Instead of waiting for Josh's response, Dana reached out and grabbed the back of Josh's thin, blue T-shirt and yanked hard, tearing his shirt and exposing at least a dozen raised round brands on his back. Some were Dharma wheels, but there were others I didn't recognize. I let out a gasp. Oddly enough, Lia, who had walked over to my side and was pressing a napkin to my forehead, was unfazed. She stared at Josh with undisguised loathing and that's when I realized she knew Josh Turner. But how?

Josh twisted away from Dana and quickly got to his feet lunging for the shovel before Dana fired a bullet at the ground between him and the shovel. He jerked to a stop and turned back to Dana, his eyes blazing with hatred.

"You act like I'm some kind of a monster when you're the same as me. Did you tell her you and me were the ones who took that Peters girl?"

"I was just supposed to be delivering herbs to that old lady's shop when you tagged along and dragged poor Mika with you. You said you had to give Brooke a message from her father. I had no idea you were going to snatch her and then a pull a gun on me to make me drive back to the farm," Dana spat out in a low menacing voice. "But it ain't no fun when the rabbit's got the gun, is it?"

"That kid was being corrupted by her mother and that weed smoking brother of hers. Mother was just trying to save her and show her a better way. She needed the discipline of the farm. She didn't want her turning to drugs like her dad had! I'd have done the same thing if she were my daughter and if it was so horrible, why didn't Nate take her back home?"

"You mean like your parents did to you? Their alcoholic teenaged son who was out of control? They sent you out here because they didn't know what else to do. Told you it was an addiction program when it was nothing but a work camp for con artists who needed free labor, and you were stupid enough to buy into all the crap your parents and the Mosebys fed you."

I was suddenly light-headed and wanted to throw up. All this time I thought strangers had taken Brooke, but the father she'd been told was dead knew where she was all along. Her own flesh and blood had betrayed her. I wanted to scream and rage on her behalf.

"That's a lie!" Josh's face was bright red and the veins in his neck bulged.

"Well, if Nate Peters was father of the year, then why did you kill him and dump his body in the trunk of the car I drove to the farm? Were you trying to frame me?" She let out a loud harsh laugh.

Josh continued to glare at her. "He breezed back into town a month ago needing a job and a place to lay low. I hired him to guard the farm. There's only one working camera on this whole property and it picked you when you showed up with that car. I came out here to see what was going on and found him rummaging through the trunk looking for stuff to sell because he'd fallen off the wagon and was using again. He needed to be punished. I shoved him into the trunk. I came back two hours later to let him out and he was already dead."

"Try again, you lying asshole. *I* was squatting in the shed; the discipline shed at that. How's that for irony? I had no place else to go because I couldn't stay at Haver House after I found out good old Mother Moseby was working there. I never saw anyone else here! That's why I came because I knew it was abandoned. Then one night you showed up here, Joshy, and you weren't alone, were you? I got scared and left the car behind because it was out of gas and booked it."

"Wait." Lia looked from Josh to Dana as astonishment widened her eyes. "Nate Peters was the body they found in the barn?"

Kerri groaned and her eyes began to flutter. I pushed Lia's hand away and knelt by Kerri's side, gently pushing the hair from her bruised face.

"You get away from her! She's still my fiancée." Before he could reach me, Dana once again struck him with the gun.

"What did you do to her?" I screamed at him.

"Nothing she didn't want me to do. She told me she wanted to transform and be the woman I wanted her to be, the woman I knew she could be without her addiction to food. All I did was show her the way!"

Kerri chose that exact moment to open her eyes wide. My body was shielding her from view. I was the only one who knew she was conscious and saw her slight shake of the head, letting me know not to react. She quickly closed her eyes again and I turned back to Josh and the others.

"You're the one who killed the Mackies and tried to kill my mom!" I lunged at him, but Lia grabbed me by the arm and pulled me back. I jerked out of her grasp and whirled to face her. "And you know both of them, don't you? How?" Indecision flitted across Lia's face, and she instantly looked over at Dana who stepped forward.

"She knows us because we're all victims of this place and of the Mackies back when they were the Mosebys. They were con artists masquerading as therapists for people desperate to cure their addictions, but there were two levels of treatment. The wealthy clients who could afford it were treated in a nice home they rented in town, while those of us who were just as broke as we were desperate were sent here to work on the farm in exchange for our treatment. Only there was no treatment, was there, Joshy? Just backbreaking work planting and harvesting herbs sunup to sundown for that old lady who owned the farm. No treatment and no escape and hardly any food, but there was plenty of punishment."

"They were geniuses!" insisted Josh. "I never touched another drop of alcohol once I completed their treatment. I even started my own practice."

"You're just as cruel and pathetic as they were." Dana let out a harsh laugh.

"Wait a minute." I turned to Lia, staring at her like I was seeing her for the very first time as Dana's words finally sank in. Lia had been here, too? I stepped towards Lia. "You aren't..." I couldn't finish as a lump formed in my throat and tears blurred my eyes. "Are you...?" I reached a hand to Lia, and she gently took it and shook her head.

"No, Ava, I'm not Brooke. I'm so sorry. But I..."

She never got to finish what she was about to say because Josh tackled Dana to the ground and the gun went flying. He began to pummel her with his fists and had already bloodied her nose. We ran to her aid when a voice rang out.

"Stop it, Josh!" Kerri was on her feet and had grabbed the gun. She pointed it at Josh. She was unsteady and almost fell, but managed to hold on to the gun.

"Kerri, honey, give me the gun." Josh straightened and took a step towards her. She stumbled back. "Give me the gun, sweetie. That's not a toy."

"My...grandma...owned this farm. It's been in our family for generations. Everyone who ran the farm...and grew the herbs, was given a share in the profits of Helen...Kay's...Herbals. She... shipped all over the world. What..." she began and then swayed on her feet again briefly before regaining her balance. "Are you all talking about? What was going on out here that you think my grandma was a part of?" She looked around wildly at all of us, swinging the gun in an arc.

"Your grandma didn't do anything wrong." Dana had gotten her feet. The blood from her nose had dripped down onto her shirt, making her a bloody mess. She took a few steps towards Kerri who swung the gun in her direction, stopping Dana in her tracks. "Your grandma never came to the farm the entire time I was living here. They purposefully kept her away. She'd call up and let us know what she needed for her remedies, and I was always the one they made pick the herbs and deliver to her shop. Sometimes, I would stay and help her pack the orders and then drop them off at the post office. She was the sweetest woman and would always give me homemade peppermint drops. The Mosebys took advantage of her kindness and turned this farm into a hellhole. She had no idea what they were doing out here."

"So, is that why Adele introduced you to Kerri?" I said to Josh who gave me a look so venomous I almost flinched. "This land is worth a lot of money, isn't it? Adele told me she and James came back here because some land they owned had grown in value, but they didn't own it. Not yet anyway."

Josh didn't answer and continued to glare at me.

"Oh my...God." A sob tore out of Kerri. "Is that...true? You just wanted...you just wanted this...farm?"

"It wasn't my fault!" he screamed. "The Mosebys found out old Helen Kay died and how much this land had grown in value. They came back to town with new names and threatened to tell the police I took the Peters girl. They were dead broke and desperate. They said if I didn't marry Kerri and kill her to get this land for them, they'd go to the police."

"All...I ever did...was love you! And you were going to...kill me?" She let out an anguished cry and the arm holding the gun fell to her side.

"I love you, too. I never meant to hurt you! But you made me so angry when you wouldn't listen to me and kept bringing up that damned prenup! I was looking at spending the rest of my life in prison if I didn't get this farm!" Josh took a step towards her.

"So, it was her or you and you picked you," I said, twisting the knife.

"Shut up!" he screamed as he took another step towards Kerri.

"You...love...me?" Kerri took a step back and pointed the gun at him again, stopping him in his tracks. "You love me, but you were going to...kill me?"

"No, I wasn't!"

"Then who's that hole for, Joshy? Because now that your supposed blackmailers are dead, you need to get rid of any connection you had to this farm, including her!" Dana had walked over to stand next to me, but Josh ignored her to focus on Kerri.

"Hon, you got sick from that diet I put you on and I just came out here because I knew there was probably something growing out here that could help you. Just put down the gun, Kerri, and we can talk about it."

Kerri shook her head as tears streamed down her face, and then she said the one word she'd probably never used the entire time she'd been with Josh Turner and the sound of it made him lose his mind.

"No!"

"Give it to me now!" he roared as he charged towards his fiancée with blood in his eyes.

The bullet hit Josh center mass in the chest, dropping him like a rabid dog before Kerri collapsed in the dirt next to him.

Hours later, when Evan arrived at the ER where they'd stitched up the wound on my forehead, he found me vomiting into a trash can because I didn't know where the restroom was. Between what happened on the farm, seeing Josh's dead body, remembering all the blood on me, Kerri, and Dana, plus the needle used to stitch my wound, it all finally caught up with me and a wave of nausea hit me hard after the nurse left the room.

"Easy," said Evan, helping me to my feet and then giving me a tissue to wipe my mouth. "Are you okay?"

"Yes, but my head is killing me." Evan guided me over to a chair next to the examining table.

"I'm going to get you some water." He turned to go when I stopped him.

"Evan, Josh is..."

"Dead. I know. The police told me. As his next of kin, I have to go to the morgue tomorrow and officially identify his body."

"I'm sorry," I said, although I wasn't sure what for.

"Don't be. I can't mourn a relationship that never existed."

Minutes later, Evan returned with a bottle of water for me and the nurse who gave me my aftercare instructions told me to come back in two weeks to get my stitches removed. I perused the instructions and noticed something was missing. I spoke up as the nurse was leaving the room.

"Hey, wait."

"Yes." She stopped and came back into the room. "Do you have a question?"

"Why can't I have any painkillers? My head is about to explode."

The nurse looked taken aback, but walked up to me and put a

hand on my shoulder. "Mrs. West, we can't prescribe you painkillers. That's standard practice for women in their first trimester."

"First...trimester?" I was instantly dizzy, and Evan had to steady me. Had I just heard this woman right?

"You...you mean you didn't know you were pregnant?"

Neither Evan nor I answered because we were suddenly sobbing in each other's arms.

FORTY-NINE

AVA

Two Weeks Later

I was eating my lunch in the playground at Haver House, sitting in one of the swings, when Lia arrived. I'd seen very little of her since what happened at Infinity Farm. I had questions. So many in fact that I wondered if she'd left town because she didn't want to tell me something I didn't want to hear about Brooke and her ultimate fate. Lia sat down on the swing next to me and gave me a smile.

"I hear congratulations are in order. How far along are you?"

"Six weeks and the morning sickness is kicking my ass."

She laughed. Of all the things that had happened to me in the last few weeks, being pregnant was the plot twist I never saw coming. Evan was still living at the town house in the basement, and we were in marriage counseling. I honestly didn't know what the future held for us, but if nothing else, we were committed to being the best parents we could be, whether we remained married or not.

"I heard Kerri's on the mend."

"She is physically, but it'll take a while for her to heal mentally and emotionally. She came in today for a few hours if you want to go say hello."

"I was relieved to hear she won't face any charges for Josh's death."

"Her being charged for his death would have been a bigger tragedy than her killing him. It was self-defense and she saved all our lives that night."

Lia nodded in agreement. "And your mom?"

"She's getting better. She's back at home and trying to put all this behind her, and thanks for not telling the police about her connection to Infinity Farm."

My mom had been lucky. Her connection to the Mosebys/Mackies bogus addiction treatment only went as far as her applying to be treated for her alcoholism, but she freaked out when they branded her, telling her it would help with her transformation. James Mackie was interested in her and offered her a job. Once she'd seen the phony degree he'd purchased for her, she quickly resigned and had never appeared in any of their brochures, but that left her with no income to pay the mortgage, so she borrowed from local drug dealers.

I'll never know if she knew Brooke was at Infinity Farm. I'm choosing to believe she didn't, and since my mom and I look alike, it was easy to convince the police that it was me Josh Turner had been after the night he attacked Mom, because he thought I was encouraging Kerri to leave him and got my mom by mistake. Me, Kerri, Lia, and Dana had told the police Josh had confessed to kidnapping Brooke and killing James and Adele because they were blackmailing him. When I thought about it, he'd never actually admitted to killing anyone, but he was a nasty piece of work and had the biggest motive. So, who else could have done it? The police closed James and Adele's murder investigation. Since Brooke's body was never found, her case was still open.

"I never once saw your mom at the farm. Her secret is safe with me."

"Thank you."

"And Dana?" she asked.

"I haven't seen her. She disappeared from the hospital where they treated us that night. I never got to tell her that none of us told the police she was involved in Brooke's abduction. I just hope she finally finds some peace."

Neither of us said anything for a few minutes as I tried to decide which of the million questions swirling around in my head I wanted answers to first.

"Who are you, Lia? How did you end up at Infinity Farm? Were you really doing a documentary on Brooke?"

She paused for a moment before giving me a sad smile. "There's plenty of time for you to hear my story. So, why don't you go ahead and ask what you really want to know?"

I'd been too afraid to ask what I really wanted to know, too afraid I'd be devastated. Lia seemed to sense this and took my hand. "She's alive."

My head whipped around so fast, and my eyes got so big Lia burst out laughing. I was speechless because it felt like all the air had been squeezed from my lungs.

"Wha...what?"

"She goes by the name Willa now. She's a married mother of two and owns a hair salon in downtown Toronto."

Willa. The name made me smile. "Do you talk to her often? Can you please tell her to call me? I'll understand if she..."

But Lia just held up her hand. "Tell her yourself." She stood up and turned around. I turned, too. And what I saw almost made me fall out of the swing.

A black couple with two kids stood several feet away. The man was tall, light-skinned, bald and built like a linebacker. He held a little boy who looked about two and was sucking his thumb, while a little girl with shoulder-length braids who looked about eight held his free hand and stared at me with undisguised curiosity.

But once my eyes fell on the brown-skinned woman, with the pixie cut and big brown eyes holding the little girl's other hand, I lost it. I knew her name was different now, but this was my Brooke. A sob tore out of me as I rushed forward. She dropped her daughter's hand and rushed towards me, meeting me halfway. We clung to each other and sobbed.

"I guess I owe you an ice-cream cone, don't I?" Tears slipped down her cheeks as she pulled away from me.

"Just...make...sure it's chocolate." I pulled her back into a tight embrace, too afraid she'd disappear again if I let her go.

We were so caught up in the moment we didn't notice that Lia had slipped away.

A few hours later, Willa and I sat on my back patio eating ice-cream sundaes while her husband Brock and their kids, Elias and Abby, watched a movie inside with Evan. I thought I'd have a million questions for her, but just being here with her and knowing she was alive and safe and sound was enough. I kept staring at her like she was going to disappear again, and there was one question I needed to know.

"Why didn't you guys come back? Why not let everyone know you were alive?"

Willa's spoon froze halfway to her mouth, and she looked at me and nodded like she'd been waiting for years to answer this question. Then she put her ice-cream bowl down on the table next to her to give me her full attention.

"We didn't come back because we were scared, Ava. When the Mosebys fled Elmhurst after I tried to get help, they took us all to another farm in Indiana. My mom always believed it was really me that had been spotted at that farm and hired a private detective to track the Mosebys to Indiana and then a private security team to extract us. Once we were out, and the Mosebys went on the run, my mom traveled back here to Elmhurst to tell the police I was alive."

"And what happened?"

Willa let out a breath and shook her head. "She quickly found out she couldn't trust the Elmhurst Police Department. We changed our names and fled the country."

"Why?"

"Because we had no idea where the Mosebys had gone or if they'd come after us and the Elmhurst PD had a corrupt cop on their payroll."

I waited for her to elaborate when another question suddenly popped into my head. "And who's we? Who were you rescued with?"

Just then Abby came bursting out of the house, with little Elias toddling after her, to tell their mom and aunt Ava what a good movie we'd missed. I knew my questions would have to wait.

FIFTY

LIA

Detective Michael Avery was surprised to see me when I turned up on his doorstep after leaving Ava and Willa at Haver House. I'm sure he had no idea I knew where he lived, but he was polite enough to invite me into his small apartment which was surprisingly neat and predictably spartan with only a black leather couch, glass coffee table with a blue ceramic ashtray in the center, and a flatscreen TV mounted on the wall over a console with a record player on top. The shelves below were crammed with vinyl records, mostly jazz and old-school hip-hop from what I could see from where I was standing. A beige leather recliner sat on the other side of the coffee table. A small kitchenette took up the opposite side of the room. Although clean, the apartment had a faint odor of cigarettes and onions.

"I'm surprised you're still here, Miss Quinn."

"Why is that?" I took a seat on the couch, and he sat down in the recliner, where, judging by the cup of coffee sitting in a cupholder on the recliner's arm, he'd been sitting when I rang his doorbell.

"I'd have thought you must have gotten all the info you needed for your documentary."

"I've actually decided to shelve the documentary on Brooke Peters' abduction. I'm focusing on a new case now."

"And what case would that be?"

"The case of another missing girl."

"Another missing girl?" His eyes narrowed and he took another sip of his coffee. "What other missing girl?"

"A little girl no one was looking for because no one knew she was missing. Her name was Tamika Clark. She arrived at Infinity Farm twenty-six years ago with her mom Nikki, who was hoping to finally overcome her addiction to cocaine. It didn't take long for Nikki to realize that the so-called treatment at Infinity Farm was a scam when she wasn't getting any better. Then one day she just disappeared, and they told Tamika her mom had left because she didn't want her anymore. Tamika still had her friend, Brooke, who meant everything to her."

"What does this have..."

"I'm not done." My voice was soft but menacing. Avery instantly shut up. "One night a couple came to the farm looking for their daughter, Crystal, and Brooke begged them for help. After the police came out to the farm as a result, they rounded them all up and took them to another farm in a remote location in rural Indiana. It was the same setup. They were there for almost two years when five men in black clothing and night-vision goggles showed up at the farm one night and tried to take Brooke."

"Is that so?" Avery replied sarcastically, but Lia's hard look shut him up.

"You see, her mom, Julia, always knew Brooke had been at that farm. That's why the Peters sold their house and disappeared. They needed the money to pay a private eye to track Brooke down and then a private security firm to extract her. She screamed and cried so much, not wanting to let Tamika go, that they had no choice but to take both of them. Two days later, the FBI showed up and raided the farm and shut it down, but the Mosebys had disappeared. Julia took Tamika in, and Brooke's family became Tamika's family, but she never forgot her real mother, Nikki. And because Julia was afraid of Nate and the Mosebys, they got new identities and emigrated to Canada. Julia died a few years ago, but she made Tamika promise her on her deathbed to find out what had happened to her mother."

Avery leaned forward in his recliner with his hands on his knees. "That's an intriguing story, but what is it you want from me...Tamika? You're the other girl in the story, right?"

I stared at him, waiting for the emotions I'd been suppressing to come surging back, but I felt nothing. Instead, I reached into my tote bag and pulled out an item from a clear plastic sleeve and held it out to him. "I want the truth, Nate. What happened to Nikki Clark? What happened to my mom?"

He stared at the one and only album of a rap group called *In the Cut* circa 1986 with its three members Tony Greer, Johnny Moseby, and Nate Peters, all dressed in black tracksuits, bucket hats, and gold chains on the cover as Mavis Brady's words from our interview echoed in my head, *"His name is Nathaniel Peters. Born and raised right here in Elmhurst. Ran off to New York City right out of high school trying to be a rapper and no one saw him for about twelve years."*

"Are you recording this?" He nodded towards my tote bag.

"You have my word that I'm not."

He reluctantly took the album from me, staring at it fondly like it was a long-lost friend. He traced a finger in the dust across the image of his younger self, absently wiping the dust on his pant leg.

"Where'd you find this?"

"It was hard to track down. I finally found it in the basement of an old record shop that was going out of business." But he'd barely heard a word I'd said.

"I remember when this came out. We thought we had made it, but the record company had no money to promote it. Radio stations wouldn't play it and six months later we were dead broke and owed the record company money for the copies that didn't sell and all of us had a nasty crack addiction. Tony got shot and killed trying to rob a bodega for drug money and Johnny and I stuck together and ended up back in Elmhurst. How'd you figure it out?"

"I could never understand why you were so eager to help me but gave me so little information. You wanted to control the amount of information I got. I had to ask myself why and went digging into you, Detective Avery. You didn't want me knowing you never worked the Brooke Peters case, did you? You didn't join the Elmhurst police force until after Brooke was abducted and that was as a rookie police officer fresh out of the academy. That's why no one ever saw Nate Peters again. You showed up back here in town a different man, Michael Avery, heavier and with a beard that covered the cut on your face that Julia gave you for what you did to Brooke when she was three."

"I had to cover that cut with stage makeup every single day when I first joined the force. No beards allowed. You have no idea how relieved I was when they allowed us to have neatly trimmed beards." He chuckled like we were old friends reminiscing and finally my anger flared to life.

"But Brooke couldn't cover the brand you gave her, you sick son of bitch! How could you do that to your own daughter? Julia told me Brooke was so traumatized she blocked the entire memory out."

"I never branded her, and I damned sure never abducted her!" He angrily jumped up from the recliner and began pacing. "Annette did!"

I continued to stare at him, not speaking until he finally calmed down and explained.

"When we got to Elmhurst from New York, the only place we could get jobs was on a herb farm out in the county run by a white farmer. We were still smoking crack, but Johnny slowly stopped. He'd be so worn out from working on the farm he stopped. He also started screwing the farmer's daughter, Annette. His getting clean was just cold turkey, but after the old man died, Johnny married Annette. The money they were getting from the old lady who owned the farm to run it wasn't enough for them anymore. Johnny had expensive tastes. So, they came up with the idea of using the farm to help other addicts get clean by pairing cold turkey with a strict diet and manual labor, meditation and a bunch of other shit to make it sound like a treatment and even passed themselves off as therapists."

"And the branding?"

"That came later, and it was strictly because of what Johnny did to Annette."

"What are you talking about?"

"Johnny never could keep it in his pants. He gave Annette chlamydia. She thought it was just a yeast infection and was taking herbal remedies that Helen woman who owned the farm was making, but it never got any better. By the time she was properly diagnosed, it was too late, she was infertile, and it broke her. She'd always wanted kids and started making us all call her mother, even Johnny. She'd lost it. The branding and the symbols were just a way for her to control us all."

"You're trying to tell me you had no clue they'd planned to kidnap your daughter?"

"None. Julia wouldn't let me see Brooke because I made the mistake of bringing her to the farm when she was three on one of her weekend visits with me, and letting Annette watch her while I went to score some drugs because I'd relapsed. Crazy ass Annette branded her to protect her from becoming like me. Julia refused to let me see her for years. Then I found out Brooke's brother Sam was selling weed and made the mistake of complaining about it to Annette. She thought my daughter needed saving. I didn't know what she'd had Josh Turner do until after Brooke was already there."

"But once you found out, why didn't you take her home? Why did you leave her there?"

"Johnny wouldn't let me! I tried to take her home and he threatened to kill me. I did the best I could for her. I even snuck into Julia's house and got her stuffed turtle because she wouldn't stop crying. Johnny went ballistic when he found out and said I was going to get us all arrested for kidnapping. We argued. I left. By the time I came back, everyone was gone. I never did know where you all went for twenty-five years until six months ago when they showed back up here as James and Adele Mackie."

"Your best wasn't good enough. You should have gotten her out of there by any means necessary!"

"I tried!" He sat back down in the recliner breathing heavily like it had cost him something to admit all of that, but I needed more from him, much more.

"What happened to my mother? And don't you dare..."

"She's dead," he blurted out, not able to meet my eyes.

"How?" My voice was barely a whisper.

I knew she was dead. I knew she'd never willingly leave me, but it was still like a knife in my heart. I had to take several deep breaths to keep the tears at bay because I refused to cry in front of this waste of space.

"Like I said. Johnny was a ladies' man. He loved the ladies and the ladies loved him. And your mom was real pretty, even for an addict. One night Adele caught your mom and Johnny messing around in the hay barn and she grabbed the nearest pitchfork and..." He couldn't finish and I didn't want him to.

"Where is she? What did they do with her?"

"When I got back and found you all gone, I noticed a boarded up well near the back of the property that hadn't been boarded up when I left. If I had to guess, she's in there."

It was getting late, and the setting sun was making the room dark. Avery reached out and turned on the lamp sitting on the table next to his chair. "Can I get you coffee or something?"

"Why, so you can poison it and kill me like you did that poor bastard in the morgue with your name on his toe tag? It probably wasn't hard to switch his fingerprints and DNA samples with yours, was it?"

"Didn't need to. Sadly, there was a mix-up, and a funeral home came and got the wrong body and cremated it before it could be fully processed and the few samples that had been taken from the body went mysteriously missing. Elmhurst PD is keeping it out of the media until they figure out how to shift the blame. More than likely, they'll make our interim medical examiner the scapegoat."

"Then who did they really find in the trunk of that car?"

Avery shrugged. "No clue. There's an alley downtown where the homeless camp out and you can throw a rock and hit a former Infinity's Child. Most of the ones who didn't run away or end up dead or in prison, wound up on the streets. There's not much any of them wouldn't do for a hot meal even go for a ride out to a deserted farm. You were getting too close. I had to do something, and Josh Turner owed me for what he did to Brooke. I told him to pick some guy who was the same height and build as me back in the day."

"You're sick."

"And your time is up, Miss Quinn. It's time for you to go. My Reds game is about to start." He picked up the remote from the table and clicked on the flatscreen on the wall.

I stared at him in disbelief. "Aren't you even going to ask where your daughter is? How she's doing? You have grandkids now. Don't you even care?"

I saw the briefest flicker of emotion in his eyes, but it was gone in an instant. "No, Miss Quinn. Nate Peters has a daughter and is a grandfather. My name is Michael Avery."

Disgusted, I got up, glaring down at him as he continued to sit there staring at the TV like I no longer existed. "You know you've been calling me Miss Quinn since we first met. I never told you I was a miss. I'm actually married."

"Then why don't you wear a ring?"

"I do when I'm not around you."

"And why is that?"

I could tell he desperately wanted me gone, but I wasn't done with him yet. "Because I didn't want you to know my married name, Mrs. Lia Quinn Lang, wife of Dr. Raymond Tate Lang, the interim medical director for Elmhurst County, my co-producer, and partner in crime."

When I'd met Ray I was an angry, emotional, self-destructive wreck over my past at Infinity Farm and not knowing what happened to my mom. He could have run away. Instead, he saw past my rage and lovingly helped me put myself back together and encouraged my healing even when it included revenge.

"What?" He stood up abruptly and swayed on his feet, sitting back down hard in the recliner looking confused as beads of sweat popped up on his forehead.

"You, Detective Michael Avery, will have the distinction of being his very last case here before your new medical examiner starts next week. He'll rule your cause of death a heart attack."

"I don't...understand. What did...you...do?" He looked around frantically.

"It was the album. That wasn't dust. It was cyanide that seeped into your skin. I'd say you've got about five minutes, give or take." I took a pair of plastic gloves out of my tote bag and picked the album up and put it back into the plastic sleeve I'd brought it in. "But don't worry, I won't let you die alone."

Avery lunged forward from the recliner and fell onto the floor. I watched him crawl towards the door before turning over on his back and clutching his chest as his eyes bulged. I watched his chest rise and fall, and his face contort in pain, like I was watching a bug die. Once he'd stopped breathing, and his eyes stared unblinking at the ceiling, I stepped over him and headed out the door. In the hallway, I took the knife I'd used to kill James and Adele, and stab Natalie Hammond, and put it down the building's garbage shoot.

James, Adele, and Josh had deserved to die. Natalie had been a gray area. While she wasn't an active participant in what went down at Infinity Farm, she knew the Mosebys were con artists taking advantage of vulnerable, desperate people and she'd said nothing. In my book, she was guilty by association. I never planned to kill her, but she did deserve punishment, I mused as I left the building to meet my husband so we could retrieve my mother's remains from the well at Infinity Farm.

FIFTY-ONE

SIMONE

One Month Later

Simone had been working double shifts at Phil's Diner and her feet and legs were killing her, but she was grateful because she owed a lot of people money. Henry, the owner, was nice enough to give her her old job back after she'd explained why she took off and who she really was. He'd even told her she could pay him back the money she stole in installments. She had already paid her landlady, Dana, the rent money she'd skipped out on. Dana even told the police she'd let Simone use her car. When the police never came for her over her involvement in Brooke Peters' abduction, she realized neither Ava nor Lia had told them. She knew she needed to thank them in person but was afraid to face them, especially Ava. But one day she'd find the courage.

On the 25th anniversary of Brooklyn Peters' abduction the Elmhurst Police Department held a press conference to announce that Brooke was alive, and she and her family were living under new identities in another country. They outlined the details of the case and what went down at Infinity Farm with the Mosebys/Mackies and Josh Turner. They asked the public to respect Brooke's privacy as she had no interest in being in the spotlight or sharing her story. Predictably, the media went nuts. But it didn't take long for a new lurid headline to capture the public's attention and knock Brooke Peters off the front page. Simone was happy for Brooke and hoped she'd be able to forgive her one day and put the nightmare of Infinity Farm behind her for good.

Simone had finally gotten her license renewed and was legally able to drive a car again for the first time in what felt like forever. Could things finally be coming together for her? It sure felt like it, but she kept waiting for the other shoe to drop. She thought back to that night months ago when she'd spotted a blast from her past and had taken off running. Now that the dust had settled, she thought back on what she'd actually seen. It had been James Mackie, formerly Johnny Moseby, in the diner that night. And, yes, he had noticed her, looking right at her and making her panic, but he hadn't been alone. He'd been with a pretty young woman Simone had never seen. He'd been on date, and she remembered how many times he'd flirted with the women at the farm.

Simone realized now that the man who'd featured so heavily in all her nightmares hadn't even recognized her. And why would he? She was no one to him. How ironic was it that his cheating had sent her trailing after him to Elmhurst and helped set in motion the downfall of people who'd caused nothing but pain to everyone who'd encountered them. Even Brooke's shady ass father, who'd been cosplaying as a cop, was dead. She knew Lia was behind it, but she didn't need to know the details. She'd recognized him when he'd come to the shelter after Adele was murdered. She didn't care how heavy he'd gotten or that he had a beard. She recognized his eyes, flat, hard, and cold like a reptile.

It had been the same with Adele. She had no idea the woman who'd forced her to call her mother all those years ago and branded her was now working for the shelter. Adele hadn't recognized her, but Simone knew who she was instantly. The same plain, round face, the same glasses, the same shoulder-length hair, albeit graying. When Ava had seen them arguing downtown it was because Simone had confronted her about being Annette Moseby and she flipped out on her, threatening to call the police on Simone for harassment.

Two days later, she was dead, and Simone had been there. She'd followed Adele with the intention of somehow making her admit to what she'd done to her and couldn't believe it when she'd pulled into the same park she had driven Josh Turner to when he'd abducted Brooke. She found Adele on the ground next to her car, bleeding out but not quite dead. When Simone had knelt down next her, she'd grabbed the front of her shirt with both her bloody hands, pleading for help. Even if Simone had called 911, it was too late. She'd lost too much blood.

Simone noticed an envelope full of money on the ground next to Adele and instinctively took it and fled. But once she'd gotten far enough away, she saw Adele's blood had soaked through the envelope staining some of the bills inside. She couldn't bring herself to spend any of it and threw it in a dumpster behind a grocery store.

Simone closed her eyes against the memory of all that blood and was instantly taken back to that shed at Infinity Farm. She'd been stripped from the waist up and she could still remember the searing pain of the brand on her back, the smell of her own burning flesh, and how she'd screamed. They'd left her lying on the dirt floor of the discipline shed, curled into the fetal position with her back on fire. At some point she must have fallen asleep because she remembered light flooding into the shed, and realized someone had opened the shed door. Was it Mother coming back to inflict more pain on her? No. It was two little girls, Brooke and Mika.

Mika pressed a cup of cold water to her lips, and she drank greedily, spilling most of it, while Brooke covered her with a towel and tucked something soft next to her. Then they were gone. When Simone woke up later, she saw that Brooke had left her stuffed turtle with her. Day turned to night and by the time she felt brave enough to leave the shed, everyone was gone. She had no idea where they'd gone, but she quickly gathered up what food she could, even finding some money in the process, before they came back, and fled. She'd been running ever since. Moving every few years and using aliases and what happened at the farm to keep everyone at a distance, even the one person that mattered to her the most.

A silver Ford Taurus pulled into the driveway of the house whose porch she'd been waiting on for nearly an hour. An older woman got out with a plastic grocery bag. When she spotted Simone waiting, a look of annoyance instantly popped up on her face and she sighed.

"Whatever you're selling, I'm not interested. I'm a retiree on a fixed income..."

"Hey, Ma." Simone took a tentative step forward so her mother could get a good look at her stopping the woman in her tracks. Her free hand flew to her mouth.

"Simone? Oh, thank God." Amelia Riley dropped her grocery bag and held her arms out wide.

"Ma!"

Simone was off the porch in three strides, launching herself into her mother's arms and inhaling the familiar scent of Shalimar, finally realizing she was home, and she was safe.

EPILOGUE

NATALIE

Two Months Later

It took Natalie two trips to bring in everything she'd bought for her future grandbaby. She knew Ava would protest when she saw all of the stuff she'd bought, but she didn't care. As a grandmother, it was her right to spoil her grandchild, and she planned on doing just that. Once she'd put everything away, she went into the kitchen. She didn't have any champagne and instead poured sparkling white grape juice into a champagne flute and carried it out into the backyard where she had a table and chairs set up next to a large flower bed.

She took a seat and looked around at her well-tended backyard, proud of how well she'd been able to maintain it on her own. Some of her other single friends who were homeowners hired a lawn care service to care for their lawns, but not Natalie. She did it all on her own. It wasn't because she loved gardening and yard work like everyone assumed. She did it all out of necessity.

Natalie knew no one could understand why she had clung so hard to this house when it would have been easier to just move to a more affordable place after Clay left her. They thought she was delusional for thinking he would come back to her, but they were wrong, because he had come back. She remembered like it was yesterday. She got a call from him to let her know he'd be home the next day, and that he had something important to talk to her about.

She'd cooked all his favorite foods, beef short ribs, garlic mashed potatoes, and parmesan and lemon roasted asparagus, and put on the red dress she knew he loved and waited. She'd even sent Ava away to Brooke's for the night so she and her husband could have some quality time alone. When he'd arrived in a taxi with a large suitcase, it had just cemented her belief that he was back for good. After dinner, which had led to dessert in bed, she'd awakened after midnight to find Clay not in bed. She found him fully dressed and, in the kitchen, packing up the expensive chef's grade cookware she'd given him for Christmas the year before.

"What are you doing?" She was so confused.

"Look, Nat, I meant to tell you this when I got here, but you went to the trouble of cooking, and I didn't want to hurt your feelings, and then we had too much wine and things just got out of hand."

"Tell me what?"

He didn't respond and instead looked at the kitchen counter where a manila envelope lay. She snatched it up, opened it and pulled out the paperwork. She quickly scanned the top page and then looked up at her husband in disbelief. They were divorce papers. When Clay wouldn't look at her, her stomach knotted up and she felt sick.

"I'm sorry, but Olivia and I want a life together. I never meant for this to happen. Please don't make this any harder than it is."

Watching him pack up the cookware, she realized the large suitcase had been empty. He'd brought it home to pack the rest of his things that he hadn't taken with him when he'd left for his new job in Seattle.

"But...what am...I supposed to tell Ava?" Her voice was thick with tears. Clay was unmoved.

"Tell her the truth. She's a big girl now. She'll understand. She can come visit us on her Christmas break."

He pushed past her to head to the garage, grabbing the keys to the Mercedes SUV, which he'd given her on their tenth wedding anniversary on his way. Everyone who knew them knew the car was a guilt gift for putting up with all his cheating. Natalie didn't care. She loved that car.

"Oh, no you don't! That's my car!" She snatched the keys out of his hand.

"Don't be a bitch! That car's in my name. I paid for it, and I need it to drive back to Seattle." He snatched the keys back and shoved her out of the way, sending her stumbling backwards into the table across from the garage door.

Natalie didn't remember picking up the heavy lead crystal vase on the table, let alone smashing into the back of Clay's head, fueled by all the lies, gaslighting, humiliation, and disappointment she'd accumulated in the years since she'd met him. What she did remember was sitting on the floor next to Clay and holding his hand as he took his last breath.

She'd tenderly wrapped him in a sheet and buried him at 3 a.m. in the flower bed, telling herself she would dig him up and put him somewhere else when she had the chance. Two days later, Brooke was abducted and the eyes of the police, the media, and the entire town were on not just the Peters family, but on her and Ava as well. As soon as she realized she liked knowing where Clay was, and that he'd never leave her, she left him where he was.

She'd texted his mistress, Olivia, from his phone, pretending to be him, and told her he'd had a change of heart and wouldn't be back. Olivia blew up his phone for weeks afterwards before she finally gave up. When Facebook became a thing several years later, Natalie found Olivia's profile and was happy to see she'd moved on, and by all appearances was happily married. She mailed a resignation letter to the restaurant where Clay had been a chef and sadly, they closed their doors four months later. Natalie drank her grape juice until there was only a mouthful left, then turned to face the flower bed.

"Guess what, Clay? You're going to be a grandpa." She smiled as she poured the remaining grape juice into the flower bed. Then she got up and went back inside the house.

A LETTER FROM THE AUTHOR

Dear reader,

Thank you for reading *Nobody Heard a Thing*. I hope you enjoyed Ava and Brooke's story. If you'd like to hear about my new and upcoming releases, you can sign up for my author newsletter.

www.stormpublishing.co/angela-henry

If you enjoyed this book and could spare a few moments to leave a review, that would be greatly appreciated. Even a short review can make all the difference in encouraging a reader to discover my books for the first time. Thank you so much!

The lives of the missing often get lost in the circumstances and details surrounding their disappearances, with missing marginalized women and girls falling through the cracks and being overlooked by the media. But for me, the same questions linger. Who were they? What was their backstory, and who did they leave behind to mourn their loss? I hope this book sparks some much-needed food for thought.

Thanks again for being part of this amazing journey with me, and I hope you'll stay in touch – I have so many more stories and ideas to entertain you with!

Angela

KEEP IN TOUCH WITH THE AUTHOR

instagram.com/angelahenry_author

facebook.com/authorangelahenry

tiktok.com/@angelahenryauthor

ACKNOWLEDGMENTS

I'd like to give a very heartfelt thank you to my awesome editor, Kate Smith. Working with you has made me a much better writer. And to Oliver Rhodes and the amazing team at Storm, you guys rock! It's been such an honor and pleasure to write for you.

9 781805 087304